To: Muffy!

For your adventures in mystery, all my best!

You Enter a Room

Nancy Avery Dafoe

Nancy Avery Dafoe

Published by Rogue Phoenix Press
Copyright © 2017

ISBN: 978-1977744630

Credits
Cover Artist: Designs by Ms G
Editor: Deborah C. Day

We are all detectives in this mystery called life—
all looking for clues.

Dedication

To Colette and Nicole Dafoe, my daughters and first readers; and to Grace and Katherine Babcock, my second readers, former students, and friends; to Karen Hempson and Judith McGinn, Pen Women and dear friends who read drafts of this novel.

Chapter One
You Enter a Room

"Poems are what? Dirt, death, fondue? Answer the question." Professor Roald Gould demanded with intensity that pinned us down from the opening of class. Silence followed. No one even took off coats or backpacks, no one adjusted seats or papers. We froze in nervous anticipation because the class could not possibly begin and end with such dramatic confusion. Our professor kept us waiting until we started to look around at each other in confusion. Were we in the right room? Roald Gould had a reputation that preceded him, but we were momentarily startled even after all of those years of schooling and every manner of introduction. Disorientation, apparently, was our lesson for the day.

"Poems are?" Gould repeated after several minutes of absolute stillness that held reticence rather than peace. In the aftermath of that interminable absence of voice, Gould spoke again; "poems are death unless they are a moving shadow, a woman making love, a boy fishing." We waited again before our instructor finally asked, "What did Leroi Jones suggest in his poem "*Black Art?*" What is his first line?"

I was again orienting myself to the Africanist presence in English Literature, but I knew Jones' work was not in the curriculum.

"I don't think he was suggesting at all," said the typically silent Michael Lawler. "Jones' lines are urgent and brutal and direct. Jones is really demanding and stating that poetry must be, must feel as critical as breath, as violent as a punch to your gut." Michael, who usually sat hunched over and pensive in class, was bolt upright for an instant. His face and confident voice were so altered that I almost didn't recognize the handsome but shy guy from my graduate level English classes.

Gould met his eyes, and the exchange happened as if no one else was in the room except the two of them. You could discern competing forces that were drawn together as the rest of us were involuntarily pulled into this tension. At the time, it was likely that none of us could define those dynamics of repulsion and attraction. Only later, would I realize that I had witnessed a struggle between independence and submission, between bravery and cowardice, between dominance and questioning, between sexual attraction and repulsion, and between good and evil. The interaction was not about knowledge or lack of knowledge as Gould framed their meeting.

"As a figure of speech, the simile by its nature is suggestive, guiding us to make the connections laid out in the construction." Gould was talking only to Michael, and the rest of us waited to see how Michael would respond. "And I note you used the word 'as' a total of four times in one sentence, apparently unaware of the signifier as simile and suggestion. Jones used the simile to *suggest* the relationship between violence of the physical world and signifiers. Read Doty's essay on metaphors." A number of students started looking through the syllabus, fearing they had missed the first day's assignment. "Don't check. It's not in the syllabus. Read Doty for your own edification; read Jones' poetry, and get a better grasp of signifiers and metaphors. Such a lack of delineation at this point in your academic careers is startling," Gould said with evident disdain.

Just as I wanted to cheer Michael for his precision about wording and poetic interpretation, as well as facing our esteemed professor on seemingly equal footing, the young man slumped in his chair and lowered his head slightly. Body language was everything. Those of us still standing, finally sat down. Michael had not simply given up the argument, but the room. No one was looking at him any longer except for me. Here there would be no wild spinning out of a disturbed magnetic order, at least not on that day.

Gould scarcely emoted in triumph but betrayed the slightest curve invading the lower corner of his lip. "Thank you for at least being aware of his poetry," he said as the rest of us wondered if we would be able to catch up. Many students fidgeted in relief that someone had dared to face the formidable instructor head on, even if the dialogue had ended poorly for him. I thought I knew Michael would regret his challenge. No one had assigned Leroi Jones, and his poetry wasn't part of the course, although I was suddenly wishing that the poem was. I wrote down the poem title as soon as I took out my pen.

Even though Michael had been humbled, as was typical in a Gould class, I was still impressed he had read *"Black Art"* somewhere along the way and could quote lines from memory as well as Gould always seemed to do.

Looking back on that time, I am reminded of Professor Gould's many lessons that were not only occasionally cruel but full of surprise and insight, even spontaneous discovery. All of the poet/educator's talent, ability, knowledge roared into rooms with him as the force of his personality was greater than a single attribute. "There are students and there are scholars," said Professor Gould, turning toward the class again. "The key difference lies in the word 'aptitude.'" He looked at all of us as if appraising which of us were merely the lesser. "What have you read lately? Do you know Charles Simic and Seamus Heaney as well as you know Robert Lowell and Berryman? Are you as familiar with Rainer Maria Rilke as Tony Hoagland?"

If having read works you were not required to know was about scholarship, then I had much work ahead of me. I recognized all of these poets' names but knew only Lowell's work well. No, wait, I had read some Heaney poems too, and I'd come across a few poems by Simic that I suddenly recalled. I started to calm down, but then I thought about the fact that our instructor only mentioned male poets. This pattern was part of a larger picture that Gould, knowingly or unknowingly betrayed, one I was slow to recognize. What did I know by Heaney? Recalling a poem entitled *"Gifts of Rain"* that I remembered liking, I thought better of mentioning it. Gould offered his own pick: "Has anyone of you read *"Strange "* by Heaney?" Most of us looked around at each other at a loss. Then Gould added, "Perhaps you should examine your heads to make sure they are still attached." He turned his own head slightly as if he was amused only with himself. I looked up the poem in the interim and discovered the related phrases in Heaney's poem. The image was macabre enough, but, at the time, I didn't connect the loss of ahead to our professor directly, only

3

wondered at his choice of lines to memorize.

I shot Michael another glance and gave him an encouraging smile. There was an attraction I had sensed on other occasions, but that morning, I grappled with his retreat before Gould. I wanted to sit down next to Michael, but he had placed his book sack on the chair beside him, and the wall was on his other side. I finally sat down two rows in front of him, turning only once to see him glaring at Gould.

Our professor had already moved on and was lecturing, speaking rapidly, as he wrote notes in shorthand on the white board, his back turned toward us. In that instant, I understood I had already fallen behind. I needed to forget about Michel and focus on Gould. Then I realized that I was in deep water and would have to start swimming faster. There were some in the class who already knew they were drowning.

Chapter Two
A Child, A Stranger

Michael Lawler was found hanging in an unlit stairwell outside his apartment door. On a Saturday of unbroken gray bone-chilling cold, the snow had stopped, but the wind picked up and I learned about Michael. Before I knew anything, Michael was struggling with a thick rope around his neck, his eyes bulging. All night, billowing snow covered tire tracks on an icy road, covered foot prints leading to and away from an old building on a side street where the trace of a man and car had noiselessly disappeared. During those early morning hours, the street never lifted its head, never blinked in astonishment, looking down so long that when lights dimmed with the approach of morning, the street had already gone blind.

He was found three stories up in a modest, but near vacant, apartment building on River Street. Hanging? I couldn't get past that. How did a brilliant, talented poet so near the end of his years of schooling suddenly decide to take his own life? His death was unacceptable on so many levels. Unimaginable, because I knew him, had read his poems, stared into his beautiful eyes, and he had placed his warm hand over mine.

Michael lived in an older neighborhood, not the best nor the worst part of Rochester, with the University of Rochester nearby. Removing himself from campus was typical of Michael in all that he did. That fact was part of the reason so few students were connected to him. The only places I might have run into him were Rush Rhees, another campus library, or classes, and I made a point of checking his favorite study carrels every time I went to a library.

Then I was hit with this information: "Forced to break down the door, police discovered the body of Michael Lawler." He'd been dead for over twenty-four hours; it was ruled a suicide.

In those early hours while Michael hung from a rope, I was sleeping fitfully but obliviously. Even years after this tragedy, the juxtaposition continued to trouble me that I could be sleeping while someone I knew was dying. Only a day after Michael's death, an accidental encounter in the campus bookstore took me to this place of growing darkness.

Going to get my morning coffee at Saxby's, I was drawn to the little crowd in the bookstore. The boy doing all the talking was tall, awkward, and looked like a freshman, but turned out he was a junior. I had my black coffee in hand and decided to look at a few books in our Barnes & Noble campus store when I saw students grouped around the tall kid. He had blonde hair that was matted together in ugly clumps as if he'd been wearing a damp wool hat and had just removed it.

Then he said, "Some graduate student here, Michael Lawler, I think they said, is dead."

"Are you sure?" a girl asked. There were probably other questions or comments, but I didn't hear them.

My mouth opened slightly; something tried to escape, my stomach twisted and my head was suddenly heavy and thick with pins and needles. I started to lose my balance, but Samantha Morris caught my arm as I headed south. "You okay?" she asked from far off while I slowly found my way back, sitting on the floor. "Vena, I think you better stay down. You don't look so good."

I sat woozily on the bookstore's floor, put my head between my crossed legs, perceived a pressure on my head with the guidance of Samantha's cool hand, until a few ounces of clarity returned. Samantha was kneeling beside me. "Oh, good. Your color's coming back. You're not going to throw up or anything, are you?"

"Did he—that kid there—say Michael is dead?" Samantha, who was not so much my friend but a classmate, nodded. We met accidentally at Saxby's. Still, she was someone I knew, a person I thought I could trust only because she worked so hard in every class, so I clung to her in those terrible seconds. I needed to get up and managed only to stumble. "Wait," I commanded the young man who had the small army around him and was now moving off, "stop him," I said rudely to Sam.

Thankfully and obediently, she went after the guy named Andrew and brought him back to me. "Please, could you tell me what you know about Michael, about what happened?" I was still on the floor with one bent knee trying to push off.

"You okay there?" he leaned over me and looked even taller up close, bending over me.

"Yes. Just tell me!" He reached out and helped me to my feet a little too quickly, and I swayed, but his hand was still gripped around my arm. "Everything, tell me everything." I jerked away, and he let go of me.

One of the store clerks was suddenly in my face, looking at me closely. "Are you all right, miss?"

"I'm fine," I said impatiently. "Thanks," then I turned to the kid with the message, looking at him intently. The store clerk disappeared or really just went back behind the counter.

"Uh, I don't know everything," he started, "Name's Andrew—."

"Okay, Andrew, but what happened?" he leaned his head to the side in deference to my rudeness.

"Like I said before, I was going for my usual morning run," I already suspected he was a runner because he was too thin for anything else unless he was sick. "I'd just made my loop to head back to campus when two cop cars pulled up across the street. I wouldn't normally stop running for a cop car, I mean, why—"

"Skip that part," I said roughly, "what did they do?" The three of us were on an island in the store. Other students, having already heard his story while I was nearly passing out, had moved on and resumed their lives. This was a big moment for Andrew. Michael wasn't exactly well-known on campus even though he'd been there for years, but Andrew made the tale exciting for his spectators. Andrew would be repeating his tale for days and weeks to come.

"Cops got out and started banging on the door of this place," Andrew used his hands to imitate the policeman's gestures. "One of them was peering in a small front window, then the other one joined him and they walked around the house looking in wherever they found a window. I wasn't really all that interested at first, but I used the excuse of a commotion to take a breather before heading back, stretching and letting my lungs fill again which is—"

"We get it. You're a runner. What happened then?" Samantha, thankfully, re-directed him so I didn't have to.

Andrew shrugged at our impolite responses. "I started to get curious as they kept trying to see into the house, going back to some of the windows they had already looked in. I coughed, but I didn't want them to hear me, so I kind of held my hand over my mouth." He replays this gesture as somehow significant.

I shook my head, finding this runner's focus on himself exasperating. Sam interrupted him for me again. "Just tell us what happened to Michael. What do you know?"

"Yeah, well, they meant business, so I knew something was going down there. After circling the house, the cops pounded on the door again, then one of them looks through a window he'd already passed and returned to, standing on his toes, and yells something. The other one comes back to the front, or I guess, really a side door, and starts kicking at it. Then both of them were smashing their boots against the door. I mean, I've seen this kind of smash in the door on TV, but to actually see these guys break something down is damned impressive."

Suddenly, I wanted him to slow up and not say the next part out loud, but Sam urged him on. "Then?"

"They went in, and I ran across the street like I was still jogging and looked in the open doorway because I guess I wasn't thinking about anybody having guns, and I realize that wasn't the smartest thing for me to do—see, I wasn't even thinking about myself at that point."

"Andrew!" I wanted to slap him.

"It was awful, really. This guy, he was hanging from the ceiling fixture at the top." I covered my face and Sam gripped my arm, her painted nails digging in and leaving little impressions. "They were trying to get him down, so they didn't see me. One cop grabbed his legs and pulled him back to the top of the stairs to check for a pulse. Then he let him go, accidentally, I think, and the guy starts swinging back and forth like a pendulum. I stepped back then because I'd never seen a dead person hanging like that, and that's when I saw his boot at the bottom just inside the door. One of his boots was still on, but the other had fallen. I was so close that I could have picked it up. I went back to the other side of the street and called my friend Jay to come get me. I was starting to feel sick."

At first the detail of the boot seemed pointless and then I saw the image as clearly as Andrew had, marking the death of the individual. Michael's boot, the worn, old leather ones that he wore every day. "How do you know the shoe or boot was Michael Lawler's?" Sam asked. "Did you know him?"

"No, never heard of him, but when an ambulance pulled up and the EMTs went in, I was still waiting for my friend. Jay had been sleeping in that morning because he didn't have class, so he wasn't there yet. See, I didn't feel like running anymore, I was nauseous, like you." He looks at me, then said, "Just like you. Another cop came and took pictures, then they brought out his body covered up like on a TV show. One of the cops said to the other, 'Anything in his pockets?'"

""License says Michael Lawler," I'm pretty sure the cop said. "Student ID on him too. University of Rochester student. Suicide." I didn't want the cops to notice me, so I stepped back further and ducked around behind a house. Thinking about what I did now, maybe it wasn't such a good idea because they might have thought I had something to do with it, like I was involved in a murder or something. I mean, he was hanging, but who knew how he got there, even if he did say suicide?"

"Oh, no," was all I could get out. Sam was crying. Looking back later, I realized Andrew might have been the one to put the word 'murder' in my head.

"You're sure?" Sam asked, and he nodded. I liked Sam a little bit more during those moments we were drawn together in horror. Whatever else life held for either of us, we experienced a temporary bond in that claustrophobic space where breathing becomes more difficult.

Andrew waited a few minutes but saw that neither one of us was up to questioning him further, so he walked off, ready to repeat his tale. He probably had friends back home who had yet to hear of his dramatic morning. That would be all the experience was for Andrew, an opportunity to enlarge his life.

Sam hugged me, and I took that solace greedily. We finally stopped holding one another. "You okay?" she asked.

I nodded, "I can't believe it."

"Me either. I'm so sorry, but I've got to go," and we parted. As soon as I left the bookstore, I was hit again, my whole body aching. By the time I reached my apartment, my head hurt so badly that I turned off the lights, pulled the curtains, and rolled into a fetal position on my bed where I stayed for hours. It didn't help and changed nothing. Hours later, I woke to restless fear and more nausea.

Although I didn't know Michael well, I was aware of his peculiarities, his withdrawn silence, his intelligence and gentleness. What was certain was I wanted to know him better. What I recognized him best for, however, was his talent. We had read each other's work on multiple occasions, wrote a few comments that were generous rather than critical. I couldn't quite believe that Michael had taken his own life, that he was gone. Logically, my search should have ended there with his death and certainty. We were told he had hanged himself. Everything should have been obvious, as related circumstances appeared to be to nearly everyone around me, but suicide and Michael did not fit, would never fit.

My mind kept seeing Michael's worn boot at the bottom of the stairs and then him swinging when the cop let go of his body either accidentally or deliberately. Unlike Andrew, I was not a witness, had not been at the crime scene, but I might as well have been because I conjured up the sight as clearly as if I had been standing outside in the snow, looking through that open doorway. My eyes followed a line of dread up narrow stairs in disbelief, but I kept turning away before seeing his distorted face, as if I couldn't bear to look at him in death, even in imagination.

Chapter Three
A Hope Thief

After Michel's death, I struggled to act on anything. Michael was at the center of that unmoving sadness, but endless winter didn't help. During my school year, the oppressive atmosphere of the City of Rochester seemed to weigh down on everyone. Even the sky was perpetually on the verge of last light. I'm told western New York is lovely in the short summer, but I've left the city by then. In autumn and endless winter, the Rochester I typically woke to was gray and cold and wet with either snow or freezing rain. Blurring lines of distinct days, I walked to class in increasing darkness before going home in a slight break in the dark attempted by the sun looking out briefly from behind a cloud before final light took back the day's struggle.

Living and working there reminded me of being held captive inside a shadow. The shadow knows! Bill, the man who let me live in his house while I was growing up, once told me about a radio program called "The Shadow" that played before and during the war years, starting in 1930 as his parents sat around with their parents and listened to the crime fighter known as 'The Shadow'.

"The fears of the Great Depression and the coming war only increased the tensions and anxiety that the show and its creepy music would build," said Bill.

"Who was the Shadow?"

"No one knows," Bill said with a wry smile. "Well, actually, he was voiced by the legendary Orson Welles." At the time, the name Orson Welles meant nothing to me, but I was captivated by the idea of a radio show playing in the darkness with everyone sitting around to listen, imagining what would come next. Perhaps that warm familial scene, which I did not have, made me somehow long for the closeness.

I liked hearing stories about my grandparents because I never knew them, both dying before my birth. But I had left those stories behind when I went off to college. Almost as if I had folded and stored my past in the old dresser I used as a kid.

But my grandparents were long gone, and the stories Bill told seemed to come up out of some ancient past, entirely unrelated to my life. Not as if Bill and I could talk about much anymore, not as if I could have told Bill that I had a crush on a guy named Michael and needed some advice as to why he was so hard to read.

"Hey, Bill, how about giving me relationship advice even though all of yours have ended badly?" I couldn't imagine saying such a thing. Bill was not the person to go to except for financial help. I would have felt guilty about U. of R. expenses except Bill was the one who encouraged me to go, told me the school's stellar reputation would be important for my future, that Rochester was a wonderful university with outstanding opportunities. He forgot to mention the part about the colder winters, the gray, and the industries that long ago left town.

A relatively old city in western New York State, Rochester had once been a 'vibrant hub'—and this is the phrase I heard used again and again—of industry and cool imagery, Kodak making its home there. There was a paradox involved in talking about Rochester as an old city in a relatively new country, by European standards, but Rochester was a city with visible wounds. By the time I arrived, however, Kodak meant nothing to me nor a lot of people of my generation, but I guess Kodak was pretty big back in the day. No, really, a giant. You'll have to trust me on this.

All of that changed years ago. The Rochester I knew was anything but a vibrant hub. Even the quality of light in this city is economically depressed. Once you leave the prestige and insulation of the campus, you find yourself staring at empty buildings, deserted factories, loss and more loss. While natives likely do not find this assessment accurate, visitors do. Rochester is the kind of city you expect nothing relevant to happen except at the universities, but I was probably wrong about it, just like I was wrong about a lot of things. This city likely had its own vibe quite apart from the universities.

To me, though, winter was the perfect metaphor for Rochester, trapped in icy fingers nearly six months a year. The dead season left its mark in the hollowed-out bones of the city with abandoned buildings boarded up left to harbor stray animals, rats, drifters, drug dealers seeking space for their deals. These wounded structures could be seen all over older American cities in the east, but that is what I saw and tried to forget until I got back to my university island.

The University of Rochester is a great university and Rochester would be a great walking campus, if the weather weren't so damn miserable all the time. Still, I walked, placing one foot in front of the other on a disappearing path, traces of my presence erased by snowfall. I kept thinking I could almost hear the footfalls of a trespassing man.

Chapter Four
Not Merely Because You're a Writer

Only two weeks earlier, I had seen Michael studying in the library and waved because we had been in a few classes together. I found Michael attractive in the way human beings who are not even remotely interested in you seem most fascinating. I also knew he was one of Gould's graduate assistants in English. We were a select breed, not merely because we were writers in a university in which almost everyone else wanted to be either a doctor or engineer. We were more than a little unusual in that we wrote poetry all the time, even when we were burdened with graduate courses that had nothing at all to do with poetry. Gould and his interest in poetry made that possible. Michael was not simply gifted but productive and sure to be published. I don't know if the attraction was his looks, his poetic genius, or something else entirely that made him so intriguing. He was also quiet and slipped under most people's radar on campus because he wanted it that way. To those of us who knew him even a little, he seemed charismatic, but he deliberately tried to disguise himself, slip away from anyone's eyes.

Let me explain my obsession with him. I was used to guys being drawn to me, so when Michael seemed perpetually preoccupied, even disinterested, I was hooked. I wasn't exactly pursuing him, but he intrigued me even when I was still going out with Jason. I realize I haven't mentioned Jason yet, but I'll get to him later. See, Jason's just not that important to me anymore. But Michael? He is dead and he has somehow, bewilderingly, become crucial.

What is also unforgivable for me is that we were on the verge of something. I intuited that with a little more time, Michael and I would have fallen in love. This is not an entirely rational claim, but I was sure of the idea that we were at a point where love was an inevitability even in the face of obstacles, Gould being one of them. After class, one afternoon, Gould asked Michael to stay. I hesitated and stared at them for an instant before Michael suggested I join them. Gould looked surprised at first, but then he seemed to accept the invitation with graciousness, even motioning for me to come with them as they left together.

"Well, I'm in the very good company of my two best students," said Gould, using unusual flattery. My head was bursting. Somehow, miraculously, I had been invited into the inner circle, and a tight one at that.

"I assume you two know each other well, but then, perhaps I shouldn't make such assumptions," Gould said, smiling the type of smile that could easily be misinterpreted as pleasant.

"Yes," said Michael quickly before I could protest. "We're friends."

I didn't want to look as surprised as I did, but then attempted to cover my initial shock with a knowing demeanor. "We read each other's poems."

Gould stopped walking and studied our faces as if he had already discerned our white lies. "Then you must share with me your analysis of one another's work."

We were standing in the cold, and I was afraid my nose was going to run and ruin everything. I shivered noticeably and then said, "Michael's work is far more sophisticated than mine."

"You're cold," Michael said, looking concerned. "Let's move on."

"Yes, indeed," said Gould, "but I would have to caution you that compliments are not analysis as you well know. I advise against close friends reading each other's work. The danger is, of course, unearned praise and worse, mistaking the work of a friend for something of value, sophisticated or not."

Michael's face was already red from the cold, but he looked stricken. "I think we are more than fair in our analysis," I said, defending myself and Michael's poetry.

"Well, we will see, won't we," said Gould, turning to face us again.

He stared at us with a strange smile for an uncomfortable interval. The look on his face appeared to be one of jealousy, but that made no sense to me. "I'm sorry," he said abruptly, "but I thought I would have more time. I realize that I have to get to a meeting. Perhaps another day, Michael." Then he walked back in the direction from which we came.

Michael and I stood there stupidly shivering and looking miserable for another instant.

"I'm sorry if I spoiled your…"

"No, no, don't apologize. He's moody like that. He might have done exactly the same thing to me even if we were alone. I'm glad you came anyway. Let's go get something warm to drink."

We did—get something to drink, but just when I thought Michael might invite me to his apartment or ask me out more formally or even lean over and kiss me, he got up and said, "I'll see you later," then hurried on his way just as I thought we were starting something again. I could never tell what exactly was standing in his way. For some reason, I thought the barrier might be Gould.

That day, months later, in Gleason, he didn't wave from where he was seated in the library, tucked away in a well-lit corner near a large window. Surrounded by stacks of books, Michael nearly had to look over the top to see me, but he nodded his head in recognition, almost smiled. I wanted to go over and ask what he was working on, but those actions seemed intrusive. Instead, I headed to my own area of Gleason, a great place to study because this library was open day and night. Michael practically lived there. He could be found in any of the campus libraries, but Gleason was his favorite, I think. That semester, I was there all the time too.

Was Michael a close friend? No. I didn't know him well enough to consider him one, but I unreasonably liked him a lot, had read his poems before classes on many occasions while we waited. As I said, we were on the verge of something, becoming more than acquaintances. Sometimes, he would ask to see my latest work first. More often, I would ask to see what he was working on, and most of the time, he shared his poetry willingly.

"Well, what do you think?"

"They are amazing." I didn't have to tell a white lie or condescend to him; his work really was that good.

"No, that's not a comment. I don't want your praise, but your critical opinion." He sounded like Gould in that moment, and I wondered if he was aware of it.

Michael was forever seeking to improve his writing, dissatisfied with good enough, even very good. If I didn't offer an honest critique in his opinion, he wouldn't offer his poems the next time.

On one occasion, I cheated by reading over his shoulder. That's right, I looked at one of his open notebooks while standing behind him. If he had turned around at that moment he probably would have found me creepy, but another student loudly dropped his book bag and I slipped over to a seat. His latest poem reminded me of a painting with which I was familiar. I wanted to tell him that but never did, just one of the many things I regret regarding my actions around him. He had read some of my work, too, but he was always kinder than he demanded from his readers.

"Your poem makes me think of the work of Louise Glück."

I was a fan of Glück's poetry, so I smiled, but then I wondered whether or not Michael meant the comparison as a compliment. "And you like Glück's work?"

"Glick," he corrected my pronunciation of the German. "Very much. She is not given enough credit."

"Wasn't she a recent Poet Laureate?"

"Yes," he said smiling, "but I was thinking of credit from Gould." We both knew Gould was the ultimate arbiter.

Still, I speculated as to whether or not Michael was trying to tell me my work was not original.

Michael and I had at least two other things in common, however. In addition to writing poetry, we'd shared the experience of being humiliated in Dr. Roald Gould's 'Construction of Authorship' class—cringe-worthy stuff, even though the savant had chosen us as graduate assistants.

Dr. Gould hit Michael on more than one occasion with his well-placed barbs, and I recollected wanting to deflect those arrows, charge across the room and stand up for him but, of course, I did nothing. No one did. Somehow, Michael, who had been one of Gould's favorites, had suddenly earned Gould's disdain. This academician ruled his classroom like a dictator, and metaphoric assassination always hung in the air. By the time graduate school came around, we weren't so much impressed or awestruck anymore as needy and willing to do anything to get that grade. Poetry was the goal even more than an escape. We had to finish with the required grade point and the time of getting on with our lives was approaching. I summed this up with Michael, too, but he seemed less concerned with his grades than the rest of us. For some reason, that too, was impressive. He also appeared indifferent to praise, even finding accolades repellant.

I asked him about the relative value of acclamation as we walked toward class, "I still feel the need to have people validate my work by saying something positive."

He nodded in understanding but then reminded me of something David Foster Wallace said: "'The more people think you're really great, actually the bigger the fear of being a fraud is.' at least, that's what I think he said. Anyway, it's how I remember it, and those words have stuck with me."

"Well, I'm feeling a little fraudulent myself." We laughed, then stopped suddenly. I thought he was going to kiss me at that moment, but he didn't. Instead, he brushed a curl from his eye and took my hand for an instant. "I will see you soon," he said before disappearing.

There is a period of time after someone dies, that the idea of their loss does not take hold. Unreality was the weird place I inhabited for a couple of weeks after they found Michael. Everything and everyone seemed to be moving around me as if there was no change in the atmosphere, but I could feel death keenly and wanted to shake everything around me. Wake up! Don't you all realize what has happened? His death changed everything. Nothing was the same or would ever be again.

Although Michael is gone, I still see his eyes. Did I mention his eyes? They were beautiful with lashes that made even me envious. His hair was slightly curly and rather long. He was a little out-of-step with current trends; still wore glasses that looked broken, at least crooked, but he exuded the kind of cool that comes from knowing yourself and not caring what anyone else thinks. Mostly, he wore sweatshirts, the same gray one over and over. The old pullover wasn't even a U of R shirt, but a non-descript one. He always wore an Army green wool jacket over his sweatshirt. I once told him I liked his coat, trying to make small talk. He shrugged and said it had been his father's but didn't elaborate beyond that.

I tried flirting in the most sophisticated way I could manage, but none of my charm really seemed to work with Michael. Once in a while, he would take the seat next to mine when there were plenty of empty ones around us. I didn't want to read too much into this simple act. Then one afternoon, Michael sat down and asked, "What are you working on?" I had my journal open, as well as my computer for class notes.

"Oh, hi. Do you mean in class?"

He shook his head and let go of a slight smile. "No, no. Your own poetry."

"I'm not that good," I said, defensive on some account, probably because I suspected that Michael was about one-hundred times better, based on comments by Gould and others in the class.

"Relative term," he answered. "Would you like to show me anything?"

"Yes!" I stated, entirely too enthusiastically, then tried to calm down and shoved my journal toward him.

He opened the pages and began reading. Professor Gould started the lecture, and I nearly forgot Michael was still reading my work until I glanced over and saw his head buried in the pages of my little book.

"Mr. Lawler, apparently there is something more fascinating for you than the subject of today's lecture. Could you give the class a summary of—."

"No, I will not be able to do that. Excuse me." Gould had called him out directly, something I don't think he'd ever done before with Michael, and I felt guilty. The way you would feel if you got your brother in trouble for something you had done, only I didn't have a brother and didn't think I had really done anything wrong.

"And Miss Goodwin, you appear to be guilty of something or you need to go to the infirmary. Your face has turned an unhealthy crimson." I tried shrinking in my chair to the extent possible, touching my face and aware of its blotchy redness.

At the end of class, Michael reached for my hand and covered it momentarily with his own. "These are beautiful. Thank you," and then he left abruptly. Gould was moving toward me. By the time Gould reached me, Michael had exited the room.

"In the future, Advena, I expect you will pay attention in class and perhaps sit in a less distracting position. This is not some silly dating game show, and I assume you will take your studies—and this class—more seriously."

"I," I stammered to explain something, but Gould had turned his magnanimous attention on Craig, praising his intelligent questions from the discussion. Craig was so surprised that he became even more effusive about the lecture, and I turned and walked out.

What did Michael's gesture mean? My hand was still warm. It was tempting to read too much into it. He hadn't really shown physical attraction to me before. He didn't seem attracted to men either, so I decided he was either psychically wounded or uninterested in people, at least sexually. No, wait, that's not true. He was a keen observer of people, took obsessive notes, but he was not particularly predisposed to interact with them. When I stop to analyze it, Michael always seemed preoccupied with events or concepts more important than whatever was going on around him at the time. And for a short time, even if only for a few days, Michael had been preoccupied with my poems or me, a feeling I would not forget.

Suicide? Maybe I shouldn't have been surprised. He did keep his own best company, but that act and the young man who scribbled lines of poetry in the margins of every book he owned did not register with me. I don't mean that he was ever cheerful. It's just that a lot of the really sensitive people I knew had talked about suicide as viability at some point in their lives, but only Michael appeared to have acted on it. What caught me and wouldn't let go was the fact he seemed so certain of one thing and that was his creative talent. The ease with which he crafted new poems made a lot of us a bit jealous of him.

After my queasiness passed that day in the book store, I just felt sadness and this profound sense of being lost. I even had to rethink how to get back to my apartment. Sam offered to walk me back, but I shrugged her off for no cause other than I couldn't bear anyone's company for a while.

Then I started to wonder about the unnaturalness of his death. Suicide is always unnatural, but hanging in a stairwell? Details floated in like refuse on the river that ran beside River Campus. Andrew said they broke his door down. Why did the cops show up at his door that morning? Who had reported anything to them? Michael didn't seem to have a lot of friends at least on campus, but maybe his family thought something was wrong. I wondered why I didn't realize that he was in trouble when he didn't come to class. Then I thought about how stupid I was, as if I knew him at all. Mostly what I thought I perceived about him was out of my own fantasizing.

Later, all of the grad students in our program were talking about his death, and the number of times these two details were reiterated; suicide by hanging and locked door seemed to give Andrew's story more credibility although probably all of the details and the telling came from just one account, Andrew's, the sophomore who had managed to gain some level of notoriety on campus simply because he was a witness to a death.

~ * ~

Why the locked door? Michael lived off campus, but he struck me as someone who scarcely thought about locking his door. He never even closed the door to class when he was last to enter and he must have known how much Gould hated that careless indifference. I always figured that Michael left every door open because he had forgotten to close it, let alone lock it.

"Mr. Lawler, I see you are fashionably late again; but you might, at least, close the door as a gesture of some civility toward the rest of us." Gould talked that way so we were used to it, except with Michael. Gould didn't treat Michael like the rest of us until then. Like I said before, things had changed between them shortly before Michael's death.

Michael typically sat in the back of the room, but one evening, he sat next to me again. I was too surprised to say much of anything. I felt him though, even looked to my left with this kind of movement of my eyes but not my head and saw that he was also looking at me. Then the kingfish at the front of the room called on someone in his intimidating manner and the moment was broken. I thought maybe Michael would continue to sit near me and we could begin talking about our work and interests, but nothing happened that way.

My experience with Michael was that he was a mystery and a compelling one. If I thought about him, I dreamed we were riding the edge of some unseen current and had just noticed it. Then he died.

The brief news account offered no illumination on Michael's death. This absence of detail caused my imagination to lift me out of melancholy to a keen sense of problem. There is not a long leap from suicide to murder in the mind of one already inclined to believe that such a thing could happen. I began to reflect on all of the murder mysteries that used the locked room as a trope—Poe to Joseph Conrad, typically the room containing a secret passage until Conan Doyle's brilliant misdirection puzzles. As macabre as it sounds, I began wondering if there was a secret passage in Michael's apartment that police had failed to notice. Maybe they weren't detectives at all, just street cops who happened on the scene.

Suppose another had been in the room, had killed Michael and made homicide look like suicide? I tried to insert some counterpoint to my line of questions. Was murder really possible? I could believe that the police never sent an investigator. Of course, they wouldn't have. Michael's hanging would look like suicide by definition. Why would the police suspect anything at odds with the obvious? So, for no discernable reason other than a gut feeling, I began to divine that something wasn't right about any of this, at least what everyone else assumed to be factual and not simply morbid speculation. Cops may have closed the case, but I was just beginning to open my own.

~ * ~

Only a year later, while I waited inside a locked room, I realized that the murder mystery of Michael Lawler was neither about misdirection nor secret passages. But what took me that long way across doubt to certainty was the separation of an ocean, further loss, and fractured time.

Chapter Five
Engaging in Weird Conversations

Shortly before Michael's death I had been agonizing over nothing more important than my dissertation topic, even though that discussion was still some time off. Trying to figure out what to write about was the kind of thing that made me want to shave my head, but I only chopped off my long blonde hair to just above my ears.

Well, my anxiousness wasn't just a reaction to a pending dissertation. I had recently ended things with Jason and Bill was being especially difficult, cutting off my regular supply of cash. Everything was coming to an end—all those long years of schooling. Really, I was kind of a wreck even before Michael's death. Within a few moments after my decisive act, however, I burst out crying. "It's all gone," I yelled to no one, then scooped up my locks and tossed them away. I even walked the waste basket down to the dumpster. I also purged many articles of clothing for no good rationale other than they no longer made me feel comfortable.

After I threw away my hair I felt guilty, because, of course, I should have donated the locks to a cancer patient undergoing chemo. A couple of hours later, I actually went down to the trash bins to see if I could take it back, but the bag got ripped open and my hair was mixed with old coffee grinds, leftover spaghetti and foul-smelling stuff I couldn't identify.

Of course, I adjusted and then dyed my hair blue. Yet another transformation, but I did not know where the disguise would take me. People told me my new style looked "cute," except Gould. He was typically sarcastic and blunt in assessment.

"Are you trying out for the part of a drug-addled boy or slightly deranged sprite in one of our dramatic productions?"

Classmates laughed uncomfortably, relieved Gould's negative attention was on someone else. Rather than unify us against him, our professor had a way of creating animosity all around him, so that classmates never really liked or trusted each other. We were like a class made up of ambitious point guards all trying out for one position on the varsity basketball team. Sam, to her credit, did shoot me a quick, somewhat sympathetic look before burying her head in her notebook again.

"Neither," I said, so quietly I doubted anyone heard me.

Gould merely went on with his lecture after thoroughly embarrassing me in the Coliseum, as I called his class in Dewey Hall. Professor Gould was either your favorite or least liked academician. Most often, he had been both at some point in time. When he was shining on you, you felt important and valued, but then there were all the other days in the semester. For a five-minute span of my academic career, I was a favorite of Gould's. At least, I thought so at the time. Looking back later, I have assessed that period rather differently.

Michael was one of Gould's favorites for much longer, at least for two semesters. We didn't talk about it, and now I wish I had asked Michael what happened between them. I wished I had asked him all kinds of things. I wish I had kissed him. I wish I had read all of the poems in his notebooks and then talked all night to him about ideas found in those abstractions, signifiers, symbols widening, deepening the world on a page. I wish we had made love.

Fear over a dissertation and bad haircut were miles from where I would go. In retrospect, those worries appear silly, mundane, but then everything was transformed after Michael's death. Everything made me sob easily for a while—even commercials on television, and, as I said, I didn't even know him that well. I wanted to know him better, but he was not easy to engage with in light conversation. He was mostly a mystery to me. I couldn't imagine how his parents must have felt about his suicide. In considering his parents, I started wondering where Michael's friends and family were. He must have had some somewhere.

No one came forward to publicly mourn on campus. Michael's was one of the quietest, tragic deaths I had ever known. Maybe his parents were as private as he was. I tried to imagine the scene in the President's office where Mr. and Mrs. Lawler sat and nodded their heads as they were told what little the police had revealed. They would visit the police station next and get no further before making final arrangements for his body, all the while saying little, only looking grief stricken. They must have loved him deeply. Was he an only child? His father must have been in the Army since he had given his son his old military coat. Why was I assuming the coat was a gift? Still, I concluded that they must have been close or Michael would not have wrapped himself in it every day.

Naturally, the University of Rochester didn't want undue publicity, so Michael's death was downplayed almost to the extent of complete absence of information. Rather than mention him as a graduate student, the discrete news report merely stated that he was a city resident living near campus and taking courses at the university, as if he didn't really exist for anyone except me and Gould and, of course, his parents. Where were his parents?

Sam said hardly anything to me after that day in the book store, as if she didn't want to bring back bad memories. If I thought we might become friends at some point, I tossed that notion aside fairly quickly. Gould also said nothing, but Michael's absence could be felt. The fact that Gould never mentioned the death of his graduate assistant made the omission only more obvious that he, too, was struggling, or was he not struggling? What was wrong with this man we had all idolized at one time or another? Our teacher came across as oddly indifferent to Michael's death, at least to me.

I didn't attend class for a few days after Michael's death, so I don't know exactly what Gould did or didn't say in the immediate aftermath. After several days of doubt and restless sadness I tried to think about other things, but Michael Lawler kept coming back. The young man who lived in relative poverty on the edge of campus and social groups, keeping to himself, writing furiously. Everyone else appeared to be able to compartmentalize Michael's death as suicide and move away from the event, far from the life of the young man.

For me, however, Michael returned as an interesting, intelligent, and living being, becoming an animated shadow that walked and talked with me far more than his mortal self ever had.

"Good-morning, Michael. Could you please tell me why you were never interested in sleeping with me?"

"I'm sorry, I just never thought about you that way. I see you cut your hair."

"Why not? Do you think—I mean; did you think I was unattractive?"

"No. I didn't find you attractive or unattractive."

"Well, that's worse, Michael." Our weird hypothetical conversations always went something like that; highly unproductive and cut off by the fact that he was dead.

They only came up because we never had the opportunity to have many intriguing conversations in real life. I had fantasized about Michael for over a year, part of the time when I was with another man, so I felt guilty even for thinking about him. Later, I just couldn't seem to find a way to get Michael to notice me, or at least that was what I thought at the time. Then before anything could be worked out or even attempted, he ended up dead. Supposedly, the act was a suicide.

Artists, writers and suicides are often considered to be a fairly natural fit, but they never are really. Michael could not have killed himself; he was a talented writer who understood what he wanted to do and how to go about it. Between the poles of a dead student and live mentor, I was about to find not simply attraction and repulsion but a force I had no idea how to control.

I will come back to Michael, obsessively return, but first I had to work things out to the extent I could at least leave my room again. I have a habit of backing up before being able to go forward. I'll start again with my fairly disastrous, dissertation consultation with my professor, advisor, mentor, Dr. Roald Gould. I'd had an appointment for over two weeks, but cancelled twice before arriving at his door.

I began steamrolling through my correspondences with someone who appeared to be a willing, even if, an unaccepting audience. At least, I discerned that he was well-versed in these works, and I didn't have to slow down to create explanations.

"Although there is no Cullen character exactly in *Light*, there is an analogous one in Bogdan, Jestor's employer, who never appears in the narrative yet is obsessively mentioned by the mistreated Jestor. Cullen and Bogdan are characters that are never substantialized, and Kieron and Jestor are constantly mistreated 'offstage.'"

"You are aware that *Light* is a novel, and therefore stage directions are irrelevant?"

I wanted to stop but decided to continue as planned. Maybe he was playing along and enjoyed my discoveries after all. "The settings are so purposefully vague yet symbolic that the actual stage in *Nightfall* is also a stage in life just as we find in *Light*."

"Breadcrumbs," Roald said, bemused as I took a breath.

"I beg your pardon?"

"Did it occur to you that perhaps Mctigue was leaving breadcrumbs for his readers, even for Baczkowski, to follow?"

I suddenly appreciated that I had come across that phrase before and realized I had been unintentionally quoting Dr. Roald Gould ever since I first took one of his classes.

Yet, I wasn't quite sure what he wanted me to do with the interruption, so I continued with my notes, as planned. "Yes, of course, Mctigue could have been leading the way for Baczkowski, but why? There's much more," I protested intent on getting to the end of my spiraling discoveries. "Both of the works exist within an intentional insipidness in which place is innocuous or largely irrelevant except, or even, the country road. Mctigue's Rian meanders on a country road while Jestor and Wislawa are also walking on a country road, asking questions about where they are as the novel opens."

"So, is the commonality of a country road enough to confirm your ideas about plagiarism?"

"Not plagiarism. Something I will get to. The tropes, too, appear identical: 'May I fart?' from the mouth of Wislawa, then there is Kieron's lament, 'You farted, and I can still smell it.' Then, 'What do you want? Want? You must want something? No, nothing. Nothing? Nothing.' The word nothing is echoed obsessively in *Light* and *Nightfall* to emphasize an existential theme of a hopeless search while arresting even the possibility of motion or continued ideation."

"I'm wondering if other authors have used the words fart and nothing?" Gould was smiling but not in a reassuring way.

I was, as yet, undeterred. "Rian and Kieron examine a dry riverbed in *Nightfall*, while Jestor and Wislawa, 'think about this empty stream,' and like their forebears in Mctigue's play, they are not sure if they have already seen it: 'Were we here before? Was the river running?'"

"'Like' their forebears?" He emphasizes and discharges my word error which I notice only after he has repeated it.

I nod my head, accepting error. "Excuse me," I correct myself but continue, "Trickles of water in Act II in a formerly dry stream seem to proffer evidence or clues of something to Rian and Kieron although they are unable to articulate even the possibility of what they are seeking. *Light* is framed around the concept of searching for clues that emerge, ultimately, as meaningless, from an empty river bed to a room that appears to be separating from the rest of the house."

"And I imagine you feel as if you are seeing connections that determine what exactly? That Baczkowski owes the entirety of his novel to Mctigue? That they both should hide in shame before Shakespeare who gave us all of these tropes, every one of their words, the roughly 3,000 new uses or new words in our language, all of these themes and symbols. So, what point are you making exactly?"

I was so frustrated with him that I blurted out, "You're a sniveling rat." It did catch him off guard, but only momentarily. I'd never seen anyone quicker on his feet than my former mentor.

"Ah, yes, *Light* gives us a similar phrase to the one Ersine uses on Kilroy."

"'Minor rat!' he yells in *Nightfall*," I say almost triumphantly, "and then there is, the word repetition in Mctigue's play as well as in *Light*, both ending their works with the word fallen. And," I add, hesitating again.

He stopped me with a sweeping motion of his hand.

Chapter Six
T.S. Eliot is Speaking

I was a Roald Gould devotee for a fairly lengthy period of time. Although I'm not making excuses, I will say that I was not alone. Gould cultivated a following based as much upon his personality as his brilliance or his teachings. I distinctly recall the first time I heard him reading before I had him as a professor in class. Poetry readings are not like rock concerts, not a big draw and free of charge, but those who attend listen carefully and are predisposed to root for the poet. The reading is, however, a big event for the poet and his or her audience. That evening, every student and faculty member, as well as the few community members in the audience, seemed a little in love with the poet on stage even before they came.

He was the myth personified: poet at the podium looking exactly like we envisioned, his shock of thick, graying hair curly and tossed about as he spoke. He moved his hands gracefully, his gestures full of expression like his voice. He seemed taller not simply because he was on a stage, but I am sure my vantage point has changed considerably since I was nineteen and seated before him. And he was smart. I don't know where some men ever got the idea that playing dumb was attractive. Professor Gould struck me as appearing like an English Lord who had left his wealth behind and gone off to become a sea captain, winds rising while he fearlessly gave the orders, the ship's sails responding to his calm but forceful commands.

Beginning with "Interiority," he performed and recited, rather than simply read, poems from his latest book. He gave credit to his inspirations, among them, he said, was Neruda who suggested, "the imminent gift of the possible turns wholly toward silence." I took notes that evening although I intended just to go for the pleasure of it. The Neruda quotation came from "Soliloquy in the Waves," said Gould. Later, of course, those generous credits would strike me as ironic, but at the time, I thought his conscience, his magnanimity were apparent to all of us.

At the end of the reading, Gould stopped and let his words sink in and take hold. The long pause, while extended, was not at all awkward. Then he said, "There is always room for at least two truths," a quotation attributed to Mitchell and found in Colum McCann's novel *Transatlantic*, he informed us. He smiled wisely and left the stage with a practiced gait, our applause raucous rather than dignified. Oddly, he did not reappear for an encore, as we expected. I remember looking around at audience members who were looking at one another quizzically, betraying momentary confusion before everyone dispersed. If they were seeking him out for a conversation after the reading, they would be disappointed.

He was more myth than man, until he fell in my eyes and became a horribly flawed mortal. The first time I had Gould as a professor, he quoted Shakespeare at opportune moments and sometimes when the relevance was lost on the rest of us. There was always an idea amusing him, however, as if he only needed an echo chamber to be pleased with his own thoughts and words.

One afternoon, a student arrived late, something we tried never to do in his class and Gould stopped his lecture and turned to the rest of the class, saying, "'But I will delve one yard below their mines, and blow them at the moon.' *Hamlet*," he said, before returning to the topic at hand. I often went back to that moment and wondered exactly who Gould wished to annihilate. Now, I suspect the target was all of us, his inferiors.

Looking back on that seemingly innocuous encounter over "The Love Song of J. Alfred Prufrock" in class, I have thought about why Gould quoted Eliot, why he inserted those words into the discussion, interrupted our train of thought or what should have been part of the planned lesson that day. Really, Gould was always in favor of disturbing the universe, and his cynicism was as pointed as Eliot's in that passage.

After class, Gould asked me how well I apprehended Eliot's poetry, and I could not help myself, bragging that I was acquainted with Eliot's literature well enough to quote sufficiently but not fluently. He laughed at

30

my immodest pretense. There was a long period of my life when I truly believed that I wanted to disturb the universe. Clearly, I had forgotten about Eliot's advisory following that braggadocio. In the days after I had relished my short-lived favor with Gould, I found excuses to stay after class, come early, meet him at his office to discuss literature. I told him my story of saving a stack of poetry books from my high school library's recycling bin.

"They were cleaning off shelves to make room for new technology, the librarian told me, and there in the refuse pile were the works of T.S. Eliot, Pablo Neruda, Kay Ryan, Emily Dickinson, and Wallace Stevens."

"What a strange grouping, but you were in rather good company," Gould said, amused. "Personally, I have never cared for the pedestrian style of Kay Ryan, but she is well recognized for her craft. And, more surprising still, no Sylvia Plath? I would have figured you for a Plath devotee, did the librarians decide to keep Plath for the melodrama?"

I was glad Ryan could not hear his insult, and I backed away from defending her poetry, feeling a bit like a Judas. Not quite sure what to make of the "Plath devotee" comment, I could only offer, "Stevens is my favorite," I blurted out for some reason, hoping that the choice would please Gould. "But I do appreciate Plath's poetry, very much so."

"The librarian clearly chose to excise some of the best. Which Stevens' poem is your 'favorite'?"

Simply the way he emphasized the word favorite made me realize my mistake. Poetry was not a fan club. I felt very silly but pushed ahead. "Peter Quince at the Clavier," I said confidently, feeling that I had chosen something with which most students were largely unfamiliar. I leaped at a few lines from the poem that I recalled about beauty's placeholder in the mind.

Gould was as much of a showoff as his eager students, I realized later, but at the time I was deeply impressed that he followed my memorized lines from Stevens' poem with lines of Stevens' that he, too, knew by heart. "And those lines you have memorized mean what to you?"

"They recall Keats' 'Ode on a Grecian Urn' but seem to subvert that poem, as well, with the idea that our immortality lies in our flesh not the imagination."

Gould nodded. "Keats, too? I take it you are far more interested in

31

poetry than in the teaching of it?"

"I'm afraid I am."

Shrugging, Gould said, "Naturally. You will have to earn a living, so don't be too hard on teaching. You like the feel of books, then?"

"I know you can probably find all of their poems online, but to have their books in my hands…"

"It's not quite the same experience, is it?" We were walking and talking, leaving the classroom and the building, and I felt as if I had finally met someone who understood me, who could challenge me. I was aware of other students looking on enviously at our casual intimacy. Walking and talking with my favorite professor in those days was akin to hanging out with your favorite rock star. "So, what happened to Neruda and Ryan in your illusory scene after the library rescue?"

"I brought them home that evening and Neruda offered Emily the couch, but she demurred, preferring a window seat to look out at the moon." Gould stopped and waited, curious as to where I was going with this fiction. I knew the risk, but I had been waiting a long time just to share my wild love of literature. "Kay sat on the arm of an old wing chair, and Wallace Stevens finally settled into the deep recesses of my best leather chair by the fireplace."

"And Eliot?"

"Eliot said he preferred to stand."

"He would," Gould laughed. "What then?"

"I suggested we read each other's poems, mine, of course, being left out in the cold. Neruda read Ryan's 'Almost Without Surface,' and Ryan read Stevens' 'The Idea of Order at Key West.'"

"Perhaps his best," said Gould, entertained.

"Eliot read several of Neruda's unnamed poems from *El mar y las campanas. The Sea and the Bells.*"

"You know Spanish then?"

"A little," I confessed, not telling him that I was very good with languages, picking them up easily.

"Be careful in translating because confusion may result due to intonation, so important to meaning. Do you know Neruda's real name?"

"No."

"He was christened Ricardo Eliecer Neftali Reyes Basoalto at birth, but Neruda is so much easier to fix in the mind."

"Oh." I suddenly felt young and stupid again. "How do you do that?" At the time, I was genuinely curious. Only later did his insertion of Neruda's real name strike me as proof that Gould was revealing his own insecurity, showing off to a student, putting her back in her assigned place.

"Recall the name of a poet?"

"Quote at will."

"Poetry and language are my areas. You will not see me fluently quote scientific articles." Both of us knew that his talent was remarkable, and I allowed his comment to pass without further remark. "But you must tell me the rest of your visiting poets story."

"We warmed the bread and uncorked the wine. Strangers at first, we got to know one another through our words."

"And lack of inhibitions, I suspect," Gould said smiling.

"Eliot and Neruda laughed at my Spanish pronunciations, a condition due to the relief of being rescued, as well as the wine. Kay fell asleep before the last poems of the evening were read and never heard Dickinson recite her new friend Kay's 'Chinese Foot Chart.'"

"Intricate little poem," said Gould. "You have her fall asleep before her own poem is read—how perfect."

"I grew tired, too, and slumped over with my head leaning on my hand, dreaming of Ryan's 'Boars of Mercy.'"

"Ah, you like the punning," he interjected.

"When I woke sometime in the pre-dawn hours, I looked for my campions who were all soundly sleeping, having given themselves in abundance of language, except the concise Emily, who brought in tea for me and sipped while I tried to defend the librarian."

"'Things shouldn't be so hard," said Kay, waking in the middle of my weak defense.

"'We are waiting," said Neruda, hoarsely but exacting as I turned on lights and handed out croissants."

"Oh, good. Imperative that you fed them and offered libations once again," said Gould. "But what about Eliot? He is much too quiet in your story. He would demand to be at the center of it, you know."

"Oh, I'd forgotten him momentarily because he'd gone out for new supplies."

"Eliot as the errand boy. No, I'm afraid not."

We both laughed. I felt connected.

My silly tale amused Gould and allowed me access and favor that few of his students received. More importantly, however, my imagined closeness with him blinded me for a long time to Gould's increasing menace and cruelty.

Chapter Seven
After Noticing Jestor's Carrot Red Hair

When you have read a book multiple times, the words seem as if they are coming from you, as if you happened to be the author all along. Aha, I thought when I came to the phrase describing Jestor's carrot red hair. There is the repeated image again. These correspondences were not so much plagiarism as bread crumbs, leaving a trail to follow, so I entered this forest without reservation. Maybe I should have been more cautious. Before I get to Gould's dismissal of my work in earnest, however, perhaps I should go back further, not so far as the moment of my birth but the one where I start trying to unravel mysteries.

I blame my fascination with literary mysteries on my English teacher parents, not only for their genetics and chosen occupation but the name they chose for me. Who gives a baby girl the name Advena? I had long since shortened my name to Vena, but whenever anyone wanted to be formal with me, Advena came back. They would have me forever an outsider. There is only one of the conative meanings of my surname that I feel attached to and that is "bird," this word flying in from the concept of migrant.

It was only years later, that I discovered that the fight over my name became one of the touchstones that led to my parents' divorce. Bill later confessed that he wanted to name me Mary.

"How utterly common," Greta told Bill, who unwisely told me.

Long before adults' awareness of my explorations, I traveled without leaving the walls of my parents' little house in Pharsalia, the town's name a return to that historic, old world battleground already fomenting seeds of rebellion in contemporary upstate New York. My parents—Greta and Bill—had their own civil war going on for years before divorcing in the aftermath, of course. Greta married again immediately—this time a stock broker—and seemed much happier moving to New York City, but Bill wound up in a series of disastrous liaisons with women who confounded him.

I lived with Bill and his parade of eccentric women friends until I was seventeen, and then I was out and on my own. Well, mostly on my own. Bill did continue to help me out. All that time with my father, and I can't recall so much as a genuine conversation about anything more than the weather and my grades. I never saw Greta. She told me she simply wasn't the maternal type. Always polite on the phone, she was impatient to hang up as soon as we said "hello." She had a very busy schedule, and "you must understand, I never intended to have children."

It's obvious I was never really comfortable with either of my parents, or, to be more precise, they were never very comfortable being parents. But that was years ago and miles apart. I have traveled far from home—at least psychologically— and found myself in one uncomfortable place after another, always the stranger even in the middle of a party. But I was at home in literature.

"What have you discovered, Advena?" Gould asked with his derision apparent, using my full name and not the shortened form Vena that my friends, acquaintances, and other professors used. Typical of Dr. Gould to ask for something and then tear apart your efforts when you thought you had arrived. He kept me so unbalanced that I never knew how to refer to him or what he really thought. Sometimes he was personal and paternal with me, at others, not so much. If the notion didn't sound so bizarre, I'd swear he was occasionally flirting when we were alone.

"Baczkowski's *Light* is *Nightfall* in another genre."

He shook his head then said, "Are you suggesting simple plagiarism?" He laughs but not in an amused sort of manner. "You are aware that one was a Nobel Laureate and the other an International Book Award winner. I'm waiting." One thing I had learned was not to keep Gould waiting. His gaze on you felt icy and hot at the same time. He, however, always looked eminently comfortable in his rumpled, light wool gray suit, the crisp white collared shirt without a tie, and the gray cashmere neck scarf that was always draped loosely around his neck. I conjectured that most older men would kill for his head of hair, definitely the curly wild but full head of a poet. He was famous and aloof, known by most on campus but indifferent to others. With a few of us, however, he decided to bring us into his intellectual light.

Instantly, that movie *Citizen Above Suspicion* came into my head, but I didn't know quite what to do with it. What was I accusing him of with that line of thought? I proceeded with the evidence I had already gathered. I thought he would be impressed with the details I had gathered, so I proceeded to lay them at his feet, rattling off my notes quickly before I started to lose confidence.

"Correlations between *Nightfall* and *Light* are more than pronounced from the first pages of both texts in which one of two male characters says to the other, 'Get out,' only to follow with a pervasive disorientation and lack of movement in largely plotless works. In Mctigue's play and Baczkowski's novel, we have two men walking in sync yet out of step with the universe, Baczkowski even employing part of that phrase in his dialogue. 'Get out,' they state again and again, yet neither of their characters can bare to be without the other."

"Thin." Gould shakes his head and is ready to dismiss me.

"There's more," I protest. "Scenes and acts are only illusions of movement here. Thematically, these two literary works suggest an inability to make meaning out of a chaotic universe, with anxiety and displacement, arbitrariness of language becoming the existential joke on humanity. Mctigue and later Baczkowski, or perhaps the other way around, proposed the unlikeliness of any freedom for their characters, or us, for that matter."

"The other way around? Are you aware of which writer produced his masterpiece first? Finding out is simply a matter of referring to recorded dates."

"But the dates don't necessarily provide the answer," I said, taking the risk. "When a literary work is published is not necessarily when the work was written or conceived."

"Really." He meant the word with a period and not a question mark.

I was determined not to be stopped by his sarcasm mid-stream.

"There is unsettling amnesia or aphasia, actual wording in Kilroy's monologue in *Nightfall* and part of the dialogue in *Light*: 'I've forgotten.'"

"I don't recall that," Roald says sarcastically, but at least he was now engaged, playing with language, too, the way he did in class that always made us strain to pick out doublets, puns, or other wordplay.

"There are also one-to-one character correspondences between Mctigue's Kilroy and Erskine as master and slave; 'my slave wishes to speak,' to Jestor in *Light*: 'I beat him like a slave.'" I couldn't help suddenly feeling like Gould's slave as his graduate assistant, an analogy that was not likely lost on him either. "Yes," I wanted to say, "Your slave wishes to speak," but I held back.

"Slave and master," he says out loud, musing on the subject as if reading my mind, "and yet, Jestor is beaten, not Wislawa. Perhaps you have lost track of the characters in your effort to force correspondence."

"No, not at all. These correspondences jump out at readers." I push on, "But the inversions work like the titles of their works." I am excited now and have to calm down before I betray my naiveté. "Wislawa and Jestor correspond to Rian and Kieron in Mctigue's play. The put-upon, misused Jestor is another Kieron who is continually brutalized offstage."

"Miss Goodwin, please try to gather your thoughts into a few coherent statements and begin again later." Cut off. Time and again, Gould stopped me from trying to articulate the connections I found as if he did not want to see them.

Chapter Eight
Observing the Symmetry

"Structurally?" Gould asks, and he expects an answer.

I thought for an instant that I had won him over, and he was prompting me not to forget all of the correlations I had discovered related to frameworks. "Mctigue's play and Baczkowski's novel were written in two, symmetrical parts. In addition, both works are thematically framed around questions that are prolific in these texts. Yet questions follow questions rather than answers. Repetition becomes a structural element, as well, the literature operating through the use of this device, not to propel action but to hold position. Baczkowski's Jestor and the narrator Wislawa are 'stuck' on the seemingly nonsensical 'tooth' and then 'nothing,' just as Rian and Kieron do nothing, their repetitions are a tedious but brutal game."

Gould sighs deeply as if tired of yet another foolish student.

"There is the rope," I say, growing desperate. "The rope and the tree that spur Rian and Kieron into contemplation of suicide/murder in *Nightfall* become the noose that hangs over the novella, with first a hanging dog that Jestor and Wislawa are confronted with and then the two hanging men at the end of *Light*, that may or may not be their future." I stopped but wanted to say, theme—check; characters—check; tropes—check; symbols—check; structure—check; exact working in dialogue—check, but I understood that would not be wise, opening myself up to further ridicule.

"'How absolute the knave is.' Have you retained that line from *Hamlet*?"

"Of course," I say, my face growing redder, the embarrassment crawling over my shoulders and up my neck before hitting full bloom.

39

"Am I to believe that in your somewhat limited comprehension of these great works of literature there are only two possibilities? Either they are unique and autarchic or one is a plagiarism of the other?"

"No, I did not," I begin stuttering slightly, "I—I didn't intend for this premise to be absolute, but the correspondences are not mere coincidence or inadvertent re-castings of ideas from an earlier work found in a later one. This moves beyond subconscious absorption of cultural tropes." I stand my ground in the face of derision, even when compared to a gravedigger in *Hamlet*. He is a clever clown, as I recall.

"I would hope that, at some point, you also came across references to Susan Glaspell's one-act play *Trifles,* in which a dead canary with a broken neck becomes a clue, so the intertextuality, indeed, continues. While Mctigue is credited with his innovative theatre and producing a work in which theatre, stage, and everything that happens on stage are metaphors for life, we need only glance back to Shakespeare to find his theatre, stage, and everything that happens in that fictive world to be metaphoric," Gould said, smirking rather than smiling at me before continuing, "It is Hamlet who says, 'There is special providence in the fall of a sparrow,' the mystery of the death of a sparrow not so far removed from The Gospel According to Saint Matthew, 10:29: 'Are not two sparrows sold for a farthing? And one of them shall not fall on the ground without your Father,' but St. Matthew follows this with, 'ye are of more value than many sparrows,' 10:31. Is Shakespeare plagiarizing St. Matthew's apotheosis of man or something else entirely?"

It was amazing how quickly Dr. Gould could turn my passion and thorough research into fool's gold, make me enact the part of Polonius to his Hamlet. I hesitated, knowing where he was going with his questions, not of Shakespeare, Mctigue, Baczkowski, or St. Matthew but of me. "I realize Shakespeare incorporated the allusion to St. Matthew while changing or reversing the relative importance of both man and the sparrow."

"Did he?"

I hated Gould's continual questioning games at that moment, his delight in playing Socrates to his ponderous students and assistants. Then I knew he was duplicating the questioning trope from both *Nightfall* and

Light. Was he suddenly agreeing with my premise or mocking me? Knowing I was not his only victim gave me what little courage I had left. I had seen him make students—adult graduate students—grow weak with rage or cry in fear of failure. "Rian has a line in *Nightfall* in which he says, 'the essential is always there waiting.' And in *Light*, there is a line, 'We spend our lives waiting for the essential.'"

"All that, without identifying an essential; you've proven you've read the literature and little else. There is no dissertation topic here. Fortunately, you have sufficient time ahead of you to come up with a topic, and you have course work to finish." He turned back to his desk; he was dismissing me as if he had slapped my face.

Before leaving, however, in the moment of bewildered hesitation, I looked down at a poem that lay on top of several student papers on his cluttered desk. I only skimmed the page because his name was unmistakably at the bottom—apparently Gould's own writing.

> *You Enter a Room*
> as stranger, hope thief;
> history and memory exiled
> from this staged tableau,
> the building like the thief
> hollowed long ago

"A new poem you're writing?" That was all I could ask before Gould cut me off. I had said enough.

He looked up, obscured the paper with his large-boned, but thin, left hand, and cleared his throat. I had already stopped reading and was trying to think of an excuse as to why I had not left. He didn't need to say anything further, but I was being obtuse, so he said curtly, "I believe we are finished today."

I nodded foolishly, turned and exited, closing the door to his claustrophobic, paper-infused office carefully. Moving, or rather, fleeing down the hall, I suddenly recognized those words were too familiar. Of course, I had read Nemerov's poem, "The Human Condition," the one to which Gould's poem might be alluding, but that was not the origin of why

I felt so unsettled. I had seen the exact wording—not merely allusions—on Gould's paper before that day. The epiphany was stark: they were Michael's words with Gould's name attached to them. How would this happen in any way that was not theft? I didn't realize until that moment that I had committed a stanza in one of Michael's poems to memory.

If the repetition had been some innocuous circumstance, then surely Gould would have mentioned it, would have stated that he was looking over an old poem of Michael's or that he had given Michael one of his own poems as a model in his teaching assistantship. I was trying to come up with scenarios in which the duplication made sense, this doubling somehow ethical, but I kept arriving back at suspicion.

Michael Lawler supposedly committed suicide. Yet, nothing was certain at that moment. All of this before I began another, far more dangerous, investigation.

Chapter Nine
You're Holding a Picture of a Painting

It was two o'clock in the morning and I couldn't sleep. Lightning kept flashing and thunder rumbled in the distance, and I could feel electricity in the air. Perhaps I exaggerate if I state the hair on my arms was raised, but there was a general feeling of everything electrified. My old desk lamp was on in the unlikely event that something wise occurred to me, and I needed to write down that epiphany. I wasn't expecting the power to go out the way it would back home, from time to time, in a good storm. I got up and went to my desk. Nothing. Not even a line I could use, not a word that hadn't been corrupted. My brain had emptied out of anything approximating original thought and was sifting aimlessly through the chaos of others' words.

Back to observation: I looked around to see what I had seen so many times before. In my cramped apartment, I sat staring at a print of "The Human Condition" as I had on evenings when my words piled up behind some imaginary dam. In 1933, Belgian Rene Magritte painted the first of his surreal paintings entitled, "The Human Condition". Magritte was well aware that his oil painting held a viewer both within and without the surface hiding the landscape behind it. Only a short time later, I found "Euclidean Walks," in which Magritte's painting of a painting again held its subject within its subject. One Magritte on my walls is sufficient, however, to extend disorientation. He had his theme and had likely given me mine, as well. But the doubles of Mctigue and Baczkowski were not nearly as troubling as the too familiar lines on Gould's desk. What did those copied lines mean?

If only Michael was there to explain it. Tell me why Gould had his poem. If only Magritte knew how much sense his works made to me, as if he created this art to allow me to see one mystery hiding inside another. I thought about how artists and writers come alive for me when I am reading or viewing their work, as if they stepped out of their canvases or their pages and entered my room.

Hello, Rene. I think I've uncovered this mystery of one author's work inside another's, and your brilliant painting has led me to this point of both discovery and indecision. I have you to thank for my suspicion and the obvious repetition. What's that? I was already keen and cynical? You're leaving because I'm boring you?

Actually, I think Magritte would find me fascinating and definitely would not have left my bedroom even though I now have short cropped, blue hair. But when I think about the man further, Magritte must have had a few sexual hang-ups. He did find his nude mother's dead body after her suicide. He did paint that strange portrait, "The Rape", of a woman's body distorted as her facial features, head and neck with phallic suggestion; he painted those hooded "lovers," but he was also married to the same woman for 45 years. I wondered what she made of him? Critics have said that his work allows for projections, and I felt I was projecting my own fantasies on his work.

I imagine that both Mctigue and Baczkowski would have liked Magritte, too, this painter who died only a few years before Baczkowski. They might have met. What do I mean, they might have met? I jump on my computer and enter a few key phrases. Surprise—all three young men were in Paris at the end of the 1920s. They had met, I felt certain of it. A line in *Light* reads, "Behind one face lies another," the pun the first thing I noticed before recognizing the connection to Magritte's themes.

Inside one work hides another. Inside one life, another slips away from view.

Nightfall.
Light.
Nightfall.
Light.
Nightfall.

I printed out the repetition of titles arranged in the way each work began and sat staring at the lines as if they could tell me something more, deliver entrance where I found only locked doors. Was the painting of a painting Magritte's response to knowing Mctigue and Baczkowski and discussing their ideas? Was *Nightfall* inside *Light*, or Mctigue's existential tropes and symbols surfacing in Baczkowski's work, only coming up for air sporadically in all that prose?

Unless, I had everything wrong. Did Baczkowski suggest his ideas to Mctigue long before? Perhaps they created them together in heady conversations, drinking late into Parisian evenings. Bottles of wine on little, cloth-covered but stained tables, animated writers, gesturing; one of the glasses is knocked over and they laugh, more than connecting, finishing each other's sentences because they'd had the same thought at precisely identical moments.

To say nothing of the radishes! Radishes, really? Baczkowski and Mctigue pepper them throughout their literature. That little red vegetable is more garnish than food substance, but in their works, radishes become sustenance and annoyance. I suddenly realized I was hungry and was trying to recall the last time I ate. Characters continually offer these radishes, grab them, eat them, discard them as scenes turn into thickets of doubt. Why radishes? I start musing on this strange little cruciferous vegetable with its glaring red face and that hair-like appendage growing at the bottom of this edible root. They are bitter, and for some reason, they are kind of funny. At least, I thought they were funny. Maybe that is all there is to it. But the fact that Baczkowski and Mctigue focus on them is enough to draw some conclusions about collusion or copying or imitation or; what else was I missing?

There was more. The aborted exchange in Gould's office left me stunned, forgetting aspects I couldn't get to because Gould was so damned intimidating. I wanted to enter the terrain of conjecture with him, but it was Gould, not me, who forced absoluteness. He was right about one matter, however, I was not ready for a thesis. I just wanted to talk about ideas and see where they might lead—the evolving thesis, I guess. He cut mine off at the knees. I should have dropped the topic and moved on to something that Gould wanted me to consider: critical theory as it related to cultural shifts, but I was not done with Mctigue or Baczkowski, or they were not done with me.

Admittedly, I could have picked a better strategist. Then again, maybe Gould was just trying to get me to recognize that I had to go further, deeper. Whenever I thought I had him figured out, he turned another direction. Was he the worst teacher I'd ever had or one of the best? I didn't know at the time. He did make me think and rethink every hypothesis, every claim, every work we read, reconsider every essay down to each particle, each noun, verb, adjective, the atoms that made up the signifiers.

What else did I want to say to the great Dr. Gould? What might have mattered in my argument? Conjecture kind of made me sick. I so wanted to please him in my early days at the university, even until those last few relatively carefree days before Michael's death. In that precious time remaining before everything felt lost, I still desperately wanted his approval.

Suppose the Polish author Baczkowski saw a production of Mctigue's play when he visited Paris? Urjasz had visited Paris on more than one occasion, spending almost two years there as a student long before Mctigue wrote *Nightfall*. Entirely conceivable that they met in the late 1920s, perhaps early in 1928, those radical young writers, exiles from home and their shared Catholicism, even in rejection of its tenants. They found a common thread and carried that line into a bar or bistro to escape the Parisian cold spring rains.

My thesis seemed largely speculative. If only I were writing a fiction, I thought, then glanced at the texts piled on my desk. Trying to come up with a coherent thesis was exhausting. Looking up from the books stacked before me, I turned to the rickety, make-shift shelf next to my bed and spotted Annie Dillard. Her *Pilgrim at Tinker Creek* was still an analogue for my time at Rochester. I flipped open the book and fortuitously landed on page 95: "What could I not do if I had the power and will of a mole!" Ah, the mole trope, I smiled—Shakespeare allusions again! If only I could be just like that mole.

Chapter Ten
Finding Mctigue and Baczkowski

Picture them literally bumping into one another as they entered a café on the Blvd. St. Jacques. Mctigue would have apologized in perfect clipped French, and Baczkowski might have hesitated, his French not as fluid as his Polish, but Baczkowski would have immediately moved into conversation with the more reserved Mctigue. Although they were fascinated with each other on some unspoken level, they parted ways, but not without at least an inkling of knowledge of each other's existence. Did they exchange addresses, agreeing to meet again at the theatre? Was coincidence or fate at work and not conscious design that led to further encounters? Were they in the company of others at the time, making collisions a competition of ideas? A group of young actors with Mctigue, who was already forming new concepts in theatre, were chatting about theatre of the absurd without naming it, without knowing how Mctigue would shape future discussions. It would have either gone further than this first speculation or not nearly so far.

While this is mere conjecture that I would not have mentioned to Dr. Gould, I made a note: entirely possible that Mctigue and Baczkowski had a brief affair, Baczkowski known to have been bi-sexual, and Mctigue not marrying a woman until very late in his life, and then in secret, only revealed shortly before his death. If these two writers had met, had some type of relationship, whatever the circumstances were, it appeared to draw no notice by other writers, their biographers focused on shaping forces of their birth countries not accidental meetings in a city of lights. Why would a legitimate biographer engage in such speculation without some definitive proof? It was not as if writers had some kind of light bulb over their heads, making them easy to spot and find each other in the crowded Paris streets. Ah, there is my future lover crossing a boulevard, deftly avoiding bicycles.

I had almost talked myself out of this obsession, but possibility created by proximity now existed. Following scant evidence, the trails took me back to their literature. If the breadcrumbs were there, then I would find more.

Had a young Mctigue and Baczkowski discussed annihilative, existential ideas that found their way into *Nightfall* and, later, *Light* when they were drinking together? Or was *Light* conceived first and only after *Nightfall* published? Even their titles suggested a yin yang completion. They might have named their works *Light* and *Dark* or *Nightfall* and *Daybreak*, but then transparency would be too obvious to all. If they were to create a puzzling pattern, the complication was primarily for their own benefit, a private correspondence that remained encoded and obtuse by design.

There was no definitive historical documentation for this premise except the works themselves and the writers' Paris residences over an approximately two-year period before Baczkowski suddenly left Paris. I wrote "suddenly." Did he really leave suddenly? Why did I choose that word? Was he psychically wounded, just broke, or both? Research suggests nothing about haste in his departure, just his leaving. Perhaps I was giving him motive—an angry or disappointed lover—when there was no motive to be discovered.

Go back to the literature, I told myself. Later, when Baczkowski sought to publish his *Anamneses* in French, perhaps he contacted Mctigue again. In any event, excerpts from *Anamneses* were published in the Paris Journal *Culture* at around the time Mctigue was staging *Nightfall* in Paris. Paris offered its own interpretations and suggestions, as Rebecca Solnit wrote in *Wanderlust*, "More than any other city, it has entered the paintings and novels of those under its sway, so that representations and reality reflect each other like a pair of facing mirrors, and walking Paris is often described as reading." Naturally, they were reading the city as they wrote and fell in love. I had underlined that passage of her marvelous treatise on walking, thinking again about my theories of doubling. Would Mctigue and

Baczkowski have found each other so easily in a city with fewer public spaces, the cafes and streets intermingling? In that small, cultured writer's world in which they existed, they were names and identities already. They each would have had a following, at least a few birds pecking at dropped breadcrumbs surrounding the writers.

At the opening of *Anamneses*, there is the curious sense of fractured time and connection:

"Hour.
You.
Day.
Absence of you.
Week.
You again.
Month.
Month.
Month.
Month.
I am alone.
Alone."

Pared down not to essentials but below them, below even staging of language into coherence.

I pulled out my well-worn copy of *Nightfall*. So many pages had been ear-marked that it was impossible to find quotations again without re-reading the entirety of the play once more. *Nightfall* is a quick read, however, and within a few moments, I came across the following passage, falling out of the gaping mouth of Kieron: "But what time? You are here. What day? You. What month? You. What year? You are not there. Day. Night. You are gone. What time? What month? This rock again. Alone."

The text reads like Baczkowski's *Anamneses* opening, but Mctigue removed even the self in his annihilative passage: a "you" without an "I." I was attempting to figure out if even that absence of pairing was mere coincidence.

I should have felt elated by these discoveries, but I, too, was alone, not a terrible sensation, however. If my conjectures had all been made by numerous others, then I would have nothing further to add to the conversation. Merely a matter of me nodding my head in agreement, but the complete absence of writing on this topic of the incredible set of correspondences between Baczkowski and Mctigue, when there should not have been any or only those related to the age and mores of the time, made me an explorer of sorts. I knew, even without Gould's approval, that I was in new territory, a good place to be when considering a dissertation topic.

Of course, my feeling of alienation also had a great deal to do with a recent breakup with my boyfriend of three years, Jason. I haven't really discussed him, have I? There was a time, not long ago, when we navigated these waters together, and now he was gone. Jason was still alive, of course, and if things had been different between us then I could have knocked on his door and invited myself in, spent the night whenever I felt the urge. At the end, I wanted him to leave as much as he wanted out, but although painful to be in each other's presence, separation was still too raw. We didn't part great friends.

The other woman in his life—and I could name her, but I've decided that action gives her more substance than she has earned—hated me, which I find funny since she broke us up, not the other way around. Maybe she didn't break us up. In truth, I was ready for someone new. Jason in all his serious, studious presence helped me as much as I helped him to get through undergrad and then grad school, so I was still grateful to him. In truth, I was still very fond of him.

But we were about to leave this insulated environment, and I think cutting all my hair off had more to do with the fact he once asked me never to cut or dye my hair than any other motivation. "You wouldn't be nearly as pretty," he said. "Promise me you won't do something stupid for attention. Your blonde hair, well, it's beautiful." The irony, of course, was that my natural hair color is mousy brown. I am only surprised now that I went with Jason as long as I did.

Jason was gone, and so was my blonde period. That was it. I was free of the burden. This discovery of embedding of one work of literature inside another was isolating but also liberating; I let the correlation surround me until I heard about a fellow student. Michael Lawler was dead in the very literal sense of the word, and now his words appeared on an instructor's cluttered desk with the name of the professor stamped at the bottom of the page.

Who was claiming authorship here? And I'm not buying into that theory that there is no solitary author, that literature is all derivative and part and parcel of cultural product. Even if everything anyone writes is part of a cultural voice, there is still that solitary act, picking up a pen and settling upon one word and then another. Not dictation. Whomever he was or wasn't influenced by, Michael Lawler wrote amazing poetry; his choices down to the last syllable, length of lines, position on the page.

There were only two possibilities I was willing to consider—were there really only two? Both of them pulled me further into some kind of intrigue. Gould had stolen Michael's poem or poems. Had Gould's unpublished words found their way into Michael's notebook, the lines I read that day looking over his shoulder? I tried to imagine the circumstances of either prospect. Had my earlier speculations been wrong?

What led me over and over to that stairwell, trying to solve the mystery of his death? I'd have to go back a long way, even before this duplication I'd discovered, with those actors who conjure up Sherlock. I'm trying to recall what Sherlock would do with an absence of evidence? I go back to my childhood.

I'm no Sherlock Holmes, nor that super smart DCI Luther, not the cool black Idris Elba who played the BBC detective so well there was no other possible John Luther inside the script. Trying to be honest here, I'm not Watson either, without even Emma Watson for moral support. I like Emma Watson, though; the actress is very cool and smart. She holds her own, but Hogwarts is still Harry Potter's world. Really, what kind of person would not like Emma? All right, I'll give you that. There are all kinds of awful people in this world who would not like her simply because she is likeable. I've met a few of them, one of whom sent me on this terrible search to solve a mystery.

Another P.I. might raise the possibility that my memory was not as accurate as I believed. That sleuth might postulate that I imagined a doubling that was only suggested by a similar word or two, and I had filled in the rest with my imagination. I have to argue on my behalf here. I am fully aware that I don't have Gould's kind of retention, but I was more than capable of recalling a handful of lines I had seen before.

If there was something benign behind the doubling, then Gould had no cause to cover the poem. He could have simply shown me his work, or said that he was helping Michael with his poetry before his death. But then those possibilities required a different character than the one owned by Professor Roald Gould.

This awful puzzle had an answer but was not to be released easily. How could I ask Gould if he had stolen Michael's words or if Michael had stolen his? There was the direct approach: "Good morning, Professor Gould. I was wondering if you stole Michael's poems and passed them off as your own because, clearly, you have lost the ability to write, and plagiarism, with all of its severe consequences, seemed to be the only way forward?"

I could imagine how that would go over. What proof did I have really? Michael's notebooks were the key, and I did not have them. I could not touch a single item that could be offered as evidence. I was quite certain that my memory was not going to be sufficient evidence. Yet, there is something that lingers. The picture of Michael carrying those notebooks everywhere, the way anxious women hold their purses, tight to their chests as if the value contained within them might be lost or stolen.

Chapter Eleven
Discovering a Dead Poet

Wherever I started, the scene came back to Michael. He kept jumping back into my life even when I was determined to move on with my focus and work. But it was my work, of course, that brought me back to them; to Michael, to Gould, to these dead poet/writers, to mystery, to an unexplained death and stolen lines. I don't really like lumping Michael in with the rest of it, so let me just separate him again. He deserved that much from me. I would have given him more, but his reserve, even in death, held me back, too.

Should I really confront Gould? The idea was ridiculous, and I couldn't give direct confrontation serious consideration. Defending myself in his presence was next to impossible, let alone attack him, accuse him of the literary crime of plagiarism and more. What was the "more" I was suggesting? Even if I was indirect, he would certainly discern my intent, read into even the subtlest of suggestions, and mock me, or worse fail me in the bargain, perhaps call me out as fool in front of everyone. Yet, I was less afraid of that last possibility since Michael's death. The weight of death removes all kinds of decorum.

From a practical standpoint, I would need to get a different advisor for my dissertation before presenting to my committee. In fact, Gould would be the one to suggest the other committee members. He held all the power in this dynamic. Never a good idea to accuse your mentor and advisor of plagiarism, theft, and other far more nefarious things before attempting to complete your doctorate.

I could envision another scene in his class where I stand up and state loudly, "Why are Michael's words on a paper with your name below them?" The entire class would turn their heads and stare first at me then Gould in horror, before Gould would stand aloof. I could hear his mocking response.

"Perhaps because I was reviewing the dead boy's project, my dear, perpetually uninformed student, and unless you plan to have another hysterical outburst, could we continue with the poetry of Charles Olson? Unless you have not bothered to read and analyze 'In Cold Hell, In Thicket?'"

No, his response would be more damaging than that. I was letting myself off too easily in this hypothetical scene of humiliation. By the end of Gould's incisive remarks that day, I would be limping out of class, my head low, my ambition and career designs destroyed. How could I write my dissertation with the man I was accusing of stealing someone else's words? Just below that lay "and more," delving "below the moon," like Hamlet who thought he had tricked his uncle, only to end up dead with the rest of the characters.

Gould's reputation for being tough and exacting was well known, and some students avoided him on those grounds. Most who wanted a challenge, however, signed up for at least one of his classes. Those of us who had served as graduate assistants knew a little more about how he operated, and the more we knew, the less we tended to like him.

In the longest conversation I ever had with Michael, he told me about a young woman in one of Gould's classes who had given her paper to Michael outside of class. She had forgotten to hand in the work earlier and was hurrying to catch a ride home. Although all of Gould's assistants had explicit instructions never to accept work outside of the classroom, everyone knew somebody who did this. Maybe Michael should not have taken her paper as she ran up to him out of breath, but he did. He told me he tucked the paper into his own notebook, and then headed to the library before going home. The next morning, he went to retrieve Tricia's paper: gone. Even in his retelling of the incident, small beads of sweat broke out on his forehead. I tried to comfort him because I realized how terrible he must have felt. How awful to lose one's own work, but to be responsible for someone else's loss was the kind of thing that kept me up at night the semester I taught.

"Not your fault," I said rather obviously but inaccurately.

"Actually, it was."

"What could you do?"

"I immediately confessed my transgression to Gould," Michael said, his eyes opened even wider. "But he would not accept the excuse. 'It's a zero for her. Already in my books,' he said, as if he wanted to punish me by hurting her, too. I told him that she could make another copy, that she very likely had the work on her computer, but he said, 'Too late. You had better inform Miss Patterson. I'm busy. You understand the consequences and should regard this as a learning experience.' He dismissed me."

"That's heinous of Gould. What did you tell her?"

"The truth. Of course, she swore, then cried, then went to the Dean. None of her words or actions did any good. Gould said he had entered grades for the semester and students needed to learn responsibility. I think even the Dean is intimidated by Gould."

"And they stuck up for him?"

"He is his own kingdom here."

"I'm so sorry, Michael. What's she going to do?"

"Take the F and put pins in the voodoo doll likeness she made of me." We both laughed in that aborted fashion where the sound catches in your throat.

"It could have happened to anyone," I said, actually meaning it, thinking about how I had lost one of my own student's papers but was grateful that I was able to make another copy. Every time I collected student work, I counted out pages meticulously and wrote down the number before enclosing them in my binder.

"I actually retraced my steps, went back to my carrel in the library, walked the same path to my apartment, and turned up nothing. Naturally, it had snowed, so the likelihood of finding the paper was infinitesimal. Still, I supposed if I looked hard enough, I should have found something, but those bound pages took off on their own."

"Did she fail the class?"

"I don't know. She won't talk with me anymore, of course. I even asked Gould if he would accept one of my papers and give me the F instead.

He looked up at me and smiled then said, 'Absolutely not. We're done here. Lesson learned. Move on.'"

Looking back, I wish I had done something more to help Michael that day and other days, as well, but I was diving into my own work. The anecdote about Gould perfectly described the man, however. He was brilliant but unforgiving.

How would anyone ever consider my conjecture about Gould's theft of Michael's work? Maybe I could get away with just making the connections between anonymous persons out loud and wait for Gould's reaction: one face behind another. Would he enter into hypothesis in the abstract with me? Not likely.

I get easily carried away. Should I play devil's advocate? Gould had not stolen Michael's notebooks and journals. Gould was already a recognized poet with several critical theory books in print, as well as two poetry chapbooks, and a full-length book of poetry to his name. There would be no good explanation for a scene to take place in which Gould would take Michael's work. I had noted a critique of Gould's poetry after we were required to read his chapbook *Frequent Tremors*, and the experts agreed that Gould's poetic, "voice shifted and moved like wind," a high compliment unless they were suggesting something else entirely. It seemed unlikely that anyone was hinting at plagiarism.

As an undergraduate, I went to my first Gould poetry reading and recalled thinking that I could hear echoes of other voices behind his words. My feeling was not the suspicion of stolen words, however, but an appreciation of chameleon qualities of his voice. I assumed the echo was intentional, involving allusions and simply demonstrated that I was not well-read enough to discover all of the references.

I had never met a well-known poet before arriving on campus, and I was not disappointed by Roald Gould. At the podium stood this tall, fairly lean but imposing man with a handsome, angular face, a mop of unruly graying hair and piercing blue-green eyes. If he needed glasses, he never wore them, contacts likely. He was both distinguished and unnerving. Always wearing an expensive looking suit jacket and collared shirt without a tie, he seemed the epitome of the intellectual, the professional poet master. His mouth was thin but sensitive in the way his lips moved, shaping language dramatically. Then Gould spoke. Deep and sonorous, his voice was commanding and also sexy. Mine was not a unique perspective.

Along with my peers and I assumed, the faculty, I believed Dr. Gould to be amazing and brilliant, and I was more than a little attracted to him. Friends in other, non-lit classes, called us the Cult of Gould. For a long while, I didn't mind this assessment even if the moniker was demeaning.

None of those qualities that I first recognized in the man had disappeared, but something had changed in my appraisal of him, and I was no longer infatuated with Roald Gould. Behind his sensitive, intelligent mask was a thinly disguised malignance, an ever-present threat that I mistakenly assumed was about grading. The threat was, rather, always about control.

All of his students wanted to please Dr. Gould, and the harder we tried, the greater his sarcasm, and the more he appeared to despise us. Occasionally, however, he would seem to step back and take us in, assess one of us in a positive manner, even befriend us for a time. In the middle of these brief respites, Gould could be completely charming and generous. During one of these interludes, I asked to be his assistant.

"Ah," he said, "the ultimate resume builder."

"I really just want to learn more," I replied. Only much later did I learn that I was his first female teaching assistant and that the decision was probably not his choice, more of a Title IX nod, according to one of my classmates who had his own issues with women in positions of authority. But back then, I was flattered that Gould considered me for the position and felt the honor.

"I would prefer my assistants already know a great deal, so they have something to offer."

Trying flattery always seemed to work with Gould. "I have learned a great deal from you, and I believe that I could help younger, less well-read students."

"Well, then you had best get started."

Chapter Twelve
Noting a Balancing Act

We grad assistants were so few. He kept us apart by design, requiring us to work on different aspects of research for him. When he published an article, three or four of us who had worked with him looked to see whose name was also credited for the scholarly article, but there was only Dr. Roald Gould's name as byline. Yet no one grumbled, at least in public. Privately, I was hurt at first. Every one of us secretly thought that Gould had chosen his next great poet/writer to mentor, to lead into glory or at least a decent college job.

I had gone to England and Italy for a semester abroad for Gould, researching Keats and his poetry, that briefest span of Keats' life flowing with sensuous, charged language. It's not that I didn't love his poetry, but I probably would have chosen another topic if Gould hadn't encouraged me to pursue my interest in Keats, which was also one of his preoccupations.

That overseas expedition was particularly difficult for me because I had very little money. Bill was fine with me going, but said I needed to pay for the trip on my own, show my emerging adulthood. To be honest, I doubt Bill had the extra money, but Greta and her third husband were loaded. She had worked her way up again from stock broker to hedge funder. After finally finding the courage to call my mother and ask for money, I ended up thanking both her and her new husband, who picked up another landline to listen. I didn't ask why he was interrupting one of my only calls to my absent mother. It was as if Greta and Richard had anticipated my call and had already worked out their arguments with claim and counter-claims built into their rhetoric. They, too, suggested I learn to stand on my own, so I hung up.

Working and going to school was a balancing act that I usually managed well. After agonizing over the expense and loans, I made the decision to go ahead with a semester abroad. What would one more job added to the load mean anyway? The loans could wait. Even back then, I presupposed skipping out on my loans or at least delaying them for years.

Jason went with me. At first, I thought the arrangement would be romantic; the two of us navigating our way around Europe, but within a very short time, our relationship started to fray and then unravel. Close and constant proximity changes dynamics between people, either pulling them together in new ways or pushing them apart. Jason complained about accommodations, the stuffy English, their "accent," visiting Stonehenge, "this bunch of big rocks,"; the French, their snobbery, their rudeness, their ridiculous scarves; long lines, "paintings that are not nearly so impressive up close," paying for water, paying for bread in restaurants; the Italians, Italian men, Italian men looking at me; touring Germans; odors on the trains, everyone's failure to speak English, hard beds, lumpy beds, bed bugs, blisters on his feet, sweating, hats; African and Arab immigrants, aggressive immigrants trying to sell umbrellas; haughty waiters, food, crowded trains, checking our bags, losing our bags temporarily, paying in local currency, everyone's failure to speak English, carrying our coats, lack of cell phone reception, buses not running on schedule, dirt, grime, the closeness of Europe, the water, every country's atmosphere!

He also began to complain about me. "Do you always have to carry a notebook and camera, looking like some goddamn tourist? Is this trip for Gould or for us? I don't think you want to wear that skirt. Why don't you put on a little make-up today? Could you do something else with your hair today? Why would you give up your seat for her? She's not really pregnant. Don't smile at that kid; he's just trying to steal from us. Really? Did you really just give that urchin money? He's coming back with all his friends. Now look what you've done. Can't you walk a little faster? We're looking at another place Keats is supposed to have stayed? Keep your hand on your passport, for Christ's sake. Don't be so naïve; that asshole wasn't being friendly, he was trying to cop a feel." Jason was the consummate teacher of the unnecessary.

By the time we flew back to the U.S., Jason was relieved to be home, and I was determined to end our relationship.

One thing I was particularly good at during our travels, however, was noticing detail, and so I returned with copious notes. Gould took them, nodded, and said nothing, not even "thank you." He did add, however, "There will be an assistantship for you in the fall." My notes, my work were the expectation, not a gift. I needed that assistantship to stay in school. Still, I suppose I thought he would be proud of me or pleased that I had so much material for his next article or book, or whatever paper he decided to write, then publish. I told him I was thinking about writing something about Keats, too.

"That wouldn't be wise. You'll end by embarrassing yourself." He noticed my chagrin. "At this point, just keep studying, reading, and taking notes. Eventually, you will be ready if you put in the time and effort," he stated, as I tried not to cry in front of him, particularly difficult because I was breaking up with Jason at the time, too.

A year later, Gould published an article in a prominent literary journal on the theme of disappointment found in Keats' poetry. When we had notice of the article coming out a few months before Michael's death, I bought a copy of the university journal and thumbed through it. Nowhere was my name to be found as a credit, but within the text, my notes were embedded everywhere in succinct phrases, dates, locations, mention of artifacts, even quoted anecdotes from people in the region where the interview took place.

Gould had used my research but not my name. I wanted to confront him about the theft but said nothing. All right, I look like a coward here, but I was not the first. Dr. Gould was always intimidating, and the idea of challenging him about anything that spoke of criticism was going down a road from which there would be no turning back. I had seen this reaction happen to others, smart young people, even poor and miserable adjuncts who disappeared from campus, or at least our program, after a negative encounter with Gould. The best I could do was promise myself not to be taken in by him again.

What I got out of my European trip was; theft by Gould, a great deal of physical discomfort, an irreparable fracture with Jason and a lasting love of Italy. Definitely worth the trip. I would return to Italy.

I could only assume Michael was tricked, as well, because he was Gould's graduate assistant for three semesters until his death. If Gould was willing to steal our notes without credit, why couldn't I imagine he would steal our actual words, our poetry, even our lives?

All right, that last one seems kind of extreme to me, too. If I managed to confirm evidence that Gould took Michael's poems, how did he get them? Gould could simply state that he had given Michael the poems to critique in order to teach him better analysis skills. Or he could say that Michael asked to read his poems and he generously shared them with his graduate assistant. Or he could remark that Michael wished to use his professor's poetry in the class he was teaching. These were all logical explanations that I would not be able to counter effectively. How to engage Gould in a conversation on these topics would be the most difficult task even though I regularly met with him. I would have to begin with some kind of fairly innocuous question and move to more insinuating ones to measure his responses.

Of course, I thought of Hamlet, the smart young man who intended to trap his murderous Uncle Claudius. Everything ended so badly for Hamlet, however, and I am fully aware that I am not nearly as clever as the young Danish prince. My idea would be to get Gould to admit something in a public way, so that the audience around him were informed, but Gould was too careful and deliberate, even in his arrogance. Somehow, I had to use that character flaw to push him further than he wanted to go. If, indeed, Gould had taken Michael's notebooks, if he had visited him, the last and most terrifying question presented itself without filter would be: was Michael alive when Gould left him? The door was locked, Michael was left hanging.

I felt stuck in a locked room. I had eliminated nothing, not even the impossible.

Chapter Thirteen
Standing in Judgement

Before I could attempt to make sense of this mystery, I pulled my new, thrift-store find over my head. The worn, checked material, once belonging to an anonymous man, was the kind of soft you only get after years of wear and washings. The shirt was comforting and the only thing I wanted to put on at night anymore. For years, I'd been pretty independent, and now I was suddenly feeling needy and alone.

I had to get some kind of definitive answer as well as plan of action. I began bravely enough with a visit to a Rochester police station. The night before I drew up a fairly silly list of how to proceed:

1. Make appointment.
2. Talk to police.
3. Try to find out if Michael definitely committed suicide.
4. Try to find out if his notebooks were in his apartment.
5. Find out what I need to do to see his notebooks if they were there.
6. Tell someone about my suspicions.
7. Talk to someone I trust.
8. Make copies of everything I find.
9. Leave copies with someone else.
10. Leave a clue of my discoveries for Gould in some subtle manner.
11. Have witness to Gould's outburst of guilt.

Numbers four, seven, ten, and eleven on the list seemed most unlikely. I realized that after two and a half years of dating Jason, I had cut myself off from a number of former friends, and my work with Dr. Gould made the idea of seeking out another professor who would be impartial or find my accusations to be an impossibility. I could, however, try to discover what the police knew or at least what they were willing to reveal. Even if they only helped confirm rumors, I had an entrance. I also had to be prepared for them to tell me unequivocally that Michael killed himself.

Somehow, I had to find what was probably laid out before me and explain my clues to the cops, but I wasn't even sure what I had. What did they need to prove something was wrong in their investigation into Michael's death? Sure, I knew something about mysteries in books and movies, but the real-life ones are not so easily unraveled.

A little over a mile or so from campus, the station house was a brisk fifteen-minute walk. The walk looked closer on a map, and I was tired and nervous when I arrived. If I'd had money for a cab, I could have entered looking less disheveled and agitated. Outside, the imposing brick building suggested the very foundation of civilization, solid walls between citizens and those who would harm us. Inside, I immediately sensed a trap. It was alarming just to walk into the place, and I unnaturally felt as if I had done something wrong, every minor infraction in my life looming up before me. Probably a lot of people come into a police station resolved not to tell them anything before breaking down, confessing crimes they weren't even sure they committed. Catching my breath and calming down, I went up to the clerk and asked to see an officer. He motioned for me to take a seat on a nearby bench.

There were three other complainants in the room, one elderly man with a large purple bruise on his cheek. With his right hand, he held an icepack to his face, taking the dripping pack away every few minutes. An older woman who might have been his wife was seated beside him, patting his veined hand with her own more wrinkled one. Standing near them was a middle-aged woman, dressed in an elegant overcoat, who could have been their daughter. She had her hand on the elderly man's shoulder, patting his bony frame distractedly now and then. The husband and wife whispered to one another and the daughter was on her cell phone, nodding her head to some unknown speaker. The four of us together felt far too intimate, as if I was a part of their group without contributing. I nearly said something to them out of unease.

I sat for a few minutes until the desk clerk motioned for me to come up.

"Now, what can we help you with, Miss?"

Why was I there? I again regretted coming, the space starting to make me feel as if I had entered a bad dream: somewhat faded yellowish walls and smells that cleaning liquids couldn't quite cover up, that undefined something worse below hard-scrubbed surfaces. The clerk was a sergeant with a large, angular nose and sharp chin, hair clipped close to his scalp, military style. I hesitated, could see his impatience, and then told him I had come to inquire about my property that was in the house of a man who had killed himself.

He took a long look at me as if sizing up my honesty and then made a note before telling me to wait again. Returning to the bench, I shifted slightly to the far end because the older couple had moved partially into my space as their daughter sat down on the other side of the man I assumed was her father. I had my pocket notebook, so I am never at a loss while in limbo, taking in details of my surroundings, odors of faded cigarette smoke and perspiration. The wife of the injured man was touching my arm accidentally every time she breathed. I didn't welcome the contact and tried to move even further away, but I was already perilously close to falling off the bench.

A young man was suddenly brought in yelling, his hands cuffed but his head swinging from side to side, his words incoherent, his face bloody. There were two cops pushing while holding him up as they passed into another corridor, the guy's twisting motions slowing their progress. I wondered what he had done and the fractured lives of that moment. He looked high on something, not scared. I questioned whether or not he even knew what he had done. When he finally came down, would he be amazed at his actions or be certain of what he had done? I hoped he'd have his wits about him enough to call a lawyer or at least a friend. I thought it would be a good idea to have a law office across from the entrance to every police station.

Almost immediately after this violent juggling act, a child of maybe eleven or twelve came in with an officer and a woman who looked like the girl's mother. The little girl was crying, and her mother looked shaken, pale, and disoriented. At least the child was alive, I thought, whatever had happened to her, she was still alive. Everything seems worse when bad happens to a kid, but there is no real protection in this world. As much sympathy as I had for the victims, I realized being a cop meant seeing the worst all the time; pain, suffering, death, abuse, cruelty, depravity at every imaginable turn. How did these officers keep their sanity? Maybe they didn't.

Sergeant Campello came up to me and introduced himself. "What can I help you with, young lady?" I nearly said that he should help the elderly man next to me first, but I got up and shook his hand. I could feel middle-aged daughter's eyes on me.

"Excuse me," she said, nearly stepping between us. "We were waiting before her. My father is injured."

I turned to witness her indignation with Officer Campello. I guessed he was used to being diplomatic. "I know, madam. We're aware. The officer already assigned to you will be right out. He knows more about your incident and is getting the report out. In fact, he is writing it up as we speak. I'm afraid you'd have to wait much longer if I worked with you." That response seemed to calm her.

Campello was clean shaven with a hint of growth darkening his face, and he held a military air about him, as did the desk sergeant. Perhaps they had both been in the Marines. The move from military to law enforcement would be a natural fit. Considering their demeanor, I was particularly glad that I was not a criminal under investigation by him, even though he was polite.

"I'm not sure where to start," I said, but then found my voice. "It's about Michael Lawler's death."

"Lawler?"

"Two weeks ago, he was found dead on River Street, just off campus. He was my friend."

He squinted then nodded in recognition of the case. "Come this way," Campello motioned for me to follow him into a dingier room, with gray walls and too many desks, loud complaints everywhere. We sat facing one another, Campello behind the desk and stacks of files. I could imagine each file contained some fresh horror.

"Now, what about Mr. Lawler?" He looked ready to arrest someone, and I was hoping he wasn't considering me in that manner.

Inexplicably, I started to cry. It wasn't an act, but my demeanor had an effect on him, changing his brusque manner.

He leaned forward. "Look, I'm sorry. How did you know the deceased?"

"He was my friend. We were in class together, and something doesn't seem right. I mean, I don't believe he killed himself."

Campello suddenly stiffened a bit. "What makes you think he killed himself?"

"It's what everyone on campus is saying. I don't care, though. I don't think they are right."

"Do you have the name of the person who gave you this report?"

I didn't want to get anyone in trouble, even annoying Andrew, so I said that I'd heard the story everywhere. People were gossips and the rumor mill was whirring. But thinking about the sophomore who claimed to have been standing outside when they brought out Michael's body, I felt suddenly protective of him. He, too, had been a victim, just out for a morning run. Andrew recounting events also made me recall Michael, and the picture was too awful to think of him as a corpse on that gurney.

Chapter Fourteen
Difficult to Accept

There was the day Michael came up behind me when I was in the campus coffee shop. He touched my arm gently, sending a shiver up it, but only to avoid running into me because a commotion had broken out behind him.

"I'm so sorry," Michael said and then he turned to see why he had been pushed. Two males were shoving and hitting each other over a girl. One punch became a flurry of close punches in what descended into a wrestling match on the floor. Security rushed over and grabbed one of them roughly by the collar of his jacket, while the other took off with another security officer in pursuit. The only reason security was on the scene so quickly was because they had stopped in for coffee, too. I thought I had seen the girl who was crying around campus before, but I didn't know either of the young men. I wasn't sure they were students, but there were plenty of people I didn't know on campus.

There was that little shock of electricity. The sudden shift from musing about a book to violence took my mind out of the philosophical and back into the physical world in less than a second. The girl sobbing pulled me in again. "Don't worry about it," I started to say to Michael, but he was gone, as surprisingly as he appeared. I questioned myself as to whether or not he had been behind me at all that day. He kept disappearing even before he fully existed for me in that scene. Why did he take off so quickly?

"Look, Miss, ah," Campello interrupted my recollections.

"Vena Smith," I said, with no idea why I just lied to a cop about my last name, it just seemed like a good idea. I could have at least invented a first name, too, realizing I had missed my chance at completely reinventing myself. There would be time for that later.

Campello kept everything formal. "Miss Smith, I'm sorry about your friend, Mr. Lawler, but I really can't discuss a case with you."

"So, it's a case? Then are you investigating his death?" I stopped crying, as if on cue.

He shook his head. "You're not family, you're a friend, right?"

I'd already told him I was a friend, so I couldn't backtrack now. I wondered if he was just trying to trick me and expose my lying.

"I'm not family, but Michael was like family to me." Here I stretched the line as far as I could reasonably go. "If I was family, could you tell me whether you suspect something other than suicide?"

"Since you're not family, I cannot, but there is no cause for anyone to conclude anything else."

Sergeant Campello had just confirmed the gossip about Michael's suicide. He knew what he was doing, so this was kindness on his part. "There's really nothing more I can tell you. If you have no more questions I can answer—" he added, leaning forward in his chair as if to escort me out of the room.

"I don't think he would kill himself. In fact, I'm sure of it. Please. If you could just go back over the scene. Look for fingerprints, an extra wine glass, DNA or something. There will be clues of something wrong at his apartment."

Campello sighed as if I was the tenth unreasonable person of his day. "For what it's worth, let me tell you that suicides are more common than murders, maybe just harder to accept."

I decided to try a different tactic. "He had some of my poems," I rattled off, "in several notebooks of mine that he borrowed." Lying again. "I was hoping to get them back. Those poems are part of my graduate program, and I spent months on them. Is there any way I could just check in his apartment?"

"No. Absolutely not. I'm afraid that's not possible. Anything at the scene is now in an evidence locker."

"Evidence? Was there an autopsy or inquest?"

Sergeant Campello looked at me suspiciously. "No purpose in

requiring either here. Now, I'm sorry, but if you believe the deceased had something of yours, there's a procedure to follow. You can petition the court to get your property back. Takes some time, but..."

I persisted. "I can't petition the court if the notebooks weren't there. Please, could I just see or ask if there were any notebooks in his apartment to check to see if they are mine? Isn't there someone who can help me?"

Campello was losing patience with me. "Listen, I won't be able to."

"They wouldn't be needed for evidence because there is no inquest. I just want a copy of my poems. They were my originals. I had no copies, so you can see why I need them. In addition to losing my friend, I lost my work. Without them, everything I've worked for this year is now gone."

He was still shaking his head and pulling his lips together in an exaggerated grimace.

"Could you at least tell me if anyone saw my notebooks? That's all I'm asking you."

Campello scratched his chin, rubbed his nose, and then said, "Just a minute." He left me and talked to another policeman a few desks away. They both turned to look at me as if my face held some kind of answer. The other officer put his lower lip out and shook his head. Campello returned. "No notebooks of any kind were found at the scene. In fact, there was no paper there at all. That's all I can say. Now, you'll have to excuse me. I've got other business."

"Thank you. I appreciate your consideration. This is kind of depressing work you do in a depressing city," I said, suddenly feeling a little sorry for him, as well as for myself.

He smiled, breaking the odd strangeness between us. "Hey, you know what they say, 'At least we're not Buffalo.'" Then he seemed to realize his comment was a little flippant for the circumstances and looked down at me again. He cleared his throat. "I'm sorry about your friend." He escorted me out. "Good luck to you."

"Good luck to you, too," I said, not knowing exactly what that meant for him. I couldn't believe a cop said that about Rochester: "not Buffalo." I mean, I'd heard the phrase enough around the city, but the joke seemed kind of lame for him too, especially under the circumstances. But I supposed that cops had heard every sob story that could be told, and they needed a little humor to get through their days.

At least he didn't say he had more important business. I could understand how the idea of an emotional college student and lost poems might not seem significant to Sergeant Campello. To be a fly on the wall near his dinner table that night. Someone, maybe his wife or kids, would be laughing over his ridiculous tales of the day at my expense; "Yeah, we got a pedophile, two rapes, an armed assault, and a violent looney tune high on some shit, and this girl wanted her poems back."

I wanted to pull a chair up to his dinner table and protest. "I don't want my poems back really. I just said that because no one would listen to me otherwise, and we have a murder here. I really wanted you to open an investigation into the death of a man whom I might have fallen in love with or at least dated."

Outside, I was a free woman again. I knew more, however, than when I went in, the notebooks were not there. What had happened to them? Who had taken them? The visit with Sergeant Campello brought me three confirmed answers. First, Michael's notebooks were gone. Second, the police had not ordered an autopsy before determining his suicide and there was nothing at the scene to make them believe otherwise. What else could I deduce from his abbreviated comments? Third, there was no struggle. If something had happened to Michael other than him deciding to take his own life, there would naturally be some obvious signs of foul play, according to the cops. They didn't know the man with whom they could be dealing.

Maybe I needed not to close that door yet. What was I thinking? There are poisons, knock out drugs. Someone could have hit him on the head from behind or choked him. If the cops weren't looking for it, they could miss almost anything. This wasn't some television show where the crime lab works for days to find the evidence with all of their high t ech gadgetry on display. And Michael's notebooks were gone.

These policemen might be good cops, but they weren't investigators out to get a killer to confess because they know immediately who did it. Just forming this last thought another came to me; could I get him to confess? Did I really believe that Gould did this? Could Gould ever be tripped up? There was the problem. I more than suspected Gould; I believed, however illogically, he had killed Michael. By then, I arrived at the more disturbing question of considering my professor and mentor as a killer. How did I expect a cop to believe this wild idea when I couldn't even swallow it? Gould killed Michael for what? For a few lines in a poem? Killing for a poem made no sense but neither did Michael's "suicide".

Michael, I need a little help here. Just give me some indication as to whether or not you took your own life. Did someone, did Gould hurt you? Michael says nothing, but I feel him get up to walk away. I can sense his disgust or despair, but perhaps that is just my own despair welling up. I must have it all wrong, and he is disappointed in me. Perhaps I have expressed his fear, and he can't believe I am giving up so easily. There is nothing I can say at the moment to restore his confidence, that I will get this right for him. This, however, will never be right for me. I returned to my tiny apartment and opened my notes. I don't know why looking at another mystery made me feel better about the more important one I couldn't solve.

Chapter Fifteen
A Red Herring

Dailan is seated with his back to Urjasz who enters *Café de la Paix* unannounced, puts his hand on Dailan's shoulder, and in his best French asks what day of the week it is. Dailan is startled for an instant, so absorbed was he in his notebook, then catches himself before responding on a Tuesday that, "Why not Thursday because it makes no difference." Urjasz Baczkowski smiles because he had already written Thursday on a note he was about to pass to the man he desired as a lover. This was only their third meeting but already the chemistry between them was apparent. Urjasz proposed they attend an opera at the Gaumont, but Dailan Mctigue declined. Mctigue was in the middle of writing a play and he wanted to get back to it. He was also nervous about his attraction to the young Pole and what the fascination would mean for him to be open about his own desires.

There was also the question of impropriety. Who was this brash man to propose and insert himself into the Parisian life of the intellectual, the Pole without connections, without cultural grace? Baczkowski laughed suddenly, disturbing the air again, and everyone in the café looked at him for a moment. Baczkowski was muscular, with a stocky build and average height, but he was charismatic with a smile that walked across the room; Mctigue was rail-thin and tall with an angular face to match. Even his nose was long and thin, while Baczkowski's wide face—with large, deep set eyes, was reminiscent of a pug. Mctigue thought as much, but declined to insult the newcomer, who did, however, have a generosity to gestures, spreading his arms wide enough to take in the world.

Baczkowski pulled up a chair and sat down next to Mctigue. He was clearly indifferent to the concept of invading personal space. "Then tell me about the play," he said, "the one you are working on."

Mctigue was reluctant at first. "I generally don't discuss work in progress. I find that all the talk stifles my creativity."

"Why? Do you intend to have an audience of one? Come now, don't be shy; perhaps I can be of help to you in working out the snares, unless, you have something that is perfection and you do not want to trifle with such *doskonałość*. I'm sorry, but Polish has a much better word. What do you have with French: la perfection?"

"I don't know Polish, but you speak English and French well," Mctigue said, suddenly uncomfortable with his own flattery.

"Ah, more compliments. I was looking for your wit. Come now, tell me about your play or the interplay within it."

Mctigue felt the sting and could feel his face reddening, but he was not entirely sure of his emotions that swung wildly between being piqued in annoyance and mixed with attraction. "Working out snares?" Mctigue was close to getting up and moving, but the man's generosity was clearly genuine. "I think it isn't wise to discuss a work so new. Right now, I need time to think without comment."

"Come now. You can't be this shy and be in theatre. Let's talk plot then characters through together. Much better here in anonymity than in front of a hostile audience later. I promise to be gentle."

Mctigue wasn't sure if Baczkowski's last statement was meant as a double entendre, and he shook his head. What followed, however, surprised him as much as he had ever been startled by his own reaction. He fell into description of his new tragi-comedy, self-correcting as he went along.

"Ah, I see, but perhaps tighter in *podsumowanie*. Oh, my Polish slips in again." Baczkowski laughed then encouraged his new friend to refine the abstract, offered a few insightful comments but was quiet during Mctigue's synopsis of the play. Mctigue generally did not want another writer's opinion of his work, but Baczkowski seemed to be so in sync with his ideas and musings that Mctigue fell into listening to the big man's critique and recognized its worth. Soon, they traded lines as if already writing together. When they both spoke the same line simultaneously, they looked at one another startled but pleased.

Perhaps that first meeting between them was also accidental but confined to American ex-pat Sylvia Beach's bookshop, "Shakespeare and Company," the most famous of the haunts of the ex-pats on 12 rue de l'Odeon in the Left Bank. Of course, they would have gone there, drawn to that intellectual hub, rubbed shoulders with other literary figures well known and those on the rise, as well as those becoming characters in their books. Mctigue reached for an Italian copy of Dante's *The Inferno*, and Baczkowski couldn't help but comment with a witty remark that normally would have been annoying to Mctigue, but that morning Mctigue was in atypically good spirits. He began to wonder if his budding friendship and attraction to Baczkowski had everything to do with his mood.

"You do realize," said Baczkowski, "we'd both be in the first circle of Hell, along with Homer and Aristotle, Cicero and Hippocrates, if Dante had anything to do with it."

Mctigue liked the conceit. "I wouldn't mind that company, but Dante is long gone and likely in that same circle arguing with Aristotle."

"Unlike Homer, I imagine he would be dreaming with a smile as if Hell suited him just fine; we'd be up all night talking, never get any sleep, growing cross, hence the inferior form of Heaven."

Mctigue nodded. "Such a Hell I could tolerate."

"My friend, I do believe you will enjoy Hell."

Something about Baczkowski's brashness was crudely appealing. Their affair began as fate, developed into friendship, and then...

~ * ~

What was Paris like at the end of the 1920s? I had done a little research and found the American Lindberg had landed in Paris in May 1927. This was the well-respected Lindberg, the one known for his aerial bravery and not some of his other qualities that became evident later, such as his anti-Semitism and elitism, the man known before his 20-month-old son was kidnapped and murdered. I imagine that, too, would change a man forever. Unlikely Baczkowski or Mctigue would have cared at all about Lindberg or his aircraft; they were neither amazed nor elated by the Spirit of St. Louis that infected much of the city at the time, immune as these two aesthetes were to the commotion around them.

Yet, they would have noticed each other. Their affinity was unmistakable, just a matter of how each would react to this instant chemistry.

"What shall we order?" asked Mctigue out of courtesy.

"I'm nearly out of currency," Baczkowski said, looking introspect.

"If you're asking if I'm paying for your meal, you had better reconsider."

"Wouldn't dream of it," Baczkowski said before offering, "I think the radishes are particularly fine this morning."

"Radishes! You don't need a lot to live on in this city," Mctigue said, before ordering an omelet with a thick slice of ham and endives.

"I'll have the radishes today," said Baczkowski grandly, "and slice them finely to savor each bite, with a touch of parsley on the side."

Chapter Sixteen
In Juxtaposition to Staged Tableau

I needed to back up, retrace my steps, go over what evidence I had gathered and what was missing. By now, Sherlock would have solved the mystery, having perceived and mentally recorded a hair left on a shirt, the tear-stained note, a missing ring, a water-stained table, whatever detail was there all the time; but no one but the great Sherlock Holmes took in details and realized the importance of each item before his discerning eyes. There were clues that I had not noticed, or if I noticed them, I did not catalog them, did not know what to do with them.

When did the suspicion first hit me? Was I doubtful of anything before seeing Gould's name on Michael Lawler's poem? I stopped in the middle of that dark corridor leading out of Morey Hall. I'd been over and over this but had solved nothing. How did Gould get Michael's poem? Not similar phrasing but exact wording, as I recall. But memory is imperfect. I could have had the words or lines all wrong. I started to wonder if Michael had stolen Gould's poem, or was I completely mistaken and only thought I had seen them before? Stopped again. Retrace steps.

Would Gould have shared his unpublished poetry with Michael? Was there a relationship I had not discerned, clouded as my emotions were around these two? If Gould was invited into Michael's home, why? Gould was an elitist unless he, unless Michael, was something more to him. Never his friend, but perhaps a lover or someone desired. Dr. Roald Gould would have no friend who was a mere student. Political imbalance made the possibility absurd. So, what was I overlooking? Michael as his lover made more sense because Michael was beautiful. I was the fool again. Here, I thought Gould was perversely interested in or attracted to me.

The curtain opened and Gould stood knocking on Michael's apartment door. No one would notice; off campus on a dimly lit street, only a few stray dogs out wandering, a cat screeching in an ally fight. Town bars were a few blocks away, even then, the patrons were mostly out-of-work men who kept their heads down, not the college crowd. Michael opens the door already knowing he will be faced with Roald; no one else coming to visit and this man, not his professor, but occasional lover, tumbles in somewhat drunk and already groping.

Was even this a ruse? Perhaps Gould only pretended to be drunk. They fight immediately because Michael expected more, too much, Roald says slurring words, but they move toward each other at the same time they raise their voices. They will have sex, but Michael is angry, tired of being used and initially tells Roald to get out. This tension of war between aversion and desire ends in an embrace. They are on the bed, and Michael forgives him because Gould is still like a god to the student.

If Gould murdered his student, how did he do it? What possible motive could he have had? No signs of struggle. A locked door. An obvious suicide. Police on the scene had made their conclusion. One glass of wine on a little table in the corner, nothing else out of place. They didn't notice a second glass of wine in the sink.

It gets tricky here with every path in the road forward blocked by debris; here a boulder, there a fallen tree, up ahead a flooded stream spilling over its banks and washing all away.

Michael would not be tricked into hanging himself, so that only left suicide or someone making the act look like suicide. If Gould managed to strangle Michael when he had fallen asleep, or was drugged, then Gould hoisted Michael's body up, after tossing the rope over the ceiling beam, finally pushing his body from the top stair. How could he have done all this and not left obvious signs of his presence? Then again, who was looking for DNA evidence or fingerprints or too many glasses on the kitchen counter? Maybe there were extra dishes in the sink, too many for a man living alone. A tie, no, a cashmere scarf thrown over a chair, used to strangle a sleeping young man, then tossed under a bed. Would Gould be that careless? No, he would go back to collect his scarf after the deed.

Locked door. Key on the table. There was no way out of this.

Tableau discovered by well-intentioned but unwitting cops. They entered the scene without awareness of intrigue, only an urgency to get the body down, rule out further investigation. A glance around the room, a few photographs, a perfunctory conversation in lowered voices. "This is as clear cut as it gets." No disturbance to note, nothing out of the ordinary for one of those bookish types with volumes stacked against the wall and near the bed. Sheets were half off, but what guy living alone makes his bed? And there was the smell. Even someone as clean and neat as Michael stinks in death. Repugnant, but they can't leave the scene, so they move quickly.

Why hadn't the cops taken the time to question the circumstances fully? If they had put on their gloves and dusted for fingerprints, pulled their shoe covers on, got out an analysis kit, turned on their flashlights pointed at oblique angles, looked under the bed for anything left behind, something that did not belong to Michael. They should have sensed that something wasn't right. A scene frozen by death, a homicide; but they missed all of the details, saw only the long body and a leather boot that had fallen to the bottom of the stairs. Someone picked up his boot and dropped it in an evidence bag, never to return to it.

Could I blame them? They were just trying to get the job done, deal with the ugly part of their work as quickly and efficiently as possible, so they could go home and sleep at night. After all, the cops didn't love him. Did I just admit that I did? That I loved Michael even though I barely registered in his consciousness? That would explain my obsession here, and my inability to start something new with any of the guys who delayed leaving class, opened the door for me, stuttered when they tried to ask me a question, offered to form a study group with me, and I had to politely decline.

If only I could have stayed in love with Jason for another year, then I was out of there free. I might have even finished my dissertation and made the late nights all work for something, at least that signed piece of paper and impressive initials after my name. I suspected that Gould would have eventually approved of my topic, even after early reluctance, if I hadn't began annoying him with misgivings about Michael's death that turned to accusations.

After the brutal attack on Michael and the staging, there was only light cleanup for Gould, the sobering duty of rinsing wine glasses, slightly straightening bed covers, arranging the scene to look as if a man alone had chosen to leave this life. No one would suspect anything. Books everywhere left in moderate disarray as they had been before; there were only Michael's notebooks to slip inside his coat and then what? Crawl out through the hidden door, secret passage with his clutch of stolen poems, leaving Michael's key in plain sight on the table. You enter a room.

Increasing disorder to scene, and the play breaks down again. Gould crawling through a secret passage? Gould on his knees? Even I was skeptical of that one. He was not the type ever to crawl.

Come back to what had been confirmed: There was a locked door. How do I know there are missing notebooks? Campello answered indirectly. All of Michael's pages of poetry were absent. He was alone and hanging in a stairwell.

Crumpling up paper in my hand, I throw the wad at a wastebasket and miss. There is an accumulating pile around the trash can. I have always had a tendency to be overly dramatic, Bill and Greta have told me on multiple occasions. Was I just getting carried away again? Suppose Michael's notebooks were nearly empty, only the first few and last pages filled with copied lines, Gould's phrases. Gould had stolen nothing from his student. Michael was practicing poetics by imitating Gould. Still possible that these conjectures were true, but I could see them leaving like the imaginary frightened bird suggested by my name.

I needed perspective while my emotions were clouding logic. Michael might have thrown away his notes and half-finished poems, discarded them in the nearest trash bin on the street, burned them in his wood stove, or hidden them in a secret crawl space. There was nothing in plain sight for the police to discover or cause suspicion.

Wait. Hidden them? Why? Wouldn't he want his work to be found after his death, catapulting his name to unlikely literary fame, as if such preposterous stuff as, "dreams are made of' actually happen? Then again, if the poetry really was Gould's work, Michael would never have wanted his notebooks found, his impersonation or plagiarism discovered. If he had merely been copying the work that his mentor had shared with him,

Michael might have felt depressed. It was possible, considering this scenario, that he couldn't write anything original anymore or that he felt origination was not even possible with cultural production filtering out of our collective brainstems. Evocative language was lost to him. He might have felt like a fraud, a fake, with the hat of a poet but not the soul. He hated Gould's class Construction of Authorship as much as I did.

Suicide began to feel possible after all. I began to doubt all of my instincts.

But if they were not his poems, Michael would have pulled away when he saw me look over his shoulder at lines on the page. Instead, he smiled. He was proud, shy but pleased I had read them. He cocked his head to the side and slightly turned to me, knew what I was doing. And if anyone ever had the soul of a poet, Michael Lawler did.

"Amazing," I said quietly.

"Thanks." He was casual. His notebook was still open. No, Michael Lawler had nothing to hide, and he believed in himself, in his "solitary creative genius."

"Could I read more of your work sometime?"

"Uh. Sure. Sometime," he nodded.

Yet, Michael never did offer to let me read his poetry after that day. I wish now that I had been more insistent. That I had taken his journals home and copied them. Then I would have proof of what exactly? Where Michael's work and Gould's stolen lines began.

Imagine Campello's face when I brought in a stack of pages, poetry that proved Michael would not have taken his life.

"This proves nothing," Sergeant Campello would respond. "They're just abstractions on a page." I could also picture Campello's retort to my protestations about "aesthetic authority" as a cultural construction and the "sacralization and desacralization of texts." Relatively unlikely the officer would have noted anything about my feminist protestations to "male-coded practice." Campello would have hated Gould's class even more than Michael and me.

Where were Michael's parents? Why weren't they demanding more answers? I didn't know anything about them, and I realized that I needed to follow that route, as well.

All the questions and speculations only led to fatigue, and I curled up on my bed and slept ten hours, missing one class and nearly a second one. When I woke, my mouth was open and lips stuck to the pillow. All right. I was going to miss the second class, too.

I was reaching the end of my time as a student, something that had gone on far too long already, graduate school immediately following undergrad studies. As an undergrad, I never skipped a class or was late to one. If there was a conscientious award, they would have given that certificate to me every year. But that ethic had changed. My grades were no longer the most important thing, and pleasing my professors had become old and tired. I still wanted something but no longer my teachers' approval.

Before all of this with Michael, there was another world out there I was anxious to reenter. Then again, I would once again feel like an alien in that other world, at least for a time. This academic environment was difficult but also insulating from so many of the world's issues. At least I thought so, until Michael's death. Now, nightmare.

Prior to his death, I was agonizing over two texts. That's too simple an answer I realized. The mystery of those lives secreted in those texts held a key to living in this world. I already thought of myself as an outsider, forever an alien in her own culture. This line of thought brought me to those other ex-pats I was studying. Instead of running to class, I turned to my notes.

After his self-imposed exile in Brazil, Baczkowski spent the last years of his life in Argentina. Mctigue died in France. Their biographers would, naturally, not make a lot of connections.

~ * ~

Yet, years earlier, over a bottle or two, they conspired in French: "They want a mystery. We'll give them one."

"Let's not make this too easy. Nothing pedestrian or irrefutable."

"And if they miss our clues entirely? Understand, they will be reluctant to question the work later."

"We're still laughing. We'll always be laughing."

"Even in death?"

"Especially in death."

"You really don't care what they think, do you?"

"I can't imagine you still do."

Baczkowski was, after all, a playwright in addition to being a novelist. He would have been intrigued by Mctigue's annihilative play, drawn to visit the theatre not once but several times, taking mental notes as he sat in the audience. The Parisians were laughing uncomfortably in the wrong places. Had they missed it, he wondered? What struck him the first time? What compelled him to layer *Light* over *Nightfall* or deeply embed his work with *Nightfall's* essence? Was there conscious collaboration between them? If so, would they have tried to hide the collusion?

If the pattern repetition was simply plagiarism, how would one get away with such theft? There was another explanation. Mctigue and Baczkowski had a conspiratorial conversation in the late 1920s in which the details that became their works were discussed together in some darkening corner of Paris.

"We could code it."

"Too obvious."

"Don't be sure of that. They're thicker than you give them credit for."

"There are always one or two who would discern…"

"Exceptions sit brooding in corners, drinking themselves into a coma."

"Aliens."

"Like us?"

"I'm not part of a tribe."

"You're in exile."

"I could go back at any time. And you?"

"Perhaps not, but I like to think I could slip in and out at will."

"You won't be back."

"It is always so definitive, so absolute, with you."

"Not with you, then?"

"We could have them talk this way."

"Gibberish."

"Perfect." A light flickered. Waiters were growing impatient to go home.

"And then they were gone."

"Just like that."

Perhaps they had planned an entire series of correspondences coded in literature. Smirking, even laughing at inept readers who would not likely discover the breadcrumbs they had left behind, but they left them, nevertheless, for someone to follow. Perhaps, simply an inside joke that would have kept them amused until their deaths, even then, they might be still laughing.

Too many details in these correspondences to arise from a conversation, even one over several bottles of good or cheap French wine. I began following another possible line; they became lovers. Or was their liaison only one night, a night Mctigue wanted to forget, embarrassed afterward, avoiding Baczkowski from that time forward. No, that kind of passion would have been more than a night, even a lust-filled one.

By then, Baczkowski had already heard from his father that he would not be further supporting Urjasz's studies. The young Pole made one last attempt to contact Dailan who had moved to another flat. Dailan wanted no visitors, particularly did not want to see Urjasz again, the heavy door closing on Urjasz's face. I could imagine Baczkowski walking back in the rain, his head lowered, his eyes catching the blurring of lines made by water distorting every surface. He would never forgive his former friend and lover, coding his work with mockery of the other man's literature. None of the repetition could be taken seriously or all of the trail was a serious parody.

With this resolve, Urjasz Baczkowski left Paris. Unlike a murderer, however, Baczkowski did not need an alibi or secret passageway to get out of the city. He simply left, not to return for years. He would not forget, however, hiding a story behind his words as in a Magritte painting of a painting.

Early in Mctigue's play *Nightfall*, there is a line by Rian that alludes to a Biblical story of two thieves who were crucified beside Christ, but the line also suggests Rian and Kieron or Kilroy and Erskine, or Mctigue and Baczkowski. Baczkowski delighted in the comparison to a thief but knew the term would sting Mctigue.

Maybe neither Baczkowski nor Mctigue was the thief of language, but two thieves together born aware of and anxious about influences in their writing to the point of deliberate deception, yet deception veiled by sensibility.

When I thought of these complications, I returned to Gould. Perhaps Gould was the thief who could not be saved. Michael knew Gould was a thief and was about to expose his mentor.

Chapter Seventeen
In Which History and Memory are Exiled

When I was thirteen, I asked Bill if I was adopted. I was blunt and so was he. Standing behind him as he graded a stack of papers on his corner desk, I felt I saw him the way Greta did before she walked out. My beautiful, cold mother would have observed his obsessive attention to detail, the balding spot on top of his graying head, usually covered with a baseball cap at home, the slight disfigurement of his left ear, pressed tightly to his skull, the injury from his old days as a wrestler, his narrow shoulders and slight build leaning into his work. He never seemed to like teaching, but he was always engaged in the act even at home.

"Bill, am I adopted?"

My father, I speculated that he was my father, stopped the motion of his hand holding a pen and looked up. "Why would you ask that?"

"Am I?"

"No, of course not. Your poor mother was in labor for fourteen hours."

"Why 'of course not?'"

He makes a coughing, sighing sound. "You're stuck with us, or I should say with me," he said with a wry look before returning to his work.

"Oh," was all I could come up with as a response. I really wanted to believe I was far too fascinating to have come from Bill. Greta, I didn't know so well because she left when I was still forming those opinions. I only knew I didn't like her very much. Fourteen hours of labor sounded quite awful, however. Maybe that was when she began to dislike me. We'd had very little contact over the years. Apparently, she divorced me along with Bill.

In books, I had discovered something for myself and the secret would not be shared easily.

You might say I first entered a book when I was eleven: Dailan Mctigue's two act play *Nightfall*, the absurdist, minimalist quality suiting my precocious cynicism, learned and honed from masters who inhabited a house with me. I sat up all night reading Mctigue's play and then read the tragi-comedy again. I understood very little of its content, but that seemed unimportant at the time. What intrigued me was the way Mctigue wound and unwound his threads, pulling me in slowly.

"What are you doing with that? You're far too young for Dailan Mctigue, although there is evidence his sarcasm will not be entirely lost on you," Bill said before roughly lifting the playbook from my little fingers and replacing it with *Heidi*, a children's book by the Swiss author Johanna Spyri. I grimaced, pouted too, but then read *Heidi*, of course, even though I resented Bill's bullying theft. "And turn on another light before you go blind."

Only a few pages into Spyri's literature, however, I decided I could relate to the child character on at least one plain of existence; she was orphaned at six and I was orphaned at birth. Of course, I had biological parents, and sometimes Bill tried to be interested in the role, but fatherhood never quite suited him. Not that he ever said anything of the sort. He tried to be kind but was mostly disinterested. Greta, that's another matter. On multiple occasions, she felt compelled to state that she never intended to become pregnant, that an accident had led to my birth, that the picture of her life and its design did not really include all these "detours." Bill told her once, when he thought I was out of earshot, that she would grow used to me; "Motherhood can mean anything you want; you can expand your definitions of self."

She told him she wanted out. Greta said she had no intention of expanding her definition of self, and, by the way, she was quite happy with herself already. I couldn't see Bill's face, but I felt his incredulous stare through the wall. I sat down and cried on the floor of my closet only once over her. Bill found me there, picked me up and carried me to bed. He read a story to me. He told me that stories were a way to escape sadness. I believed him.

Later, after Greta left for good, I heard Bill sobbing in his room one night. I listened to him outside his room for an hour before I tiptoed into my own bedroom. I am not quite sure how old I was then, but I have distinct recollections of planning to be nicer to him. I don't think of Greta as beautiful, but she is, of course. Men, in particular, find her very sensual. I know I never wanted to look like her, but I'm told that I do. I'm trying to imagine how I might have become a different person if Greta had decided to stick around and participate in the whole concept of motherhood. I lost her so long ago that I no longer feel that absence, but I did for years.

Even though Bill didn't really know how to talk to me, he used to leave me books on the little nightstand next to my bed. He would bring them home from the library, or sometimes buy me new ones. Then he would leave a cup of hot coco next to my book. "Brush your teeth after you drink it," he would say softly." Never go to bed without brushing your teeth."

We didn't go on vacations or to swimming pools and parks like other kids I knew; but Bill showed me how to cook, how to make my bed so the sheets were tucked in all around me. I slid into the narrow space like a glove. Bill also corrected my grammar. I came home from school one afternoon and threw down my papers. I intended to toss them in the trash but forgot. The next morning, I found the papers on my nightstand. They had been meticulously corrected in red ink. He drew an arrow to the back of the paper where each error was numbered and explained in detail. He was a pretty good teacher, I guess, because grammar and mechanics were never a problem for me in school.

Most of all, Bill gave me a routine of reading that allowed me not to feel completely alone because I had those books and all of their characters floating around in my head all night.

Years after my childhood foray into Spyri's book, I found that Johanna's narrative had a mirror image in the story of Hermann Adam Von Kamp, who wrote *Adelheide, das Mädchen vom Alpengebirge* before the widow conceived of her *Heidi*. I don't believe they suggested that Spyri stole Von Kamp's plot in the manner of Shakespeare's overt thefts, as that there was an indication of her reading Von Kamp's work, allowing that work to subconsciously grow into a double years later.

Turns out, I was looking into binate works of literature before I even knew what that meant. Yet, naturally, all of this was miles from where I would begin my intensive searches.

As a pre-teen, I absconded with Bill's copy of *Nightfall* and read the play repeatedly, like I said, until I nearly knew the literature by heart. You might think I couldn't wait to talk with Bill about the book since he was an English teacher, but nothing could have been further from my mind. My first reading of *Nightfall* didn't lead anywhere. I just knew I wanted to read it again, wasn't supposed to read Mctigue, and found him puzzling, therefore mysterious and inviting.

I hadn't uncovered anything approximating original thought about *Nightfall* until I opened another book years later, until I stumbled into, rather than contrived to enter Urjasz Baczkowski's novel; a labyrinth of sardonic dialogue comfortably ensconced inside Mctigue's play.

It is this place of looping doubles where I began. Of course, back then, I was searching for things such as my identity, my absent mother, my passions, love; whereas now, I'm trying to trap a murderer and a thief.

~ * ~

My issues with my parents might explain some of my cynicism when it comes to authority figures. During all my years of schooling I worked to please someone else, first teachers and later professors; all those arbiters of performance, of learning, of cultural codes. This was a continual challenge since they were demanding, and each wanted something quite different, not simply various levels of scholarship; my teachers were a compendium of messy, fallible, and ridiculous human needs and wants that spilled over into their classrooms. Only one was deadly, my personal Moriarty, but that came much later.

Gould was one more in a long succession of those who initially gave me hope, moved me to disappointment and then despair before I came to and pulled myself out of those dark places. Greta might have been good training for Gould, but I never really got to know her.

I needed something more on Gould than my suspicions and Michael's missing notebooks, if I was going to convince anyone to look into Gould's movements and possible involvement in Michael's death. What led me to suspect Gould was a slip of paper and intuition. Who would believe any connection there?

Gould and I were still in contact although he had recently suspended my teaching assistant job, stating that I appeared unable to follow through with my work responsibilities. He used my "inability to focus on readings grounded in critical theory" as evidence in an e-mail he sent to administration. I thought about protesting but knew I would lose that round, too, even if I inserted words, such as, epistemology, reciprocity, capacities, and interiority.

I confess, I went looking to find anyone who would talk about Gould or about Michael. My graduate school classes were floating islands with students generally looking only to connect with their professors, not each other.

Whether lucky or unlucky, I unexpectedly ran into Craig Sterling from my program, found myself trying to defend my assistant ship to him.

"I heard you are out," Craig said in blunt fashion, partially standing in my path as I exited a room in Rush Rhees Library.

"Out?"

"Of the class and the program. Appears you have fallen out of favor."

"Why do you care?"

"Maybe because that assistantship should have been mine to begin with," he said calmly but with a grand dash of rancor.

"Really? I would ask how you came to that conclusion, but I don't really care." I started to move past him and he stepped in my way again. Craig was built like a football player, big, but had never played the sport, he had proudly announced one afternoon as we left class. He was always fairly obnoxious but had never come after me before.

"You know the only reason you got that position in the first place is because Gould was told to fill the slot with a female. He has always chosen his own top students since offering the assistantship, that is, until he had to fill his assistantship with a girl. I suspect Title IX interference."

I shook my head. "Apparently, you are both ignorant and misogynistic. Congratulations. Now stop blocking me, or I will file bullying charges."

"You would too. Bitch."

"Ah. Your go-to insult? Good luck with it. You're clearly going places." I laughed, but he stepped aside.

After leaving, I could feel the blood rush to my face in anger. Who knew one had all these unseen enemies in the world? People who hated you for things you had no idea about until one day you ran into them in the library. My grades were definitely higher than Sterling's, but I did wonder about all of the male graduate assistants Gould had placed before me. Perhaps the pattern was not coincidental, after all. I did not so much think that I was undeserving suddenly, but it occurred to me that Gould might have had another aim in choosing male assistants. I'd have to consider this later. What was the implication? He was sexist? Easy enough to conclude, but perhaps there was more. Was he attracted to the young men he chose?

I was already aware that I had passed the dangerous point in maintaining my grades and viability in the graduate program. Someone might have intervened to save me, but then I thought of Michael and who was there to save him? Really, I just needed a friend to talk to and that was not going to happen. What would Sherlock do without Watson, without evidence, with only his instinct that told him something was not right? I had to become that kind of detective, the one who would not accept a dead end. Michael deserved that much from me, at least.

Gould was older, cleverer, more devious, politically connected, smarter, more experienced and just maybe evil. Yet, somehow, I had to beat him at his game—even though I did not know the name of the game he was playing, or risk far more than a dissertation and years in the graduate program. I needed to draw him out, but he would be aware of my attempts before I began. Gould knew the play *Hamlet* far better than me, and my professor would not be drawn into confessing, "Give me some light," like smart, but not smart enough, uncle/stepfather Claudius.

Gould was no Claudius. I would never bet on him showing signs of a guilty conscience. If I had a big enough mouse trap, however, I would have used it.

Chapter Eighteen
Authorship Constructed from Stolen Lines

I sent Gould an e-mail, trying to embed my suspicions within a discussion about his course on the construction of authorship. Initially, I thought I could try trapping him subtly, sending a note about textual questions related to course materials.

~ * ~

Dr. Gould,
You've asked us to consider Hamlet again and again, and I'm confounded by these lines: "That youth and observation copied there/...o villain, villain, smiling damned villain!" (Act I, v. 103, 108).
Vena

He would know I was accusing him of copying Michael's lines from a poem and, more, that I was stating that he was a villain for his actions.

Gould responded in a manner that was at once professional and subtly threatening. Would anyone but me see the response in that way?

~ * ~

Advena,
Shakespeare wrote about the concept of writing in that passage, as much as revealing Hamlet to be circumspect in speaking to the Ghost:

"Remember thee? / Yea, from the table of my memory/ I'll wipe away all trivial fond records (Act I, v. 99-101).

Professor Gould

~ * ~

Gould had absorbed and withstood my accusation of his villainy and thrown it back in my face, using the same passage to threaten to annihilate me and my "records." Still, who would read a Shakespeare scholar's quotation of *Hamlet* as an actual threat? Who would believe me if I made such a claim?

Perhaps foolishly, I tried again, even though I did not think I could ensnare him. This time, I added Michael's name to the quotation. I thought that he would have to respond in some telling way.

Dr. Gould,

"Within the book and volume of Michael's brain, / Unmix'd with baser matter" (Act I, v. 105-106).

Vena

He was ready as always and, once again, would not take the bait.

Advena,

You have regrettably misquoted Shakespeare. Please proofread your notes and correspondences carefully. This carelessness will be seen by others as a mark on your professional conduct. Perhaps the passage you meant to quote is the following: "My tables. Meet it is I set it down/ That one may smile, and smile, and be a villain" (Act I, v. 109-110).

Please be aware of the impression you make on others with your silly accusative words and actions.

Professor Gould

He had admitted his villainy to me, yet nothing would come of it, he knew. His chess match was going his way, so I needed a stronger tactic.

~ * ~

Dr. Gould,

"Indeed, you smile."

Returning to the theorists, Derrida claimed, "Writing shelters a little death."

On the concept of collaborative creation and authorship, do you agree with Foucault and Barthes about the "death of the author?" This seems particularly pertinent to me in light of Michael Lawler's death.

Vena

It was not as if I was sitting around waiting for an e-mail response, but I did check my computer often during the next 24 hours. Gould took his time perhaps to increase my torture.

~ * ~

Advena,

As one of your professors, I am not here to agree or disagree with your struggles over theoretical grounding but to assign required readings, guide the discussion on critical theory, and advise you to continue to read, analyze, and come to your own conclusions on the concept of authorship, at length. Please look into new electronic technologies on the way we process that formerly romantic idea of "author." Barthes and Foucault gave us frameworks for the conversation. (Also, note the considerable distinctions between their theories.)

Please try to stay up with the course readings as they will improve your academic competence. I would also advise you not to be so literal in your interpretation of language; the question and response you framed are neither professional nor sophisticated enough to warrant further consideration or conversation.

Dr. Gould

He was flawless. Nothing in that email to give me ammunition. Wiser investigators would have given up, admitted defeat and moved on.

That was not possible for me, so I went to letter format, slipping a note into his office mail. With every phrase, he annihilated any argument I may have tried to pose or offer, but I didn't give up. I don't know how I thought I was going to get him to admit something, much less to confess anything or suggest his guilt.

~ * ~

Dr. Gould,

I was acquainted with an author who was capable of origination, but he died mysteriously and tragically. He would have fit the "romantic notion of author" unless he was involved in a social construct I am unaware of at this time. Perhaps someone was writing with him at the time of his death. Perhaps they shared some of the same phrases in their writings, or perhaps someone stole the original author's work.

Vena

~ * ~

He was quick to respond in kind, placing the note in my mail.

~ * ~

Advena,

If we are discussing authors in theory and not inappropriate and questionable personal anecdotes, then please keep your queries within the pre-established boundaries of the course. I remind you of the "death of the author" as framework, not as a literal statement and advise you to stay within the parameters set out as a discussion on the "romantic idea of author as solitary creative genius." Please see me personally if you have further questions.

I have also noticed that you have not been attending classes regularly and saw you wandering around the campus somewhat directionless. You might want to become involved with a study group in order to help you appreciate and discern what you are reading. Your level

of questioning is not befitting a graduate student in our program.
Dr. Gould

He would not be baited unless that reminder about "the death of the author" could be read as a veiled threat. I took the phrase that way but was sure no one else would read into his language in that manner. There was also menace in the words suggesting he was spying on me, saw me "wandering around campus somewhat directionless." Could I use that as evidence he was threatening? Who would believe such a thing unless they had more immediate experience of Gould?

Not ready to give up, I tried writing a poem that hinted at my suspicions. For a few minutes, I must have imagined that I was as clever as Gould.

I left my poem in his mailbox.

Conceit of Crows on Authorship
Pontificating crows, forgetting their wings,
hopped along a country road and talked at length,
all at once, of course, so their identities were fused
in feathers as well as sounds of cawing
about aesthetic authority of collaborative authorship,
their raucous calls in unison designed,
their grating but crowing cackles
of etymological sense of authority in assertion:
"It's all derivative and contextual."
Startled by shots, they took to air
as a murder of crows cawing on death
of the author, contrasted with the single note
of a white-throated sparrow. "That ridiculous songbird"
believed her voice, in deconstructed wind, could be heard.
Vena

He responded curtly and disparagingly about my weak attempts at obvious, declarative prose poetry and my inability to make distinctions in critical theory. "Combining the two is at best a silly exercise, as you have demonstrated."

I finally made an appointment to talk with Gould face-to-face. I hadn't slept in days with just the thought of speaking to him again looming large. When I got to his office, I knocked on the door and he said, "enter," not "come in," or anything inviting or even civil. Everything with him was a command. We were no longer student and teacher but politically mismatched adversaries. This was a war I was going to lose, but I kept marching forward.

He looked up, then turned back to some papers on his desk as if my presence did not even require half his attention. I coughed, cleared my throat and he said, "Yes?" with his eyes half closed. I noticed he was wearing a thin scarf around his neck and loosely draped over his shoulders in the way I had seen in a photo of Colum McCann. Somehow, the thin scarf looked natural on the Irish writer McCann yet pretentious on Gould. I had begun seeing him with the unaccustomed eyes of clarity.

"I know I have missed class and not been as focused lately."

He actually snorted. Did he really make that noise? "Are you coming to ask permission to continue in our program, because I no longer see a way forward for you here," he said as he rolled a beautiful, hand-carved Koa wood pen between his index and middle fingers. I felt a certain familiarity with the pen because he had told me about it, how he acquired the instrument on a trip to Hawaii, meeting the native artist, in one of his rare, generous moves a year earlier. But I was not a threat to him back then. Everything about him now was impeccable and severe. Although I was used to his cruel comments and retorts, I was still shocked at the finality of his statement: "I no longer see a way forward for you here."

It took every ounce of strength I had not to turn and run out the door. If I was leaving Rochester without my doctorate, without completing my program, then I would at least say what I was thinking, some of the crazy thoughts that had been running through my head.

"Michael was a fine poet and scholar. He only wanted your respect."

Gould looked up again, studying me for a moment but opening his eyes wide now, his brows raised. "This isn't about Michael, and I'm not sure if that is a smart tactic to attempt to garner sympathy on your part."

"I don't want sympathy. Michael's poetry was beautiful. I read his poems, I read his notebooks, they are missing." This stopped his forward motion of thought. I could actually see hesitation across the surface of his face, his forehead, his eyes, his mouth, but he squared his shoulders further and leaned back as if mimicking ease.

"His writing was immature but held promise. I don't know about any notebooks or to what you are referring. He had not completed his project, and I understand he was considering throwing away the poems on which he was still working." Not even a quiver in his voice.

I wanted to ask him, "How do you do that? How is it possible for you to lie and take that superior tone when you have so much to hide?" But I couldn't say that, could I?

There was no turning back. Even if I had wanted to save my years of schooling, it was already too late. Desperation and despair must have given me courage. "Michael was the best poet among us." He knew I was including him, and his face flushed slightly. "He may have been depressed, I don't know, but he was never foolish. He would not have thrown away his poetry, even the versions he was unsure of. He was confident in his talent. Were you the one who called the police that morning? The morning they found his body? Someone called them. How did you know before anyone?"

"What are you babbling about? How dare you, I'm afraid you are going to have to leave immediately. Your accusations are baseless and bordering on hysterical. Leave my office now before I'm forced to call security and have you removed." Gould actually picked up a landline phone.

"Call security. Please do. I would like to talk to them about you and your threats. How is asking a question an accusation unless you have something to hide? Why weren't you concerned about Michael missing class when he never missed class?"

Still holding the phone in his hand, Gould hesitated. "Of course, I was concerned, but he was an adult with his own choices to make. I don't get into my students' personal lives."

"But you do. You know all about us. Knew that my parents were divorced. Asked me about their breakup once. What did you know about

Michael?"

He stiffened, and leaned toward me in a threatening manner, his veins at his temples suddenly noticeable. "I know only what my students wish to share, and you revealed your parents' divorce in a poem, in case you have forgotten what you have previously written."

"It was a poem not a memoir. Why do you imagine what I wrote about was autobiographical?"

"Because you are transparent and confessional in your writing just as most inexperienced and immature writers tend to be."

"But not Michael. What did you know about Michael? About his parents?" Although I was guessing, I suddenly felt like I had something to hold.

"Michael shared his family tragedies with me, and I was sympathetic, naturally, about the death of his parents, as I try to be with all my students."

New information. Michael had family tragedies. His parents were dead. That was why they didn't come to campus to bring home the body of their son. Then I laughed. I couldn't help it. His statement was so absurd. "It was you, wasn't it? Did you steal his poems?" Everything was out—not really, because I did not go as far as asking if he had killed Michael. I felt less fear than when I had entered, even as he held the phone to call security. "Go ahead and call security. I'd like to tell them some things about you, too." He put down the receiver sharply.

"Get out. You're done here, at this university," he said with rising anger, now standing and taking a step toward me.

"Maybe. But if you come closer, I will scream for help, and who knows what I might say? And who knows what they might believe? After all, some accusations, baseless or not, never go away, do they?" I was fishing now, standing on an island and casting out to sea.

"I am surprised that I never realized how shallow and small-minded you were before," he said as he stood up fully, showing his great height but not taking a step closer. "Leave now."

"I will go, but I have some things to take care of first, without interference. Because if I am prevented from finishing, leaving in my own way or you step in, maybe they won't all believe you or believe you forever.

Sooner or later, you will face what you've done. I'll make sure of it."

"You stupid little fucking bitch, I'll make sure you never...," he said with venom. Even he realized that he had gone too far.

"Just so you know, I recorded you. I wonder what the administration would think about the way you talk to your students." I held out my phone then pulled back the device quickly. I could see his Adam's apple move up and down. "You're the one who has to live with it. How does it feel to read his poems as your own? How does it feel to know you have nothing creative left inside?" I walked out and didn't look back until I reached the steps. No one was following. No security guards racing toward me. He was a coward as well as a thief and, just maybe, a murderer.

That night a letter found its way into my mailbox.

Gould had, indeed, been stalking me, keeping track of my movements.

Advena,

If you are going to continue as a student at this university, you will need to take a number of steps, including meeting with your advisors and the school psychologist. Your erratic behaviors, poor academic performance and poor attendance puts you at risk of course and program failure. Insulting your professor in an attempt to get him or her to be unprofessional in language over your failing grades is not an advisable move.

I have noticed you on campus on the days we have class. Your visitations to the library are less frequent and your continual treks to the coffee shop clearly indicate a student who is no longer a student.

You give me no recourse but to ask for your dismissal from the program.

Dr. Gould

He knew what I knew. He was now nervous about what I might say, building his alibi. I just needed to plan for a way out of town and to make a couple of stops to find out a few more details before leaving. Maybe he would get away with the theft of Michael's poetry, but I would leave with some ammunition. In a way, it would be a triumph simply to make Gould feel discomfort, and I was aware that he was arriving at that point. He had stood up threateningly. He had called me a 'bitch'. He talked about calling security. These were not the actions or words of a man nonplussed, a man innocent of a crime. Just how far would he go to silence me? I began to wonder.

Being able to penetrate the mystery was critical. My life, as well as others' lives, depended upon it. Yet, I was not ready when the task was put before me. Even after all of those years of reading in the genre, I felt at a complete loss when confronted with an unnatural and mysterious death. The sleuth is never supposed to feel that way or even to feel, really. Assuming the intellect is eminent, acumen takes over, with emotions neatly tucked away until after the case is solved. Yet I was conscious of my dominant emotions that led me in too many directions at once.

When I stopped feeling sorry for myself, I sensed an urgency — that justice was due for Michael, not out of some abstraction but that hard fist Michael had referred to in discussing Leroi Jones' poetry. I wanted to be that hard fist of vengeance.

Chapter Nineteen
You, Muted and Mad

I was back at our familiar Barnes & Noble campus bookstore, looking in the poetry section. Gould's last book of poems, the one that came out right before I arrived on campus, was displayed prominently. I'd bought a copy of his book when I took his course, but then loaned the thin text to someone and never got it back. This was the full-length book I had heard him read from but did not recall the poems. Flipping through the book in the store, I stopped at a curious one.

Catechismal
Not mythological or religious schism questions,
rather, questions philosophical: man, woman, all unnatural clowns
forming questions detached from Catholic Catechism,
unbecoming in doctrine, those questions further down,
drowning questions
intrinsic, small-minded questions only indicating tilt
of questions of the preternatural, in consideration of doom,
with weak questions of assumed innocence, of embroidered guilt,
provocative and insistent questions in bedroom or boardroom,
those sustainability questions, explicitly sexual and political,
motivated by questions hanging over crowded spheres:
those questions to be danced with, not challenged critically;
the perfunctory questions of found human skull fostering fears:
Hamlet's "To be or not to be?" no longer primary question
but raised merely as a question in sustained mockery.

~ * ~

Perhaps I had heard him read this poem years earlier, but it struck me with this reading that his poem, while erudite, was essentially hollow, devoid of feeling and cynical to the point of absence of humanity. I wondered what a psychiatrist would do with such material, yet, I had missed all this the first time, so predisposed to fascination with the man. Young and impressionable, I felt lost in his intellectual gamesmanship. I traced the word "questions" in his poem and found a pattern of question marks, something I had not noticed previously. Yet, the clever arrangement on the page gave the poem no more humanity.

I realized there would not be any of Michael's full poems or even his phrases in Gould's book, written well before he had even met Michael. With the cloud removed from my eyes, however, I was trying to discern whether or not Gould really was a decent poet. I slipped the book into my backpack for later reference.

My next step was to find a classmate who knew Michael better than I did. Rob Solnit occasionally sat with Michael and I had seen them talking on a few occasions, so I started with him. Rob was a classic scholar and would later fit the unfair stereotype of a university professor to a tee. He even looked the part with a rumpled but stately air, refined good looks, and sophistication that came as birthright of the indifferently wealthy. I caught up to him after his class.

"Rob, I need to talk to you about Michael."

Turning around slowly, he looked annoyed but still somewhat curious as to what I might say to him. "Really? Michel Lawler? What more is there to say? I'm sorry, what's your name again?" Early in the semester, Rob had tried to get my attention on multiple occasions, but I was engrossed with Michael. I suppose this nastiness was Rob's way of paying me back for the slights he must have felt.

Pretending to forget my name, of course, should be the ultimate insult, but I was beyond caring about such pettiness. Rob's rudeness could not compare to anything I'd already faced with Gould. Poor Rob. He was really going to have to work on his vituperation if he wanted to be in

Gould's league. "Vena. Rob, I'm sorry to bother you, but something Gould said made me wonder about."

"You talked to Gould? About Lawler?" He was interested now and listening, even leaning toward me slightly and slowing his pace as we continued walking. "What did he say? Gould."

"He told me that Michael had known great tragedy in his life, and I was wondering if you—"

"You're not kidding? He told you that? I'm surprised."

"About the tragedy of his parents?"

"That Gould would say anything about it. Very atypical of him."

"Do you know what happened?"

"Of course, it was awful. Michael's parents and his sister were killed in a car accident on their way home. Apparently, they had dropped Michael off after break and were heading back to wherever they lived. I've forgotten now. Over a year ago, you understand. Bad roads, naturally, icy. They ran into a truck or, rather, a tractor tailor jack-knifed into them, I think. Christ, how much tragedy is one family allotted?"

"It would seem an infinite amount. His parents and sister?" I couldn't believe what I was hearing or that Michael continued going to classes after such a horrific event. "How did he?"

"Really, his whole family in one instant. It's not like he talked about it much, but we worked on a few projects together, study groups, and he told me one afternoon without me asking anything. I don't pry into people's personal lives. There was no story the way he told it, just a statement of facts. He said they were killed as if he simply needed to say the fact out loud to make sure it was real."

"He must have told Gould then, too."

"No. Fuck. Excuse me, I mean, I didn't think they were close even though Michael was one of his grad assistants. He was so tight-lipped about it though. Of course, the administration all knew. They get notice of that kind of thing. I suppose they're expected to watch out for the student going off the deep end, and in Michael's case—sorry, that sounded a little callous. I mean Michael was predisposed to depression before that happened. I told him if he ever needed anyone, he could call me. I also suggested he get some counseling help. You know, they have those services on campus, but

I don't think he took advantage."

"That was very kind of you." Rob stopped walking and looked at me closely, trying to determine if I was being sarcastic, I supposed. Kindness wasn't an attribute most people associated with Rob. When I think of it, he might be another Gould in embryo stage.

"It wasn't much really. Looking back now, I suppose I should have done something more, but Michael was not someone to get close to, or at least I didn't think anything I said mattered to him. To be honest, I don't know how he stayed in school; I mean financially, well, really, emotionally, too. I am pretty certain he never received the counseling I suggested, and I respected his privacy."

We were facing each other now and staring at one another as if trying to read the other person. "There's something else, Rob. Did Michael ever share his poetry with you?"

"No. Why? What's all this about? Why bring up his poetry?"

"I saw some lines on Gould's desk that were from one of Michael's poems I'd seen earlier in his notebook."

Rob stepped back from me. "So? Gould had probably graded the poem and not returned it yet. You know how long he held onto our papers, particularly poems."

"No, there was no grade on the paper. Just Gould's name at the bottom of Michael's lines."

"That's nuts. What are you saying? He was probably looking at some of Michael's old work."

I repeated myself for emphasis. "Gould's name on the page with Michael's lines."

"Fuck that. Jesus, Advena, do you know what you're saying? Gould is a phenomenal poet, and he wouldn't."

"But he did. You must have seen some of Michael's poems when you studied together?"

Shaking his head, Rob studied my face a moment longer. "Look, I'm late. I think you're making a very big mistake, a serious mistake, and I wouldn't say anything about this, about Gould to anyone else. Could be detrimental. Don't mention me, either."

"Except I already confronted Gould."

"You did what? What the hell. You really are crazy, like they say."

"Who are 'they' saying I'm crazy?"

Rob turned away from me. "I'm sorry, but I have to leave, and please don't tell anyone you talked with me. I have nothing more to say to you. Ever." Practically sprinting, Rob only turned back around once to make sure I was not following him. I stood there thinking about how alone Michael must have felt; alone and betrayed. When he finally worked up the resolve to talk about the great loss of his family, there was only this prick Rob to take in his story and react unsympathetically. Again, I wished I had been more confident and walked up to Michael, thrown my arms around him, and told him that I would listen, that I would be there for him. Would I have been able to stop what happened?

How long had Michael known Gould was a thief before our professor killed him? What else had Michael discovered about Professor Roald Gould? The entire story started opening up for me in ways that I could not yet comprehend. I wondered if Michael realized that everything Gould did was part of a long set-up, a trap. I hoped Michael was not afraid at the end, that he knew nothing of his impending death before Gould struck. He was dead, but I didn't want to think of him in pain and fearful at the end, too.

Gould had everyone running scared, literally in Rob's case. I assumed that Gould felt it would be easier to steal from someone if he was no longer alive. My second epiphany: Gould had definitely killed Michael in order to steal his poems. I was certain of the theft now. He had chosen his victim, someone without a lot of allies, someone without an angry, grief-stricken family to look into the tragic death of their beloved son. I also knew that proving Gould's involvement, in any way, with Michael's death was going to be next to impossible.

That night, on my way back to my apartment, I felt someone following me. I turned around quickly and saw the shape of a man slipping or running away. Gould. Several other students appeared laughing and talking. Gould had seen them, otherwise, he might have come after me at that moment. How could I be sure? Yet, I knew that shape was his. Suddenly, I was afraid to go home or anywhere else.

Chapter Twenty
Afraid to Peer Out

Nervously pacing the room, I had no doubt that Gould would find a way to eliminate me from the program, if not the campus. No, it was worse than that. He had killed Michael, I was certain. Why wouldn't he attempt to kill me too? By now, I more than suspected that Gould had murdered, but who would listen to me? Staying on campus began to seem like tempting fate. With no one else I could turn to in that moment, I called Bill.

"Hi."

"Who's there?" I must have woken him from a deep sleep because his voice was raspy and lacked its usual control.

"It's your daughter. You know, the one you adopted."

"Advena?"

"That's right, unless you have another daughter you haven't mentioned. I'm not counting your two step-daughters even though you have to."

"So like your mother." I could almost hear his laughter beneath the words.

"Not really. And that's kind of mean, Bill. You know I'm nothing like her, and that neither of us likes her very much."

"I'm sorry. Don't forget, your mother was the love of my life. It's not really an insult."

"It just feels like one to me."

I wanted to tell him that I needed him, that I was in trouble with nowhere to go and no one to protect me. I really needed him to act like a strong, protective father for once in our lives. Maybe I was being a little dramatic, but I felt the situation called for it.

"Okay. What do you want? It's one in the morning. I'm afraid I..."

"One eleven. I know. Sorry. Really I am. I don't like waking you, and I know it's terribly rude, but," I controlled the quiver in my voice to the extent possible.

"Listen, if you need money, I'm short right now. We can't really have this conversation this time of night. You're just going to have to tighten your spending the same way I do." By now, poor Bill had two ex-wives and a couple of step-children for whom he was financially responsible. He had come up with money several times for me to enable me to stay at Rochester; another loan was not going to happen for a while again. I could hear his resolve, even when woken from sleep.

"There's something I need to tell you."

"Unless you are bleeding on the side of the road, you can wait until a decent hour, I think. Oh, my God, you're not bleeding or anything, right?"

"No. No blood. Thanks, I will call at a better time. Sound advice, as usual. Goodnight, Bill." I hung up, then sat on the edge of my bed and started rocking like a little kid, shaking. I wasn't in this weirdly fetal position for long before I thought of Jason, pulled on my shoes and coat, and headed out into the night. There was a point as to why I hadn't thought of Jason before, but I pushed it back.

By the time I got to Jason's apartment, I was shaking with cold. I really didn't know what I was doing, but I knocked on his door, tentatively at first, then more forcefully as seconds passed into minutes. This march to Jason's place was even weirder than calling poor Bill in the middle of the night. If I could have observed myself, I'd be recommending therapy.

Abruptly, he opened the door, yelling as he peered out of the blackness into light, "Who the hell? Oh, it's you. Damn, Vena. What the fuck?"

"Sorry. Sorry, it's just ....", it crossed my mind that I was saying, "sorry" a lot lately without feeling the emotion behind the words.

"What do you want? Good God, do you know what time it is?" Then something occurred to him because he changed his tone and said kindly, with a hint of old affection or concern, "Hey, what's wrong? Are you okay?" The door opened slightly wider but not all the way, so he was standing in his boxers, taking up the entire entrance. He was still entirely too cute with his wavy brown hair sticking straight up and his eyes glossed over from sleep, the way he used to look when we had a few too many glasses of wine or beer. "You're lucky I heard you. Then I wasn't going to answer the door. I thought you had to be some freak. Not you, but someone else."

"Can I come in?" I wanted to wriggled around him then into him, but I couldn't unless he moved for me. For some reason, I kept thinking about how tall he looked in the doorway.

"Vena, look, I."

"Who's there?" A disembodied voice emerged from the caliginous space behind him.

Oh, Christ. The voice was hers and I'd have to leave. How could I have forgotten about her? I hadn't really. I just refused to consider her as part of my altered new reality.

"Sorry, I didn't mean to interrupt or wake you. I was a little lonely, a lot lonely." There was no way I could bring all of this intrigue into his life now. What was I thinking when I ran over there? Jason had been the perfect boyfriend when everything was going right in my life. He just wasn't used to dealing with problems, or doubt, or well, any of the complications of life.

"Is that her? Is that the fucking bitch?" Disembodied voice rasping in the dark.

Jason let go of the door and stretched his hand to touch my shoulder. "Ah, Vena. I can't—I." He leaned toward me and I thought he was going to kiss me, so I pulled back out of instinct rather than any lack of desire.

"I know. It's okay, just out for a walk. Nice night to get some fresh air. I'll be leaving now."

"Wait." He looked down at his boxers and smiled. "Look, I'll at least walk you home. Give me a second to put something on. We can talk on the way." He reached for my hand.

"That's her? Jason, I'm asking you, is that that bitch?" Disembodied voice is getting closer, pulling sheets around her naked body, I imagined. There is a rustling noise and then a tripping sound followed by a loud thump. "Damn it. Ouch." Normally, I would have found this whole scene funny, imagining her falling over.

"No, no, that won't work," I pointed toward the voice coming from the darkness. He looks down as if ashamed. "It's okay," I told him, realizing I needed to let him off the hook. "Thanks anyway. I wasn't thinking straight, as usual."

"Let me at least give you money for a cab and maybe tomorrow," Jason said as I turned.

"Good for cab money. Got it. Thanks anyway," and I left, feeling much worse than when I arrived. I needed to stop going back to old boyfriends. Except there was one more still on my list.

On the way back to my apartment, it occurred to me that I was as likely to get killed or mugged by a stranger in the street in the dead of night as hurt by Dr. Roald Gould. Maybe I should have thought things through a bit more before rushing around like a deceived and bumbling, as well as highly emotional, amateur gumshoe. Who was I kidding? My actions were those of scared child, and nothing I was doing remotely resembled real investigative work. This was exactly the kind of thing that Sherlock would never do. He would not have followed up false leads, visited characters irrelevant to the case, left himself exposed unnecessarily, and he most certainly would not have gone to old girlfriends for help and comfort. If I was going to continue and have any hope of success in finding rectitude for Michael, I needed to stop being so amateurish and sad. When was Sherlock Holmes ever sad? Addicted to opium perhaps, but his bad habits never interfered with his ability to carefully dissect a case, analyze details, and arrive at inevitable conclusions leading to the right resolution.

I once rented an old movie, *Murder by Death*, in which the twists and turns in the mystery had all of the invited detectives thoroughly confused by their host, Truman Capote, as his character Lionel Twain. Capote had dug into more than one murder mystery, both real and fictitious, as a writer, first with his book on the actual homicides detailed *In Cold Blood*, and then with one he left all of us, regarding Harper Lee. Was Capote really the author of *To Kill a Mockingbird*? As Harper Lee's childhood friend, Capote had the means, talent, and motive to give this gift to her. I preferred, like most people, to believe that Lee had written the work, in spite of circumstantial evidence to the contrary. In a short conversation on the topic with Roald Gould, he said that Lee could never have written the novel. When I asked, "why not?" he merely scoffed as if the question was too childish to require a response.

At the end of *Murder by Death*, the fumbling P.I.s, morosely gathered for the conclusion, weren't even certain a homicide had taken place, perhaps because none had actually occurred. Turning the knob to my door with frozen fingers, I realized that I would have fit in well with that stumbling crew, but they would not be making any movies or writing any books about my none-too-clever, analytical work. And the desperation was no longer just about finding justice for Michael, but about self-preservation. Now, I was Gould's prey.

Chapter Twenty-one
The Room Echoing Emptiness

Two years before Michael Lawler's death, a graduate student b y the name of Marc Bennett jumped or fell into the Genesee River wearing work boots, dressed in fatigues and a long wool coat. When his body was recovered a day later, further downstream, it was suspected that he had been drinking heavily. Implications were that he had slipped in a drunken state, fallen into the river, and was unable to climb out due to his inebriation or from hitting his head. Friends of his stated that he left the party fairly sober, but who could really be sure?

His death stirred faculty and administrators to shake their heads and caution students about the dangers of over-imbibing. The news report was, once again, very brief, but the campus paper carried a stern warning from the president, at that time, about certain behaviors. There was no mention of suicide, and a finding of accidental death by drowning seemed obvious.

I would never have come across the story of Marc Bennett if I hadn't started looking into the deaths of University of Rochester students associated with Roald Gould. Then I overheard a professor talking with a colleague while I was waiting in the Office of Academic Records to get my records ready to send wherever I was going next. It was only a fragment, not the full story, but enough to set me searching. Apparently, Marc was a talented poet, too, according to the professor in the office.

In Rush Rhees Library, I found an old news story. In it, Bennett's relationship to the university seemed remote, as if he had only taken a few courses while working in the city. Finding the academic courses he was enrolled in would be the real search, but I set off to determine exactly what kept him at River Campus.

Any decision to swim in work boots would end badly, it would seem. Marc Bennett drowned two years before I had come as an undergraduate. No one talked about his death by the time I entered the university. After an archival search, I found a photo of him, and he looked like an intelligent young man who was destined for something better than to be caught in the branches of a downed tree and swept under muddy water. The tragedy of his death was compounded by the blame laid at his feet. He had apparently caused his own death by drinking too much and falling.

Making friends with a secretary in the Office of Academic Records is not the easiest thing to do. I had planned to arrive just before lunch. She looked at me suspiciously when I made my request. Then I launched into a story about how my father lost his job and couldn't afford to help me anymore, so I had to drop out even though I had spent all that time trying to earn my doctorate.

"Oh, dear," she said. "All your files are online, dear."

"I could use some help, please."

"I would think you would know how to do this by now." She was suspicious again, but she showed me how to access my account then told me she was going to lunch if I didn't mind. "Oh, no, please do," I said as politely as I could manage. "But I just have a couple of questions first."

She stood there while I asked about Marc Bennett, then shook her head before explaining that even if it wasn't unethical and illegal, it would not be possible to access another student's records. When I thought of my plan, I hadn't realized that everything was online, even the older records. Then, she told me student records older than five years were destroyed, except in the case of students who had not graduated or completed their programs. Dead end.

Sherlock would not give up this easily. I looked through the faculty and staff directory, trying to find someone who might have had Bennett as a student. There were names and e-mail addresses, but it wasn't the kind of question to ask via e-mail, so off I went to find people. It became my full-time job even though I scarcely believed I would discover anything from any of them. Since I had stopped going to class, I had a remarkable amount of free time on my hands.

The third door I knocked on answered, "Come in." Professor Marilyn Hamilton was a surprise. I told her I was doing an archival poetry project, trying to find poems from past students at the university in order to produce a new journal.

"What a wonderful idea," she said. "You might try our undergrad lit magazine *Logos* or the journal *Review of Contemporary Fiction*. We have Dalkey Archive Press here now, as you may know."

"Actually, I'm looking for the poems of a particular student by the name of Marc Bennett."

"Oh, dear," she said appearing distressed. "Do you know, are you aware he died several years ago?"

"I know he died while a student here. I'm wondering if you know of any professors who had him in their classes? Would you have had him as a student?"

"Of course, he was my student and Roald Gould's. Bennett was an English major, if I'm not mistaken. I only had him for one class, but he was a memorable young man, and of course his tragic death, but I certainly don't recollect any of his poems from that time; you know it was five or six years ago..."

"Seven and a half years ago that he drowned," I couldn't help correcting her error. "Do you recall the names of any of his friends or classmates? Maybe they kept a few of his poems? Perhaps his parents have some of his poetry? I have been made aware of the fact that he was a very fine poet."

"Oh, I would think not, I mean, I would think that his classmates would not have kept his work. As I recall, he was very quiet. I'm not sure if I should be saying this, but I suppose it's public record. His mother died while he was here. It was a terrible time for him, as you can imagine. I know people tried to reach out to him, but he seemed increasingly withdrawn. He seldom spoke in my class, and I might not have remembered him at all except for the tragedy, of course. My class in poetry was not one of poetry creation but, rather, of critical readings."

I waited. "There must have been someone."

She brought her head back and looked up at the ceiling as if it held a clue. Then she suddenly looked back at me. "Let me think. Maybe. There was a girl Katherine—Katherine, oh, I'm trying to think back: her last name was, it's on the tip of my tongue. I could look at my records. I think Bennett and Katherine were quite friendly." She pulled out a gradebook from the shelf behind her desk, and thumbed through pages. I tried to be as quiet as possible so she would not change her mind. "Here she is," she said delighted. "Katherine Bushnell. Lovely young woman and a good student, too. Perhaps she knew some of his poetry, or she might have seen it."

"Thank you so much," I said, wanting to hug her, but extended my hand instead. She took it in her own and held mine for an instant longer with both of hers. It's funny that you can tell a lot about a person by how they greet and leave you, how they extend a hand or hold your hands. What I could tell about Dr. Hamilton was that she was warm and generous. I never took any of her classes but knew I should have.

"I hope you find his poems or at least one and are able to honor him," she added. "That would be lovely."

"Oh, and Dr. Hamilton, I am really disappointed that I never had you as a professor. I think I would have loved your class."

"Oh, why thank you. I wish you good luck in finding the poems. You know, Marc was a favorite of Roald's. I remember now; Roald, Professor Gould, thought so highly of him he even paid for his funeral because his parents were gone. We all thought it was terribly kind of him and a bit unusual."

"He paid for his funeral?" This was startling. What professor would do such a thing? It suggested a connection far beyond that of a student-teacher relationship.

"Yes. Professor Gould is certainly dedicated. Best wishes in your search."

"Thank you." As I left the building, I thought about Marc Bennett, wondered if I would be able to find Katherine Bushnell, and I really did wish I'd had Dr. Hamilton for a professor. Gould, unfortunately, had embittered my experience at a very dynamic and excellent university. At some point in the future, I might be able to sort it out rationally. But this news about Gould paying for Bennett's funeral. What was that about?

It took me another day to locate Katherine via the Internet. She was living in New York City where she worked in the banking industry. I thought about what a long way she had come from her poetry classes. Perhaps not. Maybe she went home from her banking business all day and curled up with a book by Louise Glück, underlining phrases in "Retreating Wind" or jotting down an image of a white birch and using it as the arc of her own new creation.

"Yes?" Katherine said sharply and briskly, ready for a crank call, I suppose.

"Hello. I'm Vena Smith." I had gotten used to lying about my last name, but continued to use my first name as if that somehow made up for the deception. "I'm a student at University of Rochester in the graduate program."

"I'm sorry," she said curtly. "I don't do donations over the phone. Have the school send me a card in the mail."

"No, wait, please. It's about Marc Bennett." I could hear her sudden intake of breath, imagined the shift in her body language as she was stopped and stilled. Whatever was on her desk became lost in her transcendent state. She came to again.

"What about Marc? How did you get my number?"

"Katherine, I'm compiling an archive of Rochester student poets, and I understand Marc was a good poet."

"Good? He was a young genius. Incredible stuff, really. He made me give it up."

"Give it up? I don't understand," I said thickly.

"What I mean is that he was such a fine poet that, by comparison, my own work felt immature, really almost silly. I never wrote again after college."

"I'm sorry."

"Don't be. It was for the best."

"Do you have any of his poems or know where I could find them? I mean, for the book I'm compiling."

"Oh, God, I don't think, I-wait, could I call you back? Let me look at home. I've got a conference call in a few minutes and let me just call you later."

I gave her my number and never expected to hear from her again, but she had confirmed another suspicion. Marc Bennett was not only a poet but a fine one, and Roald Gould paid for his funeral.

Chapter Twenty-two
With Nothing Found After his Death

Katherine proved to be more helpful than I dared to consider. She called me back that night and directed me to a news account about Bennett's death. She also read a poem he had written and given to her shortly before his death. I asked her to e-mail it to me so I would be sure to get the wording right. "It's really strange," she said. "He had journals full of poems but nothing was found after his death. When the police went to his dorm room, they claimed there were no notebooks of any kind. I asked them. Marc only gave me the one poem, but he talked about his poetry all the time. I asked his roommate Brian Henderson if he stored Marc's journals, and he said there was nothing in the room. It was so odd."

I asked her if she had ever had a class with Dr. Gould.

"Oh, of course. If you were an English major, you probably had a class with Dr. Gould. He was humbling to say the least, but in his class is where I met Marc. Marc had just returned to school after being out for a while. I probably shouldn't be saying this, and please don't put any of this in your introduction or foreword or whatever, but Marc's mother died of cancer while he was in college. His father left them years earlier, and Marc was an only child he told me. I couldn't imagine how alone he must have felt. We were—listen," she said hesitating. "Don't write anything about me or that he wrote a poem for me, please. I don't want any mention of me at all, but do honor him in some way. I'd like a copy of the book when it comes out, too."

"Whatever you wish."

"It's not like I'm embarrassed, but I'm married now, and well, it's complicated. My husband knew Marc, and we, well, I don't need to go into this. I'm just glad you're going to include Marc in the journal or book you're putting together." She was crying now because I could hear sniffing and clipped wording. "It would have made him happy, I think. I'm not sure this is his best work, but I saved it. It's the only one I have."

I suddenly felt terrible that I had no intention of putting together a book of poems written by University of Rochester students and alumni. Katherine seemed to have cared deeply for or even loved Bennett. Although she had moved on with her life, she had not forgotten him. He would be the wound that never healed for her, I thought, as I considered Michael again.

Katherine's link to the news account told some of the story. There he was, Marc Bennett, a native of Pennsylvania, an honors student, whose grades must have slipped because he dropped out of the university for a year after his mother's death, then returned to try to complete his degree. After this interlude, he must have met Katherine Bushnell. He had been in a poetry class with Katherine and Dr. Roald Gould. Gould had since stopped teaching any undergraduates, but the evidence was there. Marc Bennett wrote poetry. Marc Bennett knew Dr. Gould. Marc Bennett was dead under very unusual circumstances. Marc Bennett was a prolific young poet whose journals suddenly all went missing. Gould published a new book of poetry less than a year after Bennett's death. Still, it was circumstantial, except the poem she e-mailed to me.

"This is not a love poem as you might have expected," Katherine wrote. "I don't really know why he gave the poem to me. Maybe he just wanted someone sympathetic to read this work. I guess I don't have to hide anything here since you're not going to use my name, but I was crazy about Marc. To tell the truth, though, I didn't understand his poetry and always felt kind of stupid when I read his poems. But this one is all I have left of him."

Latent
Conceive of a space
where possibility is held
not as prisoner but as invited guest,
yet inquiries remain unanswered.

The innkeeper never explaining,
and the possible politely refuses to speak.
We extrapolate from silence.
We find her in shadow even when lights outside
obfuscate rather than illuminate
what is possible
in pursuit,
beginning again in the dark
where latency
is made.
Marc Bennett

I thought it an odd poem, too, particularly strange to give to a young woman of whom Bennett was fond, but then I understood nothing of their relationship. Perhaps he intended her to consider their relationship as one held in the realm of the still possible but not yet realized. At least it was a beginning, and I had something to compare to Gould's work, even if I only found one common phrase. Of course, it hit me later that my relationship with Michael existed in that latency, too. But Gould was still the key.

I was beginning to recognize that I should have had a Gould file from the beginning. Circumstantial evidence was adding up. Not the kind, however, that was going to convince anyone but me that Gould was a murderer and a fraud, a cheat and a bastard. Well, a lot of people probably already knew he was a bastard, but he was a highly respected one, a successfully published writer and poet. Gould and Michael. Gould and Marc Bennett. Bennett's suspicious death, and Michael's supposed suicide. There was more to be weighed: Bennett's parents were divorced, and his mother died, probably about the time his grades fell into the toilet. There was no record of his father's whereabouts. Marc was on his own.

My mouth felt dry and I nearly choked. The sensation was one of fear, but I wasn't even exactly sure what I feared. Maybe it was the discovery.

Like Michael Lawler, Marc Bennett had no grieving parents asking questions first of the University of Rochester President and then the police. There was no one speaking up for him, and Marc's death notice was as quiet as he was. Gould sought out the ones who had no allies, no support system of loving family ready to ask questions, make accusations. These were smart, talented young men without wide circles of friends or fraternity brothers who might have stories to tell.

The next day, a Saturday, I ran into a classmate from Gould's authorship course, Reginald Smith-Harrison. He would make the perfect English professor, I thought. Wearing a camel colored vest and sport coat with a white shirt, this time of the morning he looked like he had stepped out of a GQ magazine. I almost expected to see him in a tie. Always impeccably dressed, he was knowledgeable but not cruel, ambitious, but interested in other people too. Both of us were getting coffee earlier than most students were awake. All of my previous college habits had been kicked to the curb since Michael's death. Reggie, behind me in the short line, asked why I hadn't been to class lately.

I didn't lie. I told him that I was dropping out and just had to take care of some business before leaving. Then he asked me something I was not prepared for: "This, your leaving, doesn't have anything to do with Lawler's death, does it?"

"It does." I was leaning with my weight on my right leg then switched to my left. How much was I going to tell him?

"I perceived there was something going on between you two. I should've known how hard you'd take it. I'm so sorry about all of it. Really, I mean, I don't think you should drop out because he died."

"What do you mean about 'something going on'?"

"C'mon, Advena. It was obvious. The guy couldn't stop staring at you in class. I thought he was going to bore a hole in your back one day. Clearly, he was in love with you." He said it and then moved on as if that was not really important.

"He didn't." Where could I go from there? How could I have been so unaware?

"He was shy. I mean really shy, but I guess it doesn't matter now."

"It does matter," I said, taking a deep breath.

"I'm sorry. That's not what I meant exactly. Gould's been on a tear lately, killing us with work. In a way, I kind of envy you, leaving I mean. Sometimes I just wish I could…"

"Don't ever envy me," I said, attempting to keep it together. He sipped his coffee, burning his lip and wincing.

"Damn, hotter than I expected. Lawsuit anyone?" He smiled, but I wasn't in the mood.

"Reggie, may I call you Reggie?"

"Sure. What else would you call me? But, it's kind of weird that we never talked before."

"I know."

"Can I call you Vena? Damn, I mean, may I call you Vena?"

"Okay. I guess we were all kind of isolated by the workload. Look, do you have any of Michael's poems, or did he ever share any of his poetry with you?"

"No, rather, yes. Let me think. I saw a couple of his poems before. They were first rate, but you know how Gould liked us to keep everything private until he had gone over it with us numerous times. Dr. Gould is always so concerned we're going to make fools of ourselves, I guess."

"I don't think that was why we were not supposed to share our work even outside of class."

"What do you mean?" Reggie had no clue that Gould was a thief and a killer and I couldn't just tell him everything, right there over coffee and our first conversation. In fact, the only time I had ever really talked with this fellow student was already almost over.

"Never mind. Could you identify any of the phrases from Michael's poems that you saw?"

"Good lord, no. I'm not a Roald Gould. Average memory for a fairly intelligent person, I would guess."

"Hey, I've got to go, but do me a small favor."

"Sure, I mean, what do you want me to do?"

"Don't forget what I said today, and, if anything happens to me, go to the police and tell them I told you that Gould is responsible."

He stood there with his mouth open, spilling his coffee down his clean shirt. I hoped his coffee didn't burn him, but I took off, unable to stop thinking about his words, about Michael being in love with me. For the first time, it occurred to me that perhaps Gould had known something about how Michael felt about me and deliberately tried to keep us apart, all of us apart. Was the cause jealousy over Michael or simply about power? I never saw Reggie again, but I was grateful to him. He had answered questions without meaning to, and I found something I didn't even realize I was looking for. Maybe I would reassess my opinion of Reggie. He had been rather nice and helpful. I had to stop judging everyone so quickly and harshly, I decided right then. Everyone, that is, except Roald Gould.

While we can never truly know another person, I understood in those lonely moments walking away from the university, that Gould was not only a dangerous man but ultimately a hollow one.

Chapter Twenty-three
You Standing Behind Legendary Writers

In my apartment I set out notecards, as if I was writing a major paper. Here was my mounting evidence, leading to my speculation that Gould had killed not only Michael, but a young man named Marc Bennet several years earlier. Suddenly, I realized I was sweating in a cold room. Fear can paralyze, and I could feel it numbing my limbs, even my will to escape. Looking around my increasingly disorganized space, I noticed an envelope on the floor near the door. How long had it been there?

Curiosity overcame inertia, and I moved to pick it up. I wondered if I had walked in my room and stepped right on it the night before. I opened the door quickly to look around. Nothing. There was no name on the outside of the envelop, no address, no indication of salutation, just a few clipped sentences: "Stop. You will regret it. I know where you were today and yesterday, you little fool. And yes, Michael was in love with you."

That was all. Who wrote the note? Was the message from Gould a threat? The diction didn't really sound like Gould and didn't appear to be his handwriting. He could certainly have disguised his writing, I decided. I kept the threat, tucking the note inside my evidence file.

Michael had been in love with me. Reggie said those exact words out loud. This clarification of something I suspected hit me the way an epiphany strikes at the end of a James Joyce short story. Michael was in love with me.

I forced myself to look at the note again. Who wrote this? How did they know? I read the words again, as if I had misplaced the note and meaning the first time. I stared at it for several more minutes. No further information or enlightenment emerged. "Stop looking," was direct. "You will regret it," was a threat. "I know where you were today and yesterday," could mean only one person and one thing. He was watching me. Again, I felt on shaky ground. Were there other logical possibilities I was not considering? Why was I a fool? Already speculating on alternatives? I checked off Jason. No, the letter wasn't from Jason who had loved me but moved on quite contentedly, even if he occasionally suffered some old longings. Some random guy, but then why the "you little fool" part? A chill moved up my arm and across my back. It had to be Gould. The imperative rather than the words sounded all Gould.

After Michael's death, I tried to think of him in the abstract. Death has a way of distancing us, maybe out of self-preservation, but I never could quite maintain the detachment needed for scientific or criminal investigation. On some buried level, I was cognizant that I had fallen in love with Michael before his death, without the slightest provocation on his part or acknowledgement on mine. I was a fool. How could Gould know this, unless…?

Gould discerned Michael's strengths and weaknesses better than I knew Michael. They had worked together over several semesters. Was it possible Gould was in love with Michael and had been rejected by him because Michael confessed his love for me? This was not something hopeful but crushing.

There was a pile of books on my desk, some I hadn't touched in weeks. Every once in a while, I had to remind myself I had been, until recently a student, one paying for most of her way, accumulating enormous debt. Looking at the books, however, I realized there was no possibility of working on a paper or doing the necessary reading. Even the titles wore me down. I ran my finger over the spines of a stack until I came to one I didn't recognize as mine.

What was *The Panda's Thumb* doing in my English lit stack? Stephen J. Gould's book of essays on biology and culture was a revelation, but why did I have it? And then I revived the memory. After class one night, Michael had handed me the book and said, "Read it. He's the 'better angels' Gould." I had something in my possession that belonged to Michael. I understood why I hadn't picked it up before: the pain of his loss would be fresh again. I pulled the book from the stack, knocking over the pile that spilled across the floor. Flipping pages, I noticed two scraps of paper fall out.

A page displaced inside a book. The concept of hiding inside something else brings me back again. The explanation for such subterfuge is part of the story, and I don't want to get too far ahead in examining my life or trying to figure out how and why Michael died. Maybe if I go over everything carefully, I will find what I was missing on first examination. Perhaps if I set out all the cards on the table and re-examine them, I will see a pattern that eluded me the first time. Reading his note, I felt as if Michael was in the room with me.

On the ripped corner of a page is one word, my name Vena, written in Michael's handwriting then a few lines of poetry:

hand wobble originates nothing
riot midafternoon in the stained mind
too late for warning, echo caught in the throat
ruin shrugged and we lay down desire

Then there was the name "Marc Bennett" in brackets. Then there were a few lines at the bottom of the paper: "The boats lay sick in the harbor, dying of love." Why did Michael write my name and Bennett's name with these lines and place them on a paper in a book? On the other folded paper, there was a poem that began, "You enter a room." I read the lines again, but the poem was rather long and felt disjointed as if Michael was leaving me with something important, but I had no entrance.

Inside the back cover of the book, Michael had written "Gould!" Of course, this was a book by Stephen Jay Gould, so he could have been just writing the author's name, but I didn't believe that explanation.

Was he trying to tell me something about Bennett and his death? I looked at the lines of Bennett's poetry again. I needed to do a search on phrases in the poem later. Maybe Michael just wanted to share the book Stephen Jay Gould had written, had forgotten about the poetry he had tucked inside, and there was nothing more to it. Even as I formed that thought, however, I had already rejected it. Michael wrote my name. Yes, Michael had been in love with me or at least he thought he might be. I slipped the paper into my jeans' front pocket. Until that moment, I had nothing of his, nothing until this random and seemingly insignificant scrap fell out of nowhere, loosened itself from secret pages in which it was hiding. Michael was not mine nor ever would be, but he might have loved me. He was still trying to reach me.

I put in my earbuds and searched for Jeff Buckley's version of "Hallelujah." I put the CD on replay, listening to Buckley's voice descend and ascend over and over until I had finally stopped sobbing. When I did stop crying, I went to my computer. If I was going to listen to this song all night, then I wanted more information than the fact Leonard Cohen wrote the song, and Jeff Buckley sang the irreverent anthem before Dylan. Buckley, like Bennett, walked into a river and drowned.

Using a few key phrases in the search engine, I discovered that Bob Dylan had recorded it, as well, and that Dylan and Cohen had met up in Paris to talk about writing in the 80s. Wait. Another set of writers meeting in Paris. So many before them and since. Paris was the island inside a European landmass, like that lake at the bottom of the ocean, a pool of denser water where seawater dissolves a layer of salt and forms depressions, or lakes of even denser water. These lakes within oceans even have waves and shorelines to trick the eye and imagination. I liked the symbolism of the whole analogy. Here is Paris, with its dense layer of poets, writers, artists of all sorts seeping through the layers around them to form an even deeper community, a secret one, far below the French city's surface.

Kindred spirits, American Bob Dylan and Canadian Leonard Cohen were sitting around sharing a couple of bottles of wine. They could afford the good stuff by end of the 80s, both already successful. Imagining this scene required relatively little effort on my part, as they discovered the best cafes, those places frequented by literary greats, some before they were well-known.

I tried to picture them sitting in one of those cafes in St-Germain-des-Pres, the quartier named after the historic church. I was always taking these kind of notes, not sure what I might need later in writing, everywhere history seeping through the pores of Paris. But Paris was different in the days when Hemingway frequented those streets; artists and writers able to share or rent cramped little spaces on the rue Visconte without it costing a small fortune. They would greet one another in their linen trousers and white shoes, women in dresses but wearing men's hats, showing their new independence, unrestricted by sexist mores. Some had money. Modigliani or Mctigue and many others didn't, however, they had to scramble and constantly find ways to support their Parisian habits.

Today, I would need a fortune to live inside such a rich and vibrant Parisian painting. But I would no longer need a beret, even Hemingway had given into the style back then, although the tam always seemed too small on his head. Was his head really as big as old photos of him suggested, or was that his ego showing itself to the world? Café du Dome is a pricey restaurant now and no more simply a gathering place for aspiring or accomplished artists who might have paid less than a franc for a meal in those days. The domed building, however, is still there and whispers its past in the bones of its architecture. I leaned in to try to hear those voices from another time, but there was only silence.

A few of the writers and artists were likely there just to meet those who already had a claim to literary or artistic fame, but the names are indelible: Hemingway being first because he seemed to visit every one of the most famous cafes and bars in Montparnasse, engaging in conversations with others, standing against the bar or over a little table at La Rotonde, La Closerie, or Les Deux Magots. Stein, Eliot, Fitzgerald were all there at various points, and of course, Beckett, Rimbaud, Gide, Sartre, and Mctigue, of course. Why would it not be natural to think that Baczkowski would have wandered in, as well? Several artists and writers were around, mixing in conversations, all hoping to connect through contact. Baczkowski might have perceived himself to be the outsider in their company, although they were all aliens in their cultures to some extent; the tragic Modigliani never to know the kind of fame and wealth his freakishly intriguing paintings would bring. But Baczkowski was not interested in Modigliani. His purpose was not casual company nor was his intent to rub up against the already famous Americans.

Then there was Harry's New York Bar in Paris, and what ex-pat would not have wandered in, if nothing else, just to get a glimpse of figurative giants Bogart and Hemingway, Picasso, Cocteau, Joyce, Breton,

Henry Miller, Degas? I suddenly wanted to go back to Paris and visit each of these cafes or the neighborhoods where the writers held court. If the conversation sprung up around Beckett, Mctigue would certainly have wandered over, with Baczkowski still standing at the bar, his head to one side, a slanted smile on his face. Mctigue noticed him but said nothing at first.

How many times did Baczkowski deliberately go to those enclaves before sitting down with the others? Perhaps he never did join them; his aloofness was what drew Mctigue to the handsome young man at the bar where they remarked on the fawning over Hemingway or some other notable of the moment. I had the distinct feeling that Mctigue would not have liked Hemingway who was far too macho an American and boisterous, too obviously bold with his loud tales of heroism and cult of followers.

Mctigue moved away from the others as Hemingway began yet another story in which he was the center of all the action. The Irishman would not have commented or openly shown his disdain but gotten up discreetly and ventured to the bar where Baczkowski was waiting. This was how they began, by separating themselves from the others and then discovering their mutual attraction. I could imagine that amorous infatuation came first, but this would lead to falling in love in that heady time, even the Paris air suggesting devotion to words, now lost to so much of the world. But whatever happened between Mctigue and Baczkowski was not explicitly stated in surviving correspondence or noted by other writers and artists curious about the defection of Mctigue to the young Pole. What was between them could only be found now in their literature, the echoes of one another's voices.

~ * ~

Buckley's high note enters my brain again and registers, pulling me back from Paris.

I suddenly understood that my love for Jason had never been a hallelujah, and the man I might have fallen for was dead. I wondered if my empty heart was always going to be like this. Wanting someone you can't have—love, the secret chord, only a "cold and broken hallelujah."

Chapter Twenty-four
As Day Falls into Night

Doing a 180, I tried to uncover Gould's past rather than Michael's or Marc Bennett's, following Dr. Gould's Curriculum Vitae like a road map. What I found was something out of a movie. Fortunately, finding biographical info on the well-known Gould was easier than the search had been on either Michael or Marc, relatively unknown young men who did not keep any kind of social media presence. Before Roald Gould came to Rochester, he worked in New York City at Fordham, where he taught undergrads English. During his tenure there, Gould was a witness to a young man, an English major, jumping from a window in Dealy Hall. Apparently, the student, Joseph Finlay, was a poet, as well. Finlay, the newspaper account quoted another classmate as saying, had been depressed after the sudden death of his father by suicide. His mother had died in an earlier boating accident. The news account stated that Gould had tried to reach the student, but Finlay fell or jumped out the window. Direct, impersonal. Gould as heroic but impotent figure.

Wondering at the angle of the fall, I thought about Joe Finlay standing against a window with Gould in his face. I could see Gould backing the young man up until he knew one push would extinguish him. Joseph must have been even more intimidated by Gould than the graduate students at Rochester. In the sophomore's hand was a journal filled with poems that Gould had seen. Gould asked to see the journal again and Joe offered up his work, his passion. They had discussed these poems, and Gould advised the young man not to show them to anyone yet because they needed work. Still, they have promise, he would have said. Finlay was only too glad to offer up his passion on the page to a man who could help them find readers.

Poor Joe. Then Gould stepped too close, and Joe couldn't back up further. He squinted, confused about the conversation and not sure of Gould's intent when a sudden arm movement unbalanced him, the shove followed by another far more powerful. Gould had previously opened the window before their walk in the hallway. The act was not a spontaneous decision but one that was calculated, cold, even meticulously designed. I didn't know Joe Finlay, but imagined I could see his face, his surprise as he tried to grab something but held only air on his way down, twisting in mid-air, fear and terror only momentary visitors before he hit.

Why would they question an English professor about a depressed student's leap out a window? Likely, campus security only talked with his roommate and other students who would have stated that Joe felt at a loss after his father's suicide. Everything lined up so perfectly, except the part that Gould was standing there, supposedly a helpless witness. Tall, strong Roald Gould, so competent in everything he did, was yet so helpless before a skinny 19-year-old sophomore bent on taking his own life.

Gould had gotten better at this, I realized, moving from being at the scene to nowhere connected to the site of the deaths. Did he have alibis or was that completely unnecessary because no one asked? Things must have been somewhat uncomfortable for Gould at Fordham because he left a little over a year later; shortly after, he published a chapbook of poetry. Young poets disappeared with Gould staying on, and no one but me seemed to be wondering about his presence in these unsettling events. He was a not only a murderer of opportunity but one who planned well in advance. His students were unpublished and unrecognized as poets but prolific. They were young men, just beyond boyhood, without guardians. Why only young men? Something else was at work, I realized.

With Gould actively plotting, I knew I had to change things up. I boxed my stuff and mailed the trunk to Bill. Before I left, I had to do a few other things first; getting out of my isolated, off-campus apartment was critical. Keeping only what I could fit in my backpack, I knocked on the door of a girl I met in my freshman year at school. She left school but we stayed in touch, at least on social media.

Melanie DeLillo was a native of Rochester and had stayed home after graduating. She was the one who introduced me to the infamous "garbage plate," Rochester's unique mix of mush food with which we stuffed our faces until I realized I had gained ten pounds my first semester. I also had Melanie to thank for showing me the worn path from campus to Wegman's, arguably the best grocery store in New York State. What I particularly liked about her was the fact she was such an unabashed fan of Rochester. She never said things like, "At least we're not Buffalo." Melanie DeLillo was certain Rochester was the best small city in America, and I thanked her for helping me navigate some of the roads along the way.

We might have stayed closer as undergraduates, but she changed majors, and I saw her less and less as time went on, but still, we talked now and then. Melanie was surprised but kind in response when I texted her about coming over. As soon as she saw my bulging backpack, she knew I was not leaving for a few days. Her boyfriend Jeff was less tolerant, but he indulged his girlfriend on pretty much everything. He was actually a nice guy.

I told her I needed to spend a couple of nights before I left school for good. She was suspicious but always too nice. I promised not to get in her way, camping out in an alcove, but incredibly grateful to take a warm shower and sleep through the night without listening for every sound outside.

"I'm sorry. I wasn't a very good friend to you," I said as she served me a glass of Earl Gray tea. "And yet you remembered I love Earl Gray."

"I drink the Earl, too. Thanks for that." Maybe she did not want me to think that she had summoned such an irrelevant detail about me. "No, you weren't, but that's okay. We were fine really. I seem to recall you editing several papers for me, definitely improving my grades. I wasn't a natural writer, like you and so many of the others there."

I resisted the urge to call out her double negative of "no" and "weren't." I had also forgotten about helping her with her papers, something I did for a lot of my fellow students. "What are you up to now?" We both looked at Jeff who was embedded in the couch watching television.

"I'm teaching third grade here in Rochester. It's a wonderful school; I mean the faculty members have been so nice, and the kids have problems, but they're so cute."

"Wow. That's great."

"Really? Thanks. I love my students, they are so sweet. I have a story every day, just something funny that Kylie or Jaquan does. All of them, really."

"Hey, I knew you'd make a wonderful teacher. You're so patient, I should know." We looked at each other, trying to figure out if either one of us understood why we weren't better friends.

"I still have to finish my Masters in Elementary Education, but we're making a go of it." We both looked at Jeff again, and this time, he looked up.

"What? Hello," he said before turning back to the TV.

"He does all the cooking. Can you believe it?"

"Of course, he's a good guy," but I didn't add, why shouldn't he?

~ * ~

Two days into my stay, I packed up again. Jeff was getting on my nerves. There was no basis for my irritation with him that I could figure out except he was content to let Melanie do everything and kept asking me questions that I didn't want to answer. I heard him whispering to Melanie, repeating my name.

I decided to confront him, politely. "Jeff, did you have something you wanted to ask me?"

He looked surprised, then said, "Not really. But there's this man standing outside our apartment the past few nights. He keeps looking up here, and I was wondering if you knew him?"

I sensed my nerves tingling, fear rolling off. "What does he look like?"

"Tall. Like a professor wearing a neck scarf. Not really threatening, but he's a little weird. He's gone now."

I went to the window and looked out but saw no one. "Like a professor?" Gould. I knew as much without having to see him for myself. How did he learn where I was?

"Melanie, did you tell anyone I was staying with you?" I tried not to sound accusing, but there was no other way for the words to come out.

"I-I," she stuttered. "Just a few old friends that we were in school together with—you know. I didn't realize that you didn't want me to tell people."

"Ah."

"I'm sorry."

"Don't worry about any of this, but I've got to get going." I have to give her credit, though. She let me stay and interrupt her life with Jeff and never said a thing to me about leaving. I tried to help out, but being in a new couple's tiny place is always a little uncomfortable. Melanie was noticeably relieved that I threw my stuff back into my backpack and was heading out. I didn't have anything to give her for her kindness, but we hugged and then I was out the door. I guess I recognized from the moment I called her that I was imposing. Now, Gould's presence made my move imperative.

"Hey, when I settle down someplace, I'd love to have you visit," I said, half meaning it.

"Thanks. That's awfully...I'd love to visit. Good luck," she said with kindness, the way she always did and would. If things had been different maybe I would have struck up my friendship with Melanie again, but, probably not. She was too accepting. That's not the word. She was too complacent. I decided I was born and would die an agitator, wherever that took me.

Gould was watching and waiting to make his move. I had to find another temporary place with someone, in some place, he would not know.

Chapter Twenty-five
In a Unlit Stairwell

On my way to another acquaintance's, actually my former boyfriend's place, I called Bill again. Time for honesty and partial disclosure: early evening and not my more typical middle of the night call. I thought he would be somewhat pleased to hear from me at a normal hour.

"Bill?"

"Advena?"

"Are you busy? I'm dropping out of school."

"What? What are you talking about? Oh, Advena. I don't think…"

"Listen, it's not an option. There is someone here trying to kill me." I started looking around as I walked and talked. If Gould was spying on me now, I needed to find a busy place where I could lose him. I decided to hop on a city bus and then make my way to another former friend's place.

"Oh, my God, Vena, what have you gotten yourself into this time? Kill you? I can't believe…"

"This time?" In all fairness, this was the first call I'd ever made to Bill to tell him someone was attempting to dispatch of me, or at least thinking about it, so I decided it was rather unfair of him to throw in the 'this time'."

"What exactly is going on? Please don't exaggerate."

"What's going on is I may know about a homicide, and the murderer is on to me. I think he is trying to kill me too."

"Lord. Go to the police."

"Can't. Actually, I already tried that, but they didn't believe me."

"Oh, Vena." Bill said this with such a profound sense of

disillusionment in me rather than concern. At least that's what I heard in his tone.

"I know. I know I've been nothing but a disappointment to you my whole life, even when I won all those awards in school, but..."

"That's not fair, and this has absolutely nothing to do with you winning awards, all of which are displayed in your room at home."

"Fair? Bill I'm not complaining about you. I'm just telling you I understand your frustration. You've been better to me than almost—no, better than anyone else even if I never exactly fit into your plans."

"I never..."

"You didn't have to, I know. But you never kicked me out or abandoned me, not once. Thank you."

"I." Even in the one word I could hear anger, not fear for me. I decided to cut our conversation short, get right to the point.

"I really hate asking you again, but I need to get out of the country not just get out of Rochester."

"My God, who are these people after you? Is this some kind of drug gang or something? Are you taking drugs again?"

"Again? Marijuana is not a dangerous drug, Bill, but no, I'm not into trouble over a joint. And I'm not 'taking drugs,' but I need a couple thousand dollars."

"A couple of thousand? I don't have that kind of..."

"You do, Bill. I know you do, and I know that this is also difficult for you. I can appreciate how many expenses you have and how large an amount I'm asking for, so I will pay you back, every last cent as soon as I am able. And while I may be a pain in the neck, I've never been a liar, and you know that in your heart. This is a loan with guaranteed interest. Think of this as an investment."

He sighed, the kind of deep, personal sigh that said he would give me the money, even though he didn't believe he would ever see any of it again. "Oh, Vena."

"Thank you, thank you," I said before he could reconsider and say something that might indicate otherwise. "Could you send a money order right away to this address?" I gave him Warren's street number slowly.

"Warren again?"

The way he said the word 'again' made me feel compelled to explain. "Not exactly. Same Warren, but we're just friends." I actually couldn't believe that Bill remembered I had dated Warren my freshman year.

"Yeah, I remember Warren. I believe you were more than friends, if I'm framing that correctly? Didn't he drop out of school a couple of years back? Got involved with too many drugs? Just friends, huh."

"Look, Bill. Stop with the drug angle. Warren is in a band and earning a living just fine. He's a good guy, and yeah, we really are just friends. He's like the only person left I trust here. Please, Bill, I need this right away. I know it's a lot to ask, and I know lending me money again is a sacrifice for you, but I promise to pay you back. Thanks." I repeated Warren's address then hung up, got off the bus and waited for another one to take me to Warren's apartment.

There was once a subway in Rochester, and the trains ran for something like thirty years before they destroyed the entire system. I thought about that subway as I waited in the cold for a late bus. There were a few people wandering around, some guy pulling a huge plastic bag of cans. He kept looking at me, but I tried to look cool and broke because I was. He had on two coats but both were ragged and ripped. His head was covered by a cap that looked like better days were a distant memory, and he smelled, even in the cold night air, his odor was unmistakable.

The man with the bag stopped and asked, "Got a dollar?"

"Nope. Less than you, I'm afraid." I started walking into the street, and he moved on, asking the next person who turned away from him, too.

I returned to the bus stop, feeling a little ashamed that I was scared of a homeless guy just down on his luck and most likely looking for a meal. Maybe he was mentally ill, I thought because so many of our homeless people have mental illness problems and can't find a way through. I looked up and saw that he was already two blocks further down the street, dragging his treasure of empty cans. Just then, the bus pulled up and I jumped on with relief.

Although it was after ten pm by the time I got there, Warren was up and texted me to come up the back stairs. He then called because he wanted to tell me that the outer door was open. I thought it was funny that he both texted and called but that was Warren. Once I'd gotten inside the outer door the hall light had blown out, so I had to hold the railing and test the height of the stairs with my foot. I stood outside his apartment door thinking about being alone in a dark stairwell, thinking of Michael hanging. I reached in my pocket for a match or lighter when I touched my phone, opened it, and had enough light to navigate when Warren opened the door and suddenly stood facing me.

"Jesus, Vena, I thought you'd left school by now. Sorry about the hall light. I keep telling that son-of-a-bitch landlord to fix it. Haven't you graduated yet?" His hair was a mess, sticking straight up in places and matted in others, but he was still adorable—not good looking, just funny and sweet.

"Leaving, but I have to wrap up a few things first. Can I?"

"Sure, get in here before you freeze. They don't heat the hallway either. Big savings for the landlord on heat and light."

Small talk was difficult during the last few weeks, but I thought I should at least attempt to be polite. "So, are you still in your band?"

"Are you still writing poetry?" We both laugh.

"Hell, yeah. The Measure."

"'Cool name. Open to all kinds of interpretations—the measure of—"

"Craig's idea, the name, I mean. We have a gig tomorrow night. Want to come?" He says this as he drapes a long leg over the arm of an old chair. Extending his hand, he offers me the couch strewn with blankets and magazines. Trying first to smooth out the lumped together old throws, I gave up and sat on mounds. An odd funky smell permeated the room, unwashed fabrics and old furniture attesting to food and wine spills in the night. Just the odor of a guy who'd lived alone for too long.

I thought I'd made a mistake in asking. "Look, Warren, I'd love to hear you play because you're damn good, but I really just need to keep a low profile for a few days until I get out of town."

"Low profile? No problem. No pressure. Get out of town, huh?"

"Are you working as a musician full-time?"

"Yeah, kind of. I mean, I'm always writing in my head and playing when I have any time, but I'm a short-order cook, should I say, a chef, four days a week, then it's all music all weekend."

"You cook?"

"Turns out I'm pretty decent, too. Say, what do you want to eat? I can whip up an omelet for you. You look starved."

"Actually, yeah, thanks, that sounds amazing."

In a few seconds, Warren was in the kitchen, efficiently mixing my omelet that looked so delicious. I hadn't realized how hungry I was until he offered. I followed him into the tiny galley kitchen, crowding him, but he seemed to enjoy it. He put me to work, handing me a wooden spoon. "Stir gently," he said, and I followed his commands, while he grated cheese.

"Do you really like cooking?"

"Pays the bills, but the long-term plan is for the music, you know, the music to sustain financially not just, well, spiritually, I guess. I want to be that guy who says he makes his living off his art."

"You're already making the music work." He looked around the tiny apartment. We both laughed again.

"Where do you go to play?"

"You mean practice? We meet in Greg's garage, literally, we're a garage band."

"Love it."

"Yeah, we do. Do you remember Greg? He quit first semester freshman year."

"No, I'm sorry. I don't remember him. I love the fact that you are doing exactly what you want in life, something that few people actually do. Life gets so messy."

"Thanks, but it's not as if anything is easy. I'm kind of scrambling all the time."

"Everyone is. Where do you play?"

"We play wherever we can get a gig, all over really, not too discriminating yet. All about the music, not the venue."

"You probably have to travel quite a bit then." Warren took the spoon from me and gestured toward a little table and two chairs. Then he tossed a plastic plate on the table and slipped the unbroken omelet expertly to the dish.

"Yep. Four musicians and our tech master in a stinking van. It got so bad last summer after one gig with everyone sweating and no place to clean up that we sped home with all the windows down. No air-conditioning in that heat. Then the same thing happened in the winter, and we rolled them down again in minus five-degree temps." He threw back his head laughing uninhibitedly, thinking about his days on the road. I could see how much he loved it. I was also glad not to be riding in the bus with them.

Already wolfing down his cheese omelet, I was delighted when he poured us both glasses of wine. "Do you ever worry about being an original?"

His eyebrows went up, and then he asked, "You mean me or the music?"

"The music, of course, God knows you're an original."

"Thanks, I think. We've got some riffs that are annexed, you could say, but I think our total sound is really ours. I guess if someone came up after a performance and said, 'You sound like Joe Bonamassa,' I wouldn't feel all that bad or insulted, but we set out to do our thing, for the most part. We are going to cut an album of our own music—not covers—in the near future."

"Are you still writing lyrics?" I was glad he was doing more of the talking, so I could relish the food and wine.

"Yeah, yeah. That's my thing. See, those English classes weren't for nothing. I'm not the best guitar player or vocalist in the group, but I earn my keep."

Chapter Twenty-six
Only a Match to Light the Room

"Do you think it's still possible for a musician or any writer/artist to be an original?'

"I get what you're saying, like subconsciously, we're so inundated with what has been produced, that it's hard not to be influenced or pull in a riff or a line from somewhere else. So, sure, I guess, we steal a little bit. Why do you want to know?"

"Just something I've been thinking about a lot lately."

After picking up my dish and grabbing the wine for us, Warren threw some magazines off the couch and motioned for me to sit down again in a more comfortable place. He poured another glass for each of us. His apartment was a disaster, filled with junk, exactly what I'd expect from a guy who was way more into music than house cleaning. He could see me looking around and suddenly seemed uncomfortable. "I know the place is kind of a pig-sty, but, you know, no women for a while and two jobs, weekends, too. I don't have much time…"

"I get it. No problem. Coming back to why I want to talk about originality, I've been considering this topic lately. At first, the idea was about a possible dissertation, but now, it has to do with why I'm leaving Rochester now rather than later."

"Right. Okay. So, you're leaving before you finish? How bad is it, if you don't mind my asking? I mean, you didn't kill anyone, or anything?" He was laughing for a second then his expression changed as he saw I wasn't kidding around. "I think you better tell me about it," he said, looking nervous and paternal.

"Long story." I sipped the wine and enjoyed being in the moment for the first time in a very long while. I leaned back and could feel a half-broken spring inching toward my lower spine.

"We've got all night. It's freaky because I'd called in sick tonight and don't have to work. How do you like that for timing? Even before you texted. Sixth sense or something. Don't get weirded out or anything, but I always felt like we had a special connection."

"We did." I quickly corrected myself. "We do."

I had a place to stay for a couple more nights and time to tell Warren my story. I almost forgot about the fact he used to love me, so the decision to seek him out and move in wasn't as difficult as I anticipated. I didn't tell him everything, just enough that he could understand why I had to leave. One of the great things about Warren is that he believed almost everything I said. It wasn't like I had to make an airtight case.

"You know, I sensed you were in trouble before you called," he moved forward and swung his long legs out in front of him.

"You always did have an uncanny ability to sense what was coming." We both smiled because he knew I also meant that he had prepared for our breakup before I'd ever said anything. Then I continued my story, my speculations and evidence trail.

"If there's intrigue anywhere, I should know you are involved, I guess," he finally said after I stopped talking. "What now? Where will you go? What can I do?"

"You aren't going to do anything right now. The last thing I want is for you or anyone else I care about to get hurt."

"Ah," he put his hand over his heart and smiled. "You do care." Then we both choked on a stifled laugh, but I pulled back quickly.

"I'm leaving the country, but first I have to get out of Rochester obviously."

To his immense credit, Warren didn't flinch. By now, we were both a little inebriated. I had let down my guard for the first time in a couple of months.

"The country? What? Where are you going?"

"I can't tell you that yet, but I will later. I will let you know when I'm safe. It's just I have to figure out a plan."

He nodded. "Okay, sure. I'll take you, I mean to the airport or wherever you want to go. I don't have a passport, though. Guess I can't take you anywhere exactly."

"No, no. I don't mean you have to take me to Europe, just as far as you can go in New York."

"Got it. When do you want to leave?" He was a little flustered because he had just accidentally revealed that he was willing to give up his band, his life in town for me, following me wherever the path led. I tried to ignore the grand gesture the best I could.

"Really? I'm flying out of New York City. JFK."

"C'mon, you knew as soon as you called me, I'd do whatever you wanted." Warren refills our glasses from another bottle he had just opened then moved next to me on the couch.

"Yeah, I guess I did, thanks."

"Just don't get us killed, okay. I mean we're not talking a mob hit or anything?" I hadn't told him Gould was after me, or I think he would have laughed again. Really, who was going to believe that your college professor is a serial killer? Warren probably imagined that some underworld drug dealers were after me.

"Not a chance. Not the mob or a gang, just one man."

Warren was also referencing our inside joke when he told me not to "get us killed." He had gotten heavily involved in drugs a few years back and almost did kill us driving on a couple of occasions. One night, we were fleeing from an angry dealer Warren had stiffed. On another night, we ended in a snow bank that blocked his little VW bug from going over a steep embankment with us still inside. I hit my head on the dash and ended up with a bruised forehead and head ache. He knew the genesis of my decision to leave him was due to his mixing of pills and alcohol. The breakup had never been about his dropping out of school, but that move also made seeing him more difficult and inconvenient.

Now, there was a difference. There was no tension. I also knew that he had been relatively clean and sober for a year or two. He was one of my only ex-boyfriends who was a better friend than boyfriend.

"One guy? Are you sure me and my bandmates can't take care of him for you? We're kind of unintimidating alone but a dark force for good when we pick up our instruments."

"No, I don't want you to have any more trouble. Besides, I can handle this guy. I just have to get out of the area. But you're sweet."

"Damn, woman. I don't want to be sweet. How about sexy?"

"That too." Then, the lights flickered and went out.

"Shit. I pay my bills," he said in the darkness. "This is just an asshole landlord who won't fix anything." I could hear Warren stumbling around in the dark, hitting his foot against something hard. "Fuck, oh, sorry, forgot that was there," he said. I thought about all the murder mysteries where the killer offs someone when the lights go out, but I wasn't nervous. I was with Warren.

Then he lit a match and held his hand to the wick of a candle. "I keep these for just such occasions." With the wick lit, I could see his smiling face again in the half light. Even in that muted shadow, he didn't look scary. "You tired?"

"Exhausted," I said, slumping.

Knowing that he was still in love with me, what I did next was crazy. When he leaned closer, I took his face in my hands and kissed him. He kissed me back. He slipped his warm hands under my shirt with such tenderness. Impossible. He wasn't even in a rush. I didn't mean to, but I slept with Warren that night. He was so nice, and I was so damn lonely and sad. For the first time in a while, I was comfortable with someone I trusted and loved.

"You know this is just for old time's sake," I finally said, pulling the sheets around me before getting up to go to the bathroom. "I forgot a toothbrush. Do you have an extra one?" I yelled to him.

"Just use mine." I took a long look at his toothbrush and decided to use my finger with toothpaste on it. I didn't want him thinking that we were back together or anything.

"For old time's sake. Sure," he said quietly when I returned, "I'll take old time's sake any day." Then he smiled broadly, rolled over, and fell back to sleep. I did too, after a few long minutes of staring at the small cracks in his ceiling. Then I slept, and slept well for the first time in a long while.

Chapter Twenty-seven
Where Spheres of Thought Collide

Warren knew better than to try to dissuade or convince me to stay on in Rochester with him, but he still let me know that I could return whenever it suited me. "Next time," he said, "I'll have the place cleaned up." He threw my backpack in the back and jumped in the driver's seat of his old Ford.

"When did you get this beauty?" I was being sarcastic, but he took the comment literally.

"Yeah, she is, isn't she? Freakin' answered an ad, bargained the guy down, and then had my buddy Steve work on it. She runs perfect now. Steve, do you know Steve?"

"No, I don't think I ever met him."

He shrugged. "Well, if you ever do—he's a genius with cars."

"I can appreciate that—never learning much about them myself."

We listened to the car motor humming for a few minutes of quiet. Warren typically had music on, so I waited for him to choose his channel. He didn't have Sirius radio, so he had to keep tapping the search button. We went through a litany of static.

"Next time, I won't be surprising you," I said, recalling his comments about cleaning up his place.

"You can surprise me anytime you want, and I really will have the place in better shape."

"Your new woman might have a say in it, and please don't change for me. I kind of love you just the way you are." I meant what I said to him, too.

"Don't be saying things like that unless you want me to come after you. What woman, by the way, are you talking about? I've got no idea."

"She's probably already waiting for you to spot her. You know, the one who shows up at every gig with those wide-open eyes and that smile anyone should notice across the room. Her skirt is a little too short, but she has nice legs. She's smart, too."

"Yeah, and she likes poetry." He looked over at me even though he was driving.

"Hey, keep your eyes on the road," I yelled.

"I'd better start paying attention. If she is already there I'm an idiot for not being aware of her, but I like fiction, too." He nodded his head in time to the music. We didn't talk for a little while. Warren was probably thinking about his imaginary girl, and I was thinking about Michael again. As Warren drove and everything raced past, I was reminded of what lay ahead of me, as well as all that I was leaving. It was the first time I grappled with sadness about leaving Rochester.

"Mind the music?" he asked me. A little metal head for my taste, but I figured he deserved to listen to whatever he wanted.

"No. Play anything you want." I anticipated Warren's eclectic tastes would allow for at least a few songs I wouldn't mind. He turned up the radio loud and started singing. I let him go without joining in because he was a much better singer than me. Besides, I wasn't quite there yet, at the point where you just let go and feel the music.

~ * ~

Out of Rochester at last. Heading east on the New York State Thruway. I paid the tolls, and he let me. I gave him my card for the gas, too. I figured that he gave up his day for me. Then we headed south on Route 81 through Syracuse. Outside the city I noticed a cyclone-like vortex of black shapes ahead of us at the side of the road. I asked Warren to pull over, so I could see more clearly, because I was in no particular hurry now that we had some distance from Rochester. The weirdness of this living tornado drew me.

"You know you're not supposed to stop on this road," Warren said, as he backed up carefully, cars zooming past us. "Good thing there's no cops around."

Once we had stopped, I could clearly see the black shapes were turkey vultures riding warm air currents that rose from some steaming heap below them. That heap was composed of carcasses of dead animals, road kill that had been collected and now was in the process of being buried in the wide median between north and south. Opposite poles, I thought, recalling the image of Michael and Gould that day in class not so long ago and looked at the vultures riding these invisible currents made visible by their hypnotic flight. I took a photo of them with my phone and then jumped back in the car.

"They're just turkey vultures," Warren said, looking at me curiously. "What did you want to stop for? You know, you still surprise me, Vena. What was that about? They're really a nasty bird."

"I guess they are. A vortex of birds, of affairs, of cosmic matter," I said quietly.

"Yeah. Okay. This some poetry project or something?"

"No, just the strangeness of life and invisible currents always moving."

"You wanna smoke?"

"Weed?"

"What do you think I meant? I'm not crazy."

"No, thanks anyway, and you shouldn't either. You're driving."

"Not turning into some moralist on me, are you?"

"Look at me, Warren. You know me better than that."

He looked over and smiled. "I don't know. I kind of like your blue spikey hair, and you seem pretty damn moral, at least highly ethical, to me." He was always saying something nice, and that made it that much harder to leave him again, but we weren't really right for each other. Both of us knew it.

By now I had a plan, and the intricacies were far more extensive than getting off campus. Gould was dangerous, and I did not question the importance of moving beyond his reach. This plan, however, was not as well-thought out as I would have liked, with amazingly constructed details like on one of those television shows where you are just trying to keep up with the high-tech design. My aim was just a kind of, get from point A to B with as little notice as possible and then reassess at point B. I did realize that I needed to have my passport and apply for a student VISA in Italy, my eventual destination.

While Warren drove, I pulled Gould's book of poetry out of my backpack. There were lines I was looking for, and we were only twenty-three miles north of Binghamton before I found them. At the center of the book, a poem with the lines: "hand wobble originates/ riot midafternoon/ too late for warning/ ruin shrugged; we lay down." There was only the slightest difference from the original.

Somehow Michael found out about Gould stealing Marc's poetry, perhaps because he, too, was already looking. I read the lines from Gould's or, rather, Marc's poem to Warren.

"Jesus, that's awful," he said, laughing. I laughed too for some reason, maybe relief that I was out of Gould's line of vision. "Just kidding about the poem," he added. "I know you love that stuff. I don't mind the poetry really." He reached over and put his hand on the back of my neck, messaging with his fingers.

"Warren!" He pulled his hand away. "What happened is awful. They were killed over a poem."

"What?"

"Gould killed them."

"Professor Gould killed Michael or Marc? Gould?" The quiver in his voice betrayed the incredulousness of it. Then, suddenly, the thought occurred to me that I had new evidence. Maybe this was something Campello could use in an investigation.

"We have to go back."

"What?"

"Really, please, we have to go back to Rochester. I need to show this to Campello, the cop I told you about."

Warren looked surprised but then shrugged. "Your wish is my command, my lady." With that, he drove into the turn around on the 81 median and then headed the other way. "Hey, that was some dumb luck," he said. "Just when we needed it, there was a U-turn and not a cop in sight. I'm feeling pretty good today."

I expected to hear sirens of a chase car but we drove on with only the radio blaring.

"Yeah, lucky," I said.

"Good sign, an omen," he added.

"Thanks for everything. I know this is really terrible of me to have you driving back and forth like this."

"No problem, darling. Long as you're paying for the gas, I don't mind you coming back at all." We drove silently for a few minutes then he began singing again. I joined him in a full out chorus.

He stopped singing suddenly. "You're sure about this, right?" he finally said.

"Absolutely," I replied. But I wasn't really certain of anything except somebody had to see this material besides Warren and me.

Figuring out the murder and the mystery all looks so perfect in a well-scripted book, movie, or television screenplay. We know who did it, how, and only have to wait for the P.I. to catch up to us. The glaring evidence is right in front of us. Sometimes we want to yell at the screen or the page because the shamus seems too slow in arriving at the obvious realization of who did what and why. We witness the murder, the killer's face often obscured, but we see his hands or his shoes, murder weapons, the moment in which a life is taken and another being is sickeningly gratified by the act. I wasn't in that movie.

But Warren and I talked about murder mysteries we had seen or read all the way back to Rochester. He was more into movies than books, but we had enough common ground to cover.

Glancing over at me as he drove, Warren said, "The murder mysteries I like are the ones where we don't care anything about the person who is killed. You know, where the shamus is always slightly cleverer than the killer, except in those rare instances when a murderer wins in the end. I don't know, those might be my favorites."

"You have one in mind?" I was trying to think of my own examples and not the real life impersonations.

"You want an example? How about the heinous father who rapes his own daughter and ends by having her killed in *Chinatown*?"

I had seen the movie and remembered poor, hapless Jake Gittes never really had a chance against the powerful force of evil that is Noah Cross. "*Chinatown* is great and annihilating—not one I want to see again."

"Really? You're kidding me. I could watch that movie ten times."

"Who doesn't want Faye Dunaway to get away with her daughter-sister in that incestuous tale of corruption-to-the-bone? I kept expecting Jake to solve the crime about the water diversion, save Evelyn Cross Mulwray and poor abused Katherine."

"Yeah, I didn't mean I liked the scene when they got offed. Just that it's cruel and funny at the same time," he said. "Hard to pull that off."

"Jake, however, gets his nose half cut off for nothing."

"I know—which is kind of great in a morbid way. But I want you not to get hurt trying to solve this crime thing with the professor."

I sure didn't want to be a Jake-kind-of-sleuth, one played and out-smarted in the end. I liked my nose, too. I was, however, betting on Campello now and evidence that was circumstantial.

"C'mon," said Warren. "Another favorite mystery, a movie."

"Raymond Chandler's *The Big Sleep,* the movie version with Bogart and Bacall."

"Yeah, yeah, I saw that one," said Warren with enthusiasm. "Great flick, and Bacall, Jesus, she was beautiful back then."

"In a story that was all about the private eye and his methods, and ultimately the sexual tension between client and private investigator. Bacall held her own against the Bogart legend."

"Bogart was so smitten he had to marry her in real life. Raymond Chandler, huh."

"Of course, William Faulkner had a hand in the screen play, so it's not that surprising the film holds up today."

"Bogart was the ultimate cool," he said, betraying envy.

"Yeah." Then I was quiet. Bogart was too cool for my sleuthing.

And lines kept echoing in my head, and I could hear Michael's voice saying, "Keep going. Don't leave the journey like this. Don't let him get away with killing me."

"I won't," I said out loud, forgetting for a half-second I was with

Warren.

"Won't what?"

"Uh, won't ever forget how cool Bogart was."

"Vena, I love you, but you're a little strange."

Chapter Twenty-eight
With Mounting Evidence

On the journey back to Rochester, I called the police station and asked for Campello. I had to wait and then finally left a message, but I was confident he would get it.

"What if he says nothing or tells you that you don't have enough evidence? I mean, I'm not trying to be difficult, but it's just a few lines from a poem," said Warren, trying to play devil's advocate.

"I will keep pestering him until he admits there is something there."

"I don't know if pestering works. That wouldn't mean much to most people or most cops," Warren offered as we trudged up the steep back stairs to his apartment. "I've watched that show on TV, you know, the real-life cops one where they've got all this evidence, and then the interrogating cop has to let the bastard go anyway. Seems like the only thing that keeps 'em is a confession, and I don't know Gould that well, but he sure doesn't look like the confessing type."

"I'll figure out something then, and I've got a feeling about him, Campello, I mean. I think he'll listen. All I need is for Campello to be suspicious of Gould and start looking at him carefully. I think once they start really looking, with all kinds of tools and technology that I don't have, well, who knows what might turn up?"

Warren shook his head. "Gould just won't give them anything. He's not the guy who breaks down."

"I know, but I don't think that's the only way they get people." At least I hoped Campello could find evidence that I didn't have on Gould.

We made it back to Warren's while still daylight, but a gray haze colored everything with deeper, denser clouds moving in like ominous waves. I was trying hard not to let the weather dampen my spirits.

"What time are you going to see the police?"

"In the morning, early, hopefully before all the crazies start arriving at the station."

"I've got to be at work tomorrow morning at five-thirty, but…"

"I don't need a ride. I know the way." Warren handed me a spare key to his apartment then opened a bottle of wine and got out two jelly jars. I decided to buy him some new glasses when I got a little extra money.

"Are we going to eat, too?"

"Darling, you have no idea how good you are going to eat. I'm a chef!" We laughed and felt good for a moment. I realized that Warren was the only person I had laughed with in a very long time.

After dinner, Warren fell asleep on the couch, but not before drinking most of the bottle and a second one by himself. I started to worry that he wasn't going to stay sober anymore. I did have him driving around all day. I tried to wake him by gently nudging his shoulder as he leaned his head over the back of the couch cushion, but gave up and crawled into his bed. Then I experienced a wave of guilt, couldn't sleep anyway, got up and covered him with a blanket, took off his boots, and lifted his feet up on the couch. By then his head was in a better position and I went back into the bedroom. I squirmed right to the middle of his old double bed where the long indentation from his body was most pronounced.

By the time I woke, he was gone, but he left a note on his old Formica table.

"Good luck with the cops today. If they don't believe you, just come back to my place because you know I do. Bagels on the counter were fresh yesterday and cream cheese in frig. Coffee is at the back of the frig, and I washed out the pot for you this morning. No mold, I promise. I'll bring dinner home tonight. Love, Warren."

Suddenly, I discerned I was just using Warren and that he was falling in love with me all over again. I didn't want to hurt him, and the thought made me feel really lousy on top of being nervous and scared.

I took a bus part of the way and then, pulling up my coat collar around my ears, walked the rest of the way to the police station. Trudging through the sloshy snow in the cold helped somehow, almost as a kind of penance.

"I need to speak to officer Campello, please," I said in my most urgent voice.

The desk sergeant looked up at me and squinted for an instant, trying to recall where he had seen me before. "Hey, I know you."

"Yeah, it's me again, but I'm back with evidence this time."

He puffed his cheeks, blew the air out, but then almost smiled; he motioned for me to take a seat. This time the bench was empty, and I perceived the absence as a hopeful sign. The focus would be on Michael's murder and reopening the case, or really, getting them to declare it a case at all would be a victory. I was trying not to have expectations that were too high. I just wanted him to listen and consider the evidence.

Campello walked in and scratched his head when he saw me, but I sensed he held the scene in his head of our last encounter. "Miss, Miss Smith, right? What have you got today?" I could hear his exasperation and had to be careful not to annoy him further.

Squinting, I realized that I had to tell him the truth about everything I knew, including my name. "Officer Campello, my name is Advena Goodwin, and I'm sorry for not telling you my real name the first time. I was a little intimidated just being in a police station."

"Well, at least we're starting with a little honesty this time." He shrugged, not in the least angry with me. "Advena, huh, and Good-win. Could be a good sign."

I caught myself before starting to tell him the etymology of my name, meaning friend of gods and stranger. That would be going a little too far. "I hope so, a good sign, and thanks for seeing me."

"So, what have you got besides a real name?"

"Evidence," I said steadily.

"Evidence?"

"In the Michael Lawler case."

Campello scrunched his face as if he had just chewed on a lemon, but then said, "C'mon back." He wasn't formal this time and seemed resigned to my wasting his time, but there was something else, too. Maybe he was a bit amused by me. I decided a cop's day probably had a lot of boring stuff wadded up inside, and maybe I wasn't the worst part of his day.

When we sat down, I laid out my notecards as if preparing to write a term paper. I was hoping my meticulous attention to detail would impress him enough to consider what I was asking. Campello raised his eyebrows but said nothing for a moment.

"This card shows Michael Lawler's words from his poem that I read in his notebook. This card holds the lines found in the poem on Professor Roald Gould's desk with Gould's name on the paper." Campello raised his eyebrows again in a gesture that I couldn't get a read on, either irony or genuine surprise.

I went through every card, making connections between Michael's and Gould's identical phrases and lines and then Marc's and Gould's duplicate lines. I also set out Gould's chapbook with the underlined passages and the poem that Katherine Bushnell had sent to me, written by Marc Bennett. Then the arrow to the same lines in Gould's poetry book. Then I set out my motive card, proximity notes, and an opportunity card, along with an index card listing each additional piece of evidence or circumstance. I had bits of string cut to just the right length and laid them down to make the connections between the cards with the people's names and topics. At the center, I placed a card with the name Gould on it. Every piece of string was also connecting Gould to all of the other cards.

"Easier to read if you come around this side of the desk," I said to Campello who was already turning to stand over my shoulder. Then I pointed out my other new evidence. "Did you know Gould paid for Marc Bennett's funeral? Do you know if Gould was involved with paying for Michael's? Something beyond compassion is going on here."

Campello looked pained at first, but I could feel the slight change in his interest as he leaned over the desk. Then he picked up the cards individually for more careful reading. I started to speak again, but he held his index finger in front of my face, letting me know he was considering what I had placed before him and needed a moment to concentrate. He turned every card over and moved them around on the table, organizing them in his own fashion but leaving Gould in the center.

Finally, after what appeared to be an hour but was probably only about 10 minutes, he brought his hand to his chin and stroked it. He looked at me directly again, then said, "I'm not saying there is nothing here," making my heart jump to my throat, "but it's highly circumstantial, and I could see a decent defense lawyer ripping all of this to shreds." He changed his voice to imitate the defense lawyer's remarks: "'Inference, inference, inference, with multiple and possibly reasonable explanations behind each one.'" Then he frowned and said in his normal tone, "Not enough for an arrest, or even…"

"There's got to be a way," I interrupted him, but he was shaking his head while looking thoughtful.

"Suspicion is one thing. Insufficient evidence is another. If we went around arresting everyone on merely our suspicions, well, you can imagine…"

I had already promised myself that I would not cry or get to discouraged, so I took a deep breath and prepared to collect my evidence cards. Campello put his hand over mine and drew the card away. "Suspicion is not necessarily the starting point for me," he said. "Curiosity is. Can I keep these?"

I almost reached over to hug him but stopped myself before looking even more foolish. "Of course." He gathered up my index cards in a neat stack and secured them with a rubber band from his drawer. He wrote across the top, "Gould."

"If anything happens to me, you'll know where to start looking?" I asked him without sarcasm.

"Nothing is going to happen to you, Miss Goodwin. But let's just say that you've put this Professor Gould on my radar."

"That's good, right?"

"That could be very bad for Gould," he said smiling for the first time. "Stay in touch."

I gave him Warren's address in the event he found anything new. I told him Warren was a family friend and that I was leaving school for a while.

"A family friend, eh?"

I could tell he didn't believe me. "All right. He's my old boyfriend, but he's an honest, good man and trustworthy."

Campello released a broad smile. "Honesty feels good, doesn't it? Miss Goodwin." He then shook my hand, and I left with some weight lifted. Maybe he was just telling me what I wanted to hear to get me out of the office, but it appeared more genuine than that. Maybe Campello was just another actor, but then again, he was interested enough to start poking around in places to which I had no access.

In some stories and movies, the camera or scene moves quickly, and our eyes miss a detail here and there that only the gumshoe or cop is able to link back to the murderer. We rewind and watch again, trying to catch what our eyes did not consciously connect to our brains on first viewing. This is every Sherlock Holmes' mystery. Only Holmes has that photographic memory at work from the outset. I had little confidence that Campello had Holmes' acuity.

Gould was still dangerous, specifically dangerous to me, but I also began to believe that he might be caught if he went after me. I had no idea until a couple of years later that Campello was known by his fellow officers as 'Bulldog'.

~ * ~

I went back to Warren's third floor apartment to eat, rest, and plan the next steps, and those steps that would lead me out of the country. Even if Campello was on his case, Gould still had freedom to move around and come after me. I was not going to underestimate him again. By this time, I was certain someone had told Gould that I was staying with an ex-Rochester student by the name of Warren Taylor. I ran into a classmate getting coffee off campus and he asked me about Warren out of the blue. How did all of this get around anyway? I then realized that maybe Warren was a little too pleased to see me and mentioned our living arrangement to an old friend or friends.

"Yeah, heard you dropped out, and then here you are. You and Warren dating?" Josh said.

"No. No. He just drove me somewhere. Where did you hear that?"

"I don't know. Around. So, are you coming back to school?"

"Sure, but I've got to go now." Josh waved as if he would see me the next day, but I never saw him again. If Josh knew, who else knew? When I got back to Warren's place, I locked the door, pushed a chair up against the handle and waited. I was even getting jumpy waiting for Warren.

When he got home late that night with our dinner, I immediately disappointed him by saying I had to leave again.

He took the statement well. "What's with the furniture next to the door?"

"A little insurance. And Warren, please don't tell anyone that I was staying with you. It's not safe for either of us." I also made him promise to get a roommate and stay away from Gould.

"I saw someone hanging around across the street last night," said Warren.

"Oh, no."

"I couldn't tell who he was, but he looked like he was watching the house."

"Damn."

"Don't worry," he said. Warren reached behind the door and came out with a baseball bat, gripping the wood with both hands. "Just for such occasions."

Chapter Twenty-nine
Of Nothing and Nothing More

Leaving the country with no immediate plans to return, I called Bill to let him know where I was going, but I didn't want a lot of people aware, people whom Gould could track down and find out where I headed. Even with Bill, I told him only enough so he wouldn't worry, should the thought of me ever occur to him again. I left with next to nothing, figuring I could always buy what I needed when I got wherever I ended up, eventually. The flight out of JFK took me to London, but I would not stay there, intending to head to Italy as inconspicuously as possible, destination Rome.

Dying my hair again that last night at Warren's, I chose a light brown—my natural mousy color that Warren said was beautiful—and styled it for the first time in years. He loved the color because that was how I looked when he first met me. I already appeared like a different person. In fact, airport security personnel checked my passport several times, looking back up at me, checking my old blonde messy locks in the photo against my new brown wavy ones, before letting me through to board. Imagine if my short, blue, spikey hair image had landed on my passport? I kind of considered myself an imposter, too, as if I was peeking out from behind someone else's life.

Poor Warren had to drive me east and south again, this time all the way to New York City. When he dropped me off, I was frozen for an instant, uncertain and scared. Then I looked up at his wide eyes that were a little watery.

"Hey, you take care of yourself," he said, breathing funny. I had to leave before we both started balling. Reaching over, he hugged me tight.

Then he told me that he had a friend who lived outside New York where he could stay the night. I'd grilled him on the details because I didn't want him turning around and driving all the way back to Rochester in one long journey.

"You, too, and thanks, thanks for everything." I leaned over just as he moved toward me again at the same moment, and we bumped heads pretty hard. Intending to give him a little kiss, I yelled, and we parted rubbing our sore foreheads, then started laughing.

"Don't remember me this way."

"It's exactly how I want to remember you." Then I kissed him full on the lips, leaning in through the open car window.

"Damn," he said in the way that meant something else.

I didn't want to look back and do something crazy like change my mind, so I tried disappearing into the crowd. I was struggling. At that moment, all I really wanted to do was run back and jump in Warren's car. Something kept me moving forward. He honked the horn, and then I turned and waved. He shook his head but smiled, I think. I couldn't actually see his face well.

I was leaving everything that was familiar except my theories. Still fearful for my life, I had taken almost nothing except my passport, enough cash to get me a few places, and stay in a few more after cashing Bill's check; and let's be honest, a change of underwear and toothbrush. I hate it when I can't brush my teeth in the morning. In Warren's car, in the airport, even on the plane, I shifted into a patient gear, settling in for long periods of waiting and the suspended life of airports.

Almost any airport is its own domain, but JFK is so crazy huge and with so many people from all over the world, you really feel invisible in this sea of humanity. I bought a coffee and sat down to wait for my plane, listening to the announcements in thick, almost unintelligible accents calling for passage to distant ports. For a few seconds, I wondered if I should just jump on one of those planes to more distant ports—to Istanbul, to Manila.

Weird, but when I got in line to board, I started looking around to see if I knew anyone, as if the world really is as small as my circle. Then I try to figure out who these people are, why they are heading to England or

Europe. Who are they traveling with, and before long, I have numerous stories about each little family unit and the travelers' galaxies.

~ * ~

Once settled on the plane, I took out a novel that I bought in the airport, along with a journal. I wouldn't be able to sleep, so I decided to make use of the time. I hadn't read more than a few pages of the pop culture book, something about a woman who finds a younger lover on holiday, before I noticed phrasing from another book. Here we are again, I thought. With plot and characters, it's easy to identify borrowing, less so with themes, images, tropes, and symbols. You have to know the works well to spot this subtler type of piracy. Exact wording? No problem calling out plagiarism except when the theft is done in parody.

How do these scales tip when reputations of the authors are above suspicion? Was Baczkowski above suspicion? Was Gould? No matter what I thought I had proven, no one would consider my accusations because of the prestige of the subjects. Gould could not possibly be a killer, yet he was. He was the citizen above suspicion. I started thinking about other serial killers who, after they were finally caught, surprised everyone. Those white guys with glasses, short hair, wives and nice-looking children, neighbors who said they were quiet and never caused any trouble, except, of course, the various heinous murders they committed.

Unable even to read any longer, I got up and went to the tiny restroom just to stretch my legs on the long aisle. The jostling walk down the narrow path gave me an opportunity to look around at the other passengers, too. On the Atlantic crossing, an elderly woman and man sat in the seat next to me in the middle row. At first, I was just glad to have an aisle seat, but the man kept poking me accidentally as the woman haplessly flailed at him, yelled at him, and then struck him rather solidly.

"Sorry," he said. "I'm so sorry. She doesn't know what she's doing. She's my wife, see, and a good woman, but she has a brain disease."

"Oh," was all I could manage. After a few hours, I felt so badly for him, knew too much of their life story together, but still had not had five minutes of sleep, so I took a risk and went to the back of the plane to talk to the stewardess.

"See, that man being hit by that woman?"

The stewardess, who appeared to be in her 50s, most likely had to lower her standards to take this position due to budgetary cuts, looked out over the dark rows half way up the coach section and then spotted the elderly woman taking her hat as a weapon to her husband. Estelle, her name plate gave away, nodded but seemed bored.

"I'm not trying to get them in trouble or anything, but it's really hard to sit with them. Do you think I could sit in that empty seat?" I had already scouted out the empty one on my way back to the tiny lavatory earlier in the flight.

Estelle shook her head. "I'm sorry." An awful lot of people said they were sorry for things they either could not control or didn't really care about. "You'll have to take your own seat. I will speak to them." The tone was sharper than her words.

"No, no, don't do that. Forget it, please. He has enough trouble." Miserably tired, I made my way back, buckled my seat belt obediently, and leaned out over the aisle as far as I could, only occasionally getting a scarf, hat, or sweater in the face.

The poor man must have said, "I'm sorry," or some variation about fifty times to me, and I just shrugged, telling him once that I was used to it. I don't even know what I meant by that, except that I was used to feeling put upon by someone else.

Near the end of the flight, he leaned over conspiratorially to me and whispered, "I've thought about ending it, smothering her with a pillow." Even though the plane was quiet for a plane because most of the passengers were asleep, I wasn't sure if I heard him correctly.

I turned my head and looked at him, but he was cradling her head lovingly with his arm because she had fallen asleep. He was studying my face. "Excuse me?"

"Only joking," he said. "She's so dear to me, but we never know what we're capable of, do we?" He sighed wearily and closed his eyes.

Closing mine as well for a few minutes, I saw an image of him holding a pillow over his wife's head and her brief struggle. I woke with a start, finding myself sympathizing with her at the end, but then realized we were landing. What had this interaction meant? I supposed, this sad exchange meant nothing at all.

~ * ~

I could have stayed in London for a few days but decided to go right to Rome. I wasn't intending to be a tourist but, rather, start a new life far from home.

On my second plane ride, I tried sleeping again, gave up, and took out my notes on Baczkowski. I made a graphic organizer in my pocket notebook, aligning and crisscrossing Baczkowski and Mctigue and their works. Then I wrote a few statements. I wasn't sure if what I had written would all come to nothing again, but I kept returning. After writing, I read it over.

~ * ~

Urjasz Baczkowski was a highly respected and decorated Polish author. The idea that his works should call up other literary works in the absurdist milieu is not strange. It is odd, however, that one of his most acclaimed works, the novel *Light,* should not only elicit the absurdist feel of a Sartre or Mctigue work but should start to read as if trapped in a mirror image of *Nightfall.* Does Baczkowski transform something mundane into something extraordinary? No. Mctigue's play is already a phenomenal, bizarre, and curious great work of literature that won for its author the Nobel Prize. *Light* won the International Prize for Literature shortly after its publication.

There is a little over ten years separating these works' publications, but the gap –that missing space between them— must be important. That gap was the mystery where all my speculation lay but would not be disturbed.

~ * ~

I tucked my scarf under my head and leaned back, imagining

Mctigue and Baczkowski conspiring. Maybe I thought their plan would come to me in that state between waking and sleep. In the beginning of R.E.M. sleep, I discerned Michael's presence rather than Mctigue's. The feeling was not haunting but comforting. He was flying with me.

Falling asleep for just a short time, I woke with my neck bent awkwardly and sore, and the woman in the middle seat leaning her head on my shoulder, drooling. Still, she was a nice woman, and I was not about to wake her up. Nothing really happened on the plane, and I came to no new decisions. Everything was still suspended as if I had never landed.

Chapter Thirty
Then Opening the Door

Sometime after arriving in Rome and finding my way to my hotel in the heart of the city, I went to the window and pushed back the curtains, looking out on the ancient and modern. I was exhausted from two flights and very little sleep, but I stood looking through the window and recalled everything from what I thought was a safe distance. I finally fell back on the bed and slept well for the first time in days. I woke again thirsty and then deduced something Gould had said in the last days we parried: "Their words were mere skeletons. I covered their ugly bones with sinew, muscle, organs; I animated them and created poetry." Fitting he used the imagery of death and dismemberment in describing his actions.

Gould was still in my head, all those miles apart. I recalled, too, Gould's response to my admission of a fondness for mysteries over three years earlier. "Which ones in particular?" he asked, ready to analyze then judge. I should have recognized his penchant for quick assessment.

Proud of my versatility, I named Arthur Conan Doyle first, candidly, then John le Carre's *The Spy Who Came in From the Cold* and Dorothy Sayer's *The Nine Tailors*. Those were the days when I was still trying desperately hard to impress Gould, so I also said, "Naturally, Poe, too, and Umberto Eco's *The Name of the Rose.*" I hadn't actually finished Eco's historically based mystery novel, even though I had started the book three times. I hoped Gould would not quiz me.

But Gould looked at me with amusement. "Not Dostoyevsky's *Crime and Punishment*? I would have thought you would have chosen that first."

I felt foolish and not for the first time. Of course, I should have named Dostoyevsky, and I remembered Gould's first choice much later. Back then, I was trying too hard. "What are your other favorites?" I inquired innocently enough.

"My favorites? I don't classify literature in terms of personal favorites, but Dostoyevsky was one of the first masters of the genre." Just the way he said the word "favorites" made me feel ridiculous. Tone was everything with Gould, and he could decimate an individual or entire classroom with a phrase.

Gould always made everyone feel less than, and I should have been annoyed, but I kept trying. "What I meant to say is, what other mysteries are ones you want to return to?"

Without hesitation, which I now find odd, considering the breadth and width of his reading—he said, "A Taste for Death," Lady James novel in the Dalgliesh series." Gould folded his long, thin fingers together in repose.

"A Taste for Death?" I repeated unnecessarily.

"Are you aware the title is taken from A. E. Houseman's four-line poem?"

"I'm afraid I haven't read it yet, but I will." I had read neither P.D. James nor much of Houseman's work, other than the required reading of "To An Athlete Dying Young" in my tenth grade English class in high school. Bill liked that poem, but I found nothing memorable about the Houseman poem at the time. All I recalled was the word lintel because I did not know what a lintel meant and had to look up the definition. Surprisingly, the word denotes an architectural support. Of course, there would be ways to play with this concept of "support" in the poem. The definition was impressed upon me because Mrs. Slade asked us the following morning to discuss the architectural motif in the sixth stanza. I was the only one who had a clue as to what to answer.

Early on, I recognized that I wasn't any smarter than anyone around me, just curious and willing to follow the path of curiosity to some kind of answer. In those days, I was such an obedient pup that wanted to please, particularly my teachers. Later, I looked up the Houseman poem and found the quotation to which Roald Gould and P.D. James alluded was about death and acquiring a desire for it. In the same series of short poems, Houseman suggested that none of us had much worth living for anyway.

Whether it was James or Houseman of whom Gould was so fond, I wasn't sure, but I appreciated by then that Gould, too, had an unnatural affinity for death. Just when he first acquired his taste for death would be impossible for me to determine, but I suspected his affair with death began long before even poor Joe Finley. Serial killers seem to leave the backroads littered with tortured animals long before they move up the evolutionary chain to human beings.

Gould wanted what he could not have, as well as what he was able to steal. "We're not so terribly different," he said on the last occasion I saw him on campus. He was still smirking, knowing that I was aware he had killed Michael and, perhaps, Marc Bennett, too, but he did not fear me, was not really nervous. Gould was certain that I was powerless, and if not, he would eliminate me efficiently, as well.

"We are poles apart," I said and walked away from him in the crowded hallway, trying not to look back.

~ * ~

Once upon a time, Roald Gould was my mentor and teacher. I respected him, idolized him, really, was infatuated with him. He could talk for hours and his students thronged around him. But toward the end, near the beginning of my slow realization of the kind of monster he is, I saw the cracks appearing. Rebecca Solnit wrote in her book *Wanderlust*, "Nobody remains heroic forever," but I had come to realize that Gould was never heroic, that I, along with his many acolytes, had mistaken his conceit and his acumen. An uncanny ability to recall lines of others was neither heroic nor scholarship.

There was an afternoon, back and forth with him early in the year, that I recalled because I began to feel something was insinuating itself into his criticism. I said to him in my naïve manner, "Eliot is not quite stating the same concept as Foucault, though, in remarking, 'no poet, no artist of any art, has his complete meaning alone.'"

"You read Eliot's essay 'Tradition and the Individual Talent,' and are able to quote from it. I like seeing students pursue readings that are difficult for them on their own."

At the time, I think I was flattered by his words, and now, I realize the degree to which he was insulting or at least condescending to me.

"I'm fascinated with his poetry."

"Separate from his literary criticism, he would claim that creating art and analyzing art are different functions but both impersonal: 'The emotion of art is impersonal. And the poet cannot reach this impersonality without surrendering himself wholly to the work to be done,' also a quotation from his essay."

Gould had to make sure I grasped he could not only quote the same essay but at greater length and by heart. In my open notebook were a series of quotations from T.S. Eliot's essay on tradition and the individual, yet here was Gould quoting again without crib notes, without hints, purely from memory. I recall wanting to avoid sycophant flattery but let him know that I appreciated the intellect behind such a feat.

"You know this essay by heart?"

"Let's just say that I have a familiarity with her." He saw my eyes widen at his use of the feminine pronoun. "I say 'her' because Eliot's writing has always struck me as having a feminine quality in spite of the masculine constructions and his subtle misogyny."

Blushing at his remark without a clear understanding of why, I stood in amazement before him. It was difficult not to be conscious of how handsome he was, commanding, and authoritative. But I tried to offer a counterpoint. "His work as feminine?"

"Indeed. Signifiers such as 'surrendering' and 'continual self-sacrifice,' as well as 'continual extinction of personality.'"

I should have argued that self-sacrifice and extinction of personality were no more feminine than masculine, but at that point, I was still enthralled by him. In retrospect, I realize that Gould was sexist as well as manipulative.

How far I had come, around the world and in this beautiful, historical city, yet here was Gould in my head again.

I returned to Eliot's famed essay and underlined the lines: "You cannot value him alone; you must set him, for contrast and comparison, among the dead." There was Michael and Marc, and Joe beneath Gould's lines and lies.

Setting out, I left my hotel room and shut Gould out, as well. Rome, I have arrived.

Chapter Thirty-one
You Venture Out

The first day in Rome I headed to the Spanish Steps in the area of the city even the Romans call, "The English Quarter", because so many English poets and writers had found their way to this place of ancient beauty and history. This little quarter of Rome belonged to the Italians, of course, but the locale had also been home to Englishmen and other expats who wandered in and never left. Shelley, like Keats, died there. I knew from a previous visit that viewing the room where John Keats took his last breath, struggling from tuberculosis, would not be impossible for me. The Keats-Shelley House at the foot of the Spanish Steps was not a prime tourist destination, but I was drawn there again. I also knew that Gould had gone to this place of particular interest to poet's years earlier. He had suggested I visit Keats' deathbed before my first trip overseas.

As I stood in that little room, looking at that narrow daybed where Keats had slept and died just off the street of *Piazza di Spagna* 26, I was aware of an involuntary shudder. Strangely, the sensation was not the ghost of the twenty-five-year old English poet that blew upon my neck, but the eerie whiff of being in the room with Gould. Turning suddenly, I half expected to find him standing there glaring at me in contempt. Only after several minutes did my heart stop racing, and I set out to visit other parts of the city. The tingle of hairs on my arms and the breath on my neck were caused by unnatural fears, I reasoned with myself. But the thought of Gould stalking me was present too, however unlikely.

Wearing a woven nylon hat with a striped band, I tipped it slightly toward the angle of the sun. I bought the cool hat from a most persistent street vendor and was grateful that it kept the hot sun off my face. Really, the vendor was more than a little annoying, following me for two blocks before I relented. Then, I was glad he had trailed me. I never wore a hat back home, but here, the sun beat down with a different kind of intensity.

After standing at a counter with other patrons on their way to work, having our espressos, I walked briskly to the Basilica Santa Maria degli Angeli, designed by Michelangelo. Very quickly I learned to move rapidly in Rome to avoid looking like an easy target. I suddenly thought of Solnit's book *Wanderlust* again. Weirdly, I was starting to feel like Gould, able to recite recollected lines in their entirety. In her chapter "Walking After Midnight," Solnit said of women's physical presence in the city, "It equates visibility with sexual accessibility, and it requires a material barrier rather than a woman's morality or will to make her inaccessible to passersby." The "it" in her construction was the very act of being alive in social constructs that attempt to imprison women in the home for thousands of years. I was making my statement for freedom, but not unaware of the dangers of doing so.

Tucking my guide map discreetly away, I was forced to take out my phone for directions several times as I race-walked along. Even if I had to backtrack, better to look resolute in the streets. Although I was breathing the dust of ancient and modern Rome, I wanted to laugh. The irony of being chased to Rome by Gould struck me. He had once sent me to Italy and England to do his research, and here I was fleeing to this place. If I could admit it to myself, I had left school not only to get away from a murderous Gould but to try to find myself. To be a stranger in my own skin was to discover myself again, so I willingly entered another kind of peril.

I had heard of the church built inside the walls of the Baths of Diocletian, but nothing in my tour guide book or online Wikipedia source could do fair treatment to the spectacle. History seeped through walls, even weeping at points, ancient brick revealed outside this building that it was so much more than structure alone. Inside, the ceiling was all Michelangelo in its arched perfection: there were faint echoes in imagining cries of martyrs and men of science; older still, commands of an efficient and well-organizer emperor who had perfected the torture and deaths of thousands of Christians. Those Christians later made martyrs of thinking men, the vicious cycles of human depravity and enlightenment in the name of empire building eerily similar to the building of religious institutions. The space where I stood was yet another example of doubling.

While I looked up at the larger than life sculpture of Galileo, I considered that here was evidence of his science, his pendulum and here his near martyrdom, as the Christians who had once been split at the feet of Diocletian made sacrifice of men of science, calling them heretics. The church had long ago made its penance, however, and had the sculpture of Galileo erected within their sphere. Galileo would have, undoubtedly, found his huge likeness in such a place to be ironic but satisfying. Somehow just standing before the statue of Galileo made me forget Gould and my fears temporarily. In that moment of calm, transported to another point in history, someone spoke to me.

Which is more incongruous?" a young man asked directly behind as I stared at the stern face of Galileo. I turned to see to whom he was talking. There was no one else in the immediate vicinity except the two of us. A group of Chinese tourists had moved off together. I should have been nervous, but I wasn't. He was entirely too good looking and charming. In fact, he was exactly the sort of character you find in a movie, the one you're sure could not possibly exist in real life. He was without blemish, stylishly, but casually dressed and his eyes beautiful.

"Excuse me?"

"I was just wondering what you thought of Galileo's presence looming so large in the place where he had been condemned." His quick smile and easy manner were infectious, but I had cautioned myself against this type of encounter, then promptly tossed caution away. I had not come all this way just to be afraid again.

"If he were not bronzed, Galileo's stern face would break into laughter."

"Ah, I think you are quite right. American, yes?"

"I am an American. And you?"

"Italian who speaks very good English, no?"

"Yes. You're an accomplished speaker. I'm afraid my Italian is still halting and not nearly so precise."

"I promise not to laugh. Please." He put his hands out as if taking my words with an embrace.

"*Mi inchino davanti a questo luogo di tanta storia,*" I said a bit hesitantly.

"She speaks Italian. Excellent."

"Well, I must be going, good day."

"Elio," he yelled, catching up to me. "Elio Canestrini. And your name?"

I shook my head and left the young man, walking away quickly, but I also smiled. I really had no idea that he was following me all the way to my next stop. I promised myself not to be an easy target, but to remain open to new adventures as well. That would prove to be a difficult, if not impossible, balancing act.

~ * ~

In the *Museo Centrale Del Risorcimento*, I was searching for a Caravaggio painting I hoped to see. Turning around twice, I couldn't help looking for the handsome young man again but did not spot him. I was paradoxically both relieved and disappointed. I had learned the trick of looking as if I was expecting someone at any moment and appearing occupied in order to keep unwelcome strangers at bay.

After wandering around the museum, I was getting tired, and my feet were sore, but I promised not to retreat until I had found it. Then, suddenly, as I walked through an opening to another small room there she was: Judith beheading Holofernes as large as life pinned against the wall. Caravaggio's masterpiece was more powerful than I could have anticipated. The strength and mystery of Judith, her extraordinary bravery made me feel her vitality, as well as her tension. I expected to love the painting but not to be viscerally moved by it.

"She is beautiful, no?" I looked to the side, and there was Elio smiling but looking at the painting not me.

"Where did you come from? Are you spying on me?"

"Spying? No, no, no. But you are young and beautiful, and unaccompanied in our glorious city that has more than its share of nefarious characters. I could not let you wander alone without some escort. You have no idea how dangerous that could be for you, so I am here to escort you."

"I think I have a pretty good idea about the city. What do you mean? You have been following me? For how long?"

"Ah, since you left the train station. Lots of pickpockets and thieves, some disagreeable, is that the right word, men?"

"Disreputable, I think you mean, but, disagreeable will do. You've been following me since the station? Why shouldn't I be nervous about you?"

He bowed. "Because I am an honorable man. I am at your service and welcome you to Rome."

"Were you at the hotel?"

"Your hotel is well-known for accommodating tourists, and therefore, an easy mark for those who might consider lightening you of your valuables."

"And did you see any of these nefarious characters?"

"No, just a Tunisian selling you a hat, and it looks very nice on you."

I recognized then that he truly had been following me all along. I should have been nervous but wasn't. "I could yell for the police."

He laughed. "Ah, my oldest brother is with the Carabinieri. I will call him and ask him to, ah, how do you say, tell you I am a good guy?"

I shrugged. "You might as well be my guide, but that is all. And not too close."

"I accept this assignment. You like Caravaggio?" We looked at the painting again.

"Not quite as obsessed as Artemisia Gentileschi who painted this violence many times, Judith always so calm. And then there was Bigot, but..."

"None were Caravaggio," he finished my sentence.

"No, none quite so marvelous as this painting, but I am rather fond of Artemisia too, and, of course, a woman painting this powerful statement in a man's art world."

"And some would say, 'a man's world,' too, but not me. I like this Artemisia, if you do." Elio nodded approvingly. "She is Italian, too. And your name? We're friends now."

"Not yet we aren't. Perhaps I will tell you. We will see. What intrigues you about this painting? The beheading?"

Excited and nervous that we were talking, Elio said, "It is the worry in her eyes, not just the triumph. See that crease in her forehead. She is very smart and has defeated her enemy but a victory with costs." I liked his answer.

"Vena," I said and could see the smile lines at the corners of his eyes. "And in her lips, between her brows, the lines of tension."

"Yet her hair is perfectly in place and not a drop of blood touches her after the act."

"She has saved her people but, as you said, at a cost." I was foolishly seeing myself in this woman on canvas, but I had not defeated the monster Gould. I was no Judith. I had run as far away as possible from Gould. My cowardice loomed as large as the canvas.

"What do you think of the serving woman?"

"She is aptly hideous. Yet her intense satisfaction is most perfect and unsettling."

"You can almost hear her whispering to Judith before the act, encouraging Judith; the old one has a lust for blood."

"Where do you see this?"

"In my mind, but Caravaggio took me there. Look at their gestures. Judith determined but wrestling with a conscience, the old woman, and I wonder if, perhaps, she was really an old man disguised as woman, clutches the bag with an eagerness to accept the head of Holofernes, and the general's spayed fingers, his last movements—open in shock."

"Do you come here often? You know the painting almost too well."

"Yes, but this is my city. Of course, I come and linger. I am in love with Judith in the painting."

"What do you love about her?"

"Everything. Her strength but distaste for what she knows she must do. I imagine that even the seduction of Holofernes was most disagreeable to her. Slicing through his head should have been pure pleasure, but you see, she is troubled. This is a woman of great bravery and great conscience, necessity that wrestles with her compassion."

"And do you find young women to impress with your knowledge

and charm each time?"

Elio turns his head to look at me. "Anything I say here you will not like."

"Try honesty." I remembered Campello's words to me.

"Then, my answer must be, many young women, but I am seldom interested for long. Either they do like this painting or they run away, afraid of their own shadows."

"Perhaps the problem is you and not the women?"

"Most likely, but this is yet to be confirmed. Great work, no?"

"Caravaggio or Judith?" He was standing closer to me now, near enough to touch my hand at my side. I could have moved away but didn't.

"Ah, both. Where to next, Vena? By the way, I do like your hat."

His remark reminded me of a P. D. Eastman children's book, *Go, Dog, Go,* on the page where the male dog says to the female dog, "Yes, I do. I like your party hat." I started to laugh.

"Thanks, I think. I don't know; I mean, I have no idea where to go next." In other circumstances, I might have broken down and started crying, but looking vulnerable was not possible in his presence.

"Then you are most fortunate because I do. You must see our Quattro Fontane. But first, we will sit down and relax, find a good café, and eat something. Okay? Shall we go?" He led the way, and I followed, constantly looking around to make sure I was in a crowd. Although I was immediately attracted to this brash young man, I was not completely unaware that he could be dangerous to me. At least I was aware for an hour or two, but then I fell for the Italian art on display in every archway, curves of the public forums, the way light filtered down, moving between colorful clothes on a line strung between narrow spaces, until we arrived at the four fountains where rivers, air, ancient stone, and roads converged. In such a place, even the most cynical lose their distrust of the world.

"Listen, and you can hear the river gods speaking," Elio said with a finger to his lips.

In spite of the traffic, human noise, and rush of the city, I could sense whispers of long ago ages when politicians, a Pope, an Italian nobleman, and old gods fought as rivals. "See, Diana whisper to the River Tiber while Juno looks on jealously?"

"Why not have Tiber jealous of his rival Tererone for Diana's affections?"

"Oh, you know them then? I like you more every minute."

"Not as intimately as you. I suppose you know the history of how they came to be here." Elio took my hand, and I allowed my fingers to slip between his without concern or distrust. The bravest thing I had done was not face Gould, but let myself fall so easily for a stranger in a foreign land.

"Yes, but here we have a long story filled with politics of the architect Borromini, a Cardinal, Barberini, a Saint, and a Pope. I can tell you while we eat and drink."

"They are so beautiful," I said, "but so covered in street grime." Such a busy intersection, and the exhaust from cars and motorbikes settled heavily on these ancient statues.

"Part of their charm. Come, let's get a cool drink and find a trattoria."

"I was hoping to visit the *Antico Caffe Greco Via Condotti*," I said, by now flirting and wanting to get my way.

"Then, that is where we will go. Some English author you are researching, perhaps?"

"Keats. How did you know?"

"Ah, you English and Americans!" He laughed. We walked together, and his index finger sensuously brushed across my palm which I allowed to vacation there.

That is how I met the generous, playful, flirtatious, and very smart Elio Canestrini.

Chapter Thirty-two
Apprehensive but Determined

Other than with Warren and now Elio, I too often experienced the sensation of being a stranger in the company of all those around me, perhaps the way my estranged mother had always intended by naming me Advena. But I wasn't my mother's daughter. Even if every once-in-a-while I wondered what she might think about me, I never went so far as to wish she was still in my life. Although I was continually reminded I looked like her when I was younger, few people mentioned my similarity to her any longer. Of course, we were never together, so any comparisons were next to impossible from anyone except, perhaps Bill, and he no more wanted to bring up Greta than I did.

Toying with giving myself a new name, I finally settled upon shortening it, something I had always wanted to do. Disguise is central to this discovery, even self-discovery. I had considered renaming myself Celia when I arrived in Italy and believed that Shakespeare would have liked it. I was not hiding in the Forest of Arden, however, but in a Mediterranean country which is so much warmer, and Rome offered the opportunities as well as anonymity that I was seeking.

Even though Elio was more than amusing and intriguing to me, and the sites of Rome were spectacular, I kept seeing that Caravaggio painting in my head and knew I had to find a way to take Gould down. I simply couldn't live peacefully or happily knowing that he had murdered Michael and others and gotten away with it. I knew, and I couldn't un-know this terrible thing that had happened. Even if I braved going back to Rochester, what would I do? I had already confronted the man I once held in such high esteem. I had gone to the police, tried to arouse suspicion of Gould in others, all to no avail.

Unexpectedly one afternoon, Elio suggested we travel to the Amalfi coast where his father was renovating a couple of rental properties. "You could stay in one apartment, and I will manage the others," he said. By then we were already making love, and in love, so agreement was easy. Also, the end of the summer was so hot in Rome that even its beauty was constrictive, oppressive. Going to the beautiful Amalfi coast was something I had long wished to do, and being able to get to water easily was on my mind every afternoon as the sun pushed down upon young and old alike.

"I am going to have to get a work VISA because my student one will run out," I told him, "and if you want me to work, I think I need something to make the proposal official."

"No worries. You are fortunate you met me." I thought about his statement a great deal. "My father is a very influential man, with many friends in high places, as you say in English. He will get you something quickly."

"Why is your father so generous?" I asked Elio.

"He's rich. And I suppose because he feels a little guilty," Elio smiled at that as he drove, looking over at me until I reminded him to keep his eyes on the road.

"Guilty? Of what?"

"For leaving me and my brothers to grow up with our mother alone and with limited support. She worked until near the end when her illness no longer permitted it. You see, I'm not really spoiled. Do you think I'm spoiled?"

"Yes, no, I don't know. You seem to have everything, but you're also generous."

"I'm not spoiled, you see, because I didn't know I was rich until I was all grown up."

"You're rich, too?"

"See, you like me better already."

"I liked you fine before, as if you didn't know. How did you get rich?"

"Vincenzo, my father, told me he wished he could have taken me with him when he left, but my mother would not hear of it. Quite rightly, she didn't like his lifestyle. I am not sure I believe him about wanting to take me with him, but ah, all is forgiven. Too many years ago now."

"What happened to your mother?" His mother's absence immediately struck me that Elio's circumstances of growing up were an inversion of my own.

"She died of cancer when I was thirteen. I was a disaster, of course. Then Vincenzo swooped in and brought me to live with him. He had a housekeeper who I saw far more frequently than my father, but when I saw him, the experience was always pleasant, fun. My older brothers had already gone off on their own, so they didn't forgive our father. Ha, to this day, they curse his name when we get together, as if this curse becomes a blessing in our greeting, a ritual we share; curse the name of the father."

"Do you get along with your brothers?"

"Of course, but they were several years older than me and had other interests, not wanting to spend time with a scrawny little brother tied to his mother's apron strings."

"It must have been terrible for you when she died."

Elio nodded his head. "She was a saint. That is why I understand my brothers' anger. But after I went to live with my father I lacked for nothing and he treated me very well. I thought, why not forgive but not forget? My mother raised me, loved me, was patient and encouraging. She stayed up all night when I was sick as a little boy, ran six blocks one night to get medicine for me, read to me, talked to me. She was there for me every day. My father? He indulged my whims with expensive gifts when I was thirteen. He sees no difference, but, naturally, I do." I realized that I, too, had forgiven my absent mother but would never forget.

In a stone house in the village built between the sea and hillside, I found a little home; moved in on the first floor and helped Elio manage the upper two floors guests rented from his father. We painted the walls and decorated with items we had brought from Rome. I planned to stay at least for several months, so I set up the closest thing to my own house I had in a very long time. Elio had moved into the third-floor apartment of one of his father's other houses further up the hill. The separate quarters gave us space even though we were often at each other's apartments.

"You see, I do not crowd you," he said cheerfully. "When you are ready to tell me your story, you will."

Part of me did not want to bring up the past, but I finally sat next to Elio and poured us each a glass of wine. "This is a long story," I said to him.

"Good. I love stories and wine, naturally."

"Not this one." Then I proceeded to tell him everything that had happened. He was quiet throughout my digressions, only nodding or looking concerned.

He interrupted me only once to say, "This Gould is a very bad man. I am glad you are here and not in America."

"And then I met you," I said, coming to the end of my tale and my journey.

"But you are safe now," he answered, pulling me to him to kiss me.

I pushed away only slightly. "I can't be. Do you understand?"

"No. He is far away, and I wouldn't let him touch you even if he showed up at your door."

"I don't want to be saved. I want revenge or at least some kind of reckoning, but I am no Judith. I am not brave or strong. And I'm not clever like Sherlock Holmes. I can't even find all the clues that will lead to his arrest. Still, I can't let this go, as if it never happened. I have allowed Gould to get away with it. Do you understand?" I had started walking around the room as I spoke, unable to simply sit there.

Elio got up and followed me as if we were walking to some destination yet unknown. "What do you want to do? What can you do? You are so far away from him."

"I want to trap him, trick him into confessing. I want him to pay for what he did."

"Then I will help you as long as the plan doesn't include going back to America. Tell me what you wish me to do. What is your plan?" I shook my head, told him I needed to be alone for a while.

"I think I understand, but perhaps you will think of something. You are very smart. I have confidence in you." He was the smart one on this and I kissed him, which led to him kissing me, which led to falling into bed together and more kissing and making love again. Hours later, he woke and finally headed back up the hill. "I have to get up early to work on that place up there," he whispered to me. "No more making love tonight. I need my rest." We giggled like children. One of the wonderful qualities I adored about Elio was his confidence, his sense of self.

Lying in bed, I had already decided to lure Gould to me, but how much to put in or leave out? Would he really come? After Elio left, I forced myself to get up and sat at my desk to write a letter. There was a line between temptation and blatantly begging. Gould was typically too clever for me, but I had only one advantage, and that was his conceit. Balancing the fine line between appearing confident in my safety and vulnerable enough to tempt Gould was not going to be easy.

~ * ~

Dear Dr. Gould,

I expect that this letter finds you well, writing and teaching. Your students are most fortunate, and I mean that sincerely. They will learn more in a semester with you than a year with any other teacher.

It was the right decision for me to leave the University of Rochester; I realize now how irrational I had become, how unfocused.

Surprisingly, I have rented a lovely little yellow house in this quaint village on the Amalfi Coast of Italy. Dark green shutters mark her soulful eyes. Living on the first floor is an ideal vantage point to look out at the Tyrrhenian Sea, but I will move upstairs. The scene is as beautiful here in Santa Maria di Castellabate as any postcard the imagination can conceive.

Within the next year or two, I am hoping to be able to finish my doctorate or at least continue my pursuit of it. Until then, I am reading and researching in this paradise. I will be leaving for Rome to find another apartment in a little over a month, so if you would like to write to me, please do so as soon as possible. As one of your former teaching assistants, I hope you will give me a good recommendation when the time comes.

I also would like to apologize for my earlier behavior and accusations. I realize that you could not have had anything to do with Michael's death. Grief and confusion caused me to act out of character and with great rudeness toward you. I hope you can forgive me.

At some point, I expect you will release my remaining files and poems in your possession in order for me to finish my dissertation and continue my work in Italy. I would love to hear from you and truly wish you the best.

Sincerely,

Advena

I never used the name Advena except with Gould, so signing with my given name was most appropriate. Even as I wrote Advena, I no longer recognized it. Then I neatly printed my new address in the top left corner. The trap seemed too easy, but we were thousands of miles apart. There was nothing easy or remotely feasible about any of this. Suddenly, I was filled with doubt. My intention to lure him would never work. I vacillated between these extremes. Would he take the bait? How could I assume he would still want to hurt me after all this time and great distance? I was not threatening him, and he could let the invitation go, laughing. Yet, if I had learned one thing about Gould with absolute certainty: he was perverse. Flying to Rome was no small journey even for a wealthy man like Roald Gould. He might just revel in the challenge, however. If this was my mousetrap, I had to offer myself as bait and the trap had to feel genuine. My letter must ring true, and I had to sound contrite.

The outcome was uncertain, but I could imagine Judith preparing for Holofernes' visit, her seduction a sacrifice; arranging her hair, perfuming her soft skin, closing the revealing garment that the giant would rip away.

Chapter Thirty-three
To Straighten out a Few Things

Someone, probably Campello, had driven Gould from his citadel. Warren wrote in an e-mail to tell me that Gould had left the university suddenly, and 'unofficial word' was that the police were 'looking at him for something sleazy'. "Well, actually, Campello sent me a note to tell you that he and Gould had an interesting conversation." I thought of Campello and was grateful for his persistence. To be a fly on the wall in the interview or 'interesting conversation' between Campello and Gould:

"Professor Roald Gould? We'd like you to come down to the station to straighten out a few things for us."

Gould wouldn't have panicked; he was too sure of himself, too careful, but he would have been curious enough to meet with Campello to see what the cop knew or didn't know. Gould, with his superior attitude, his disdain for Italians and cops barely concealed, would have strolled in ready to annihilate the questioner, but he would have found Campello a surprising match. Campello was far more intelligent than Gould had initially given him credit for, and Gould would have had to adjust his tactics.

They measured each other and immediately found the other lacking in some critical aspect. Campello saw through Gould's impeccable styling and found moral bankruptcy. Gould knew the cop had likely finished his schooling at a state school and was on a fishing expedition. Pre-determining not to speak first, Gould waited to counterattack. Campello was all about the gestures below language that would reveal far more than the professor believed possible. He had studied people's body language as long as Gould had been studying the English language, its syntax and grammar, its styling and history.

"See, we've got some strange circumstances, possibly coincidences, that we have to align," said Campello, carefully taking off the rubber band and spreading out my index cards like a Vegas dealer practiced at winning for the House.

"Are you attempting to organize your notes for a high school paper of some sort?" Gould couldn't resist insulting the cop across the desk from him.

But Campello was no star-struck rookie looking for a good grade or an assistantship.

"No. I've been out of high school for a long time now, learned a thing or two about human behavior along the way. I'm done with writing papers. These cards, see, were given to me by a young lady who is convinced that you might be able to help us with this puzzling set of circumstances."

Wait. Would Campello really betray me like that? No. He'd leave out the "young lady" part.

Gould smirks at this. "By its definition, circumstances or a coincidence…"

"That's the thing here," Campello said, interrupting Gould who was entirely unused to interruptions. "We don't really think they're coincidences or just oddly aligned circumstances. So, if we follow what we know, we come to you, as both starting point and, maybe, ending." Campello paused for effect and watched Gould raise his chin higher in defiance but also defense. He also noted Gould move his left hand from the top of the desk, a sign that he was hiding a twitch or moving fingers. Nerves were struck.

"Ridiculous. You don't have anything and know even less. Your starting point, I'm afraid, is also ending right here." Gould was determined not to show his impatience but arriving at that point in spite of his seemingly calm demeanor.

"There's where you're wrong, Professor. See, we already know who called us about checking into Michael Lawler's absence from class. At first, the gesture might seem magnanimous of you, but then…"

Would Gould have been thrown by the cop's use of the word "magnanimous" as much as he was by the underlying accusation? He couldn't show his surprise. Of course, they could have traced his phone call. Although he did not consider the call at the time, he was prepared for that question.

"Then it would seem I have a choice to either walk out in the middle of your absurd insults or stay and listen to you make a fool of yourself. Of course, my lawyer may be less amused by your harassment than me. Should I call him now?"

Campello is unruffled. "Call him or not. That's up to you. We're just having a little conversation. But I will tell you that I'm going to ignore your threat of a harassment lawsuit because you don't have one. So, let's back up a bit to the day you called in about a missing student. Then we start thinking about why an esteemed but very busy professor—such as yourself—and I understand you are quite well known in your circles—would call us after a student misses a single class. I'm guessing that students miss class all the time, and no one is calling about their whereabouts."

Catching the insult "in your circles," Gould knew he had made a mistake with the call the morning after his act, but he figured that one phone call would prove nothing except the fact he was a concerned teacher.

"Never having attended graduate school, you would be unaware of how infrequently graduate students at our university miss classes. They take their scholarship quite seriously, and I think I previously explained the foundations of my concern: my student's instability, his desperate attempts to get attention, any kind of attention, and obvious suicidal hints in his writing," Gould said, fairly nonplussed. As he explained the circumstances, he even appeared fairly generous to both Michael and Campello. His retelling of the experience was so believable that he had fashioned a new reality.

"You did, but the more these puzzle pieces start to fit a pattern, the closer we get to something we didn't recognize before. See, there are these pieces that just don't fit your convenient story."

"Are you implying I had something other than concern for a troubled student?"

"Implying? I'm just having a talk with you. See, it's just that we keep finding Professor Gould in the middle of things, like Michael Lawler's death, so it's natural that we have to ask, why?"

"I'm hardly in the middle of things with Lawler, and what I was aware of was information that his family had been tragically killed, and he walked around with enormous guilt, survivor's guilt. As I said before, I could discern all this from his writing."

"You seem to have known a great deal about the young man. You don't happen to have a copy of his writing, in his hand, that addresses his depression directly, do you?"

"Officer—Sergeant? Excuse me, I seem to have forgotten your name."

"Sergeant Campello. You're fortunate because I am well aware of your name. Now about Michael Lawler's writing?"

"Campello, students don't hand in work that is not composed on a computer anymore. In fact, something hand written would not be accepted by me or anyone else. And I'm afraid, I don't keep student work once that work is graded. The papers are promptly returned or discarded."

"So, your evidence of Lawler's depression has vanished?"

"That's a ridiculous comment. You are obviously not aware that I have eidetic memory or what you would call photographic memory, so I do have evidence of Michael's writing revealing his deep depression, his struggles with reality and psychic pain."

"And evidence of your calls to the university's counseling and medical staff about your concerns for a student who might have been suicidal? We would just need the time and date of each call."

This information in the hands of the police caught Gould off guard only momentarily, and then he recalled his note to the campus health center in which he expressed his concerns for Michael. He had written the note only two days before climbing Michael's stairs for the last time.

"I expressed my concerns to the UHS staff in writing. You are welcome to check with them."

Campello made a note to verify Gould's claim. "Then there's Marc Bennett's drowning, and—"

"Bennett? Why bring up that unfortunate young man?"

"You knew him, too."

"Knew him?"

"See, I already know you knew him."

"Well, you are nothing if not repetitive. He was a student at one point and a very troubled one with a drinking problem. I believe he had attended some party, drank too much, and fell in the Genesee River, as I recall."

"You recall pretty quickly after seven years."

"I've already told you about my near perfect memory."

"Well, see, your comments about Bennett drowning? That's what was assumed at the time because no one was really looking at that incident as closely as maybe we should have, but here's the thing, even after someone's dead and buried, an autopsy can tell us all kinds of stories, say, for instance, how a bruise was caused antemortem, perimortem, or postmortem. With a little work and even less luck, we could determine what made a blow to the head. Drag marks on a body still struggling as opposed to one that is already dead, and fortunately, we still have the photographs from the scene. Of course, no one was looking at them carefully at the time because assumptions were made."

"You're rather skilled at making inaccurate assumptions, I understand." Gould knew he should have said nothing but could not help himself from insulting the cop who was prolonging the scene. "I'm sure you imagine yourself as a TV cop when nothing out of the ordinary comes across your desk." Gould congratulated himself for resisting the temptation to say, "TV dick," the thought alone produced the smile creeping across his face.

"Then you show up, and here we are."

"I was asked to come, and I am about to leave."

Campello didn't let Gould's insults phase him. He'd heard far worse on the streets on a daily basis. "Well, that is the interesting thing about reopening a file; you suddenly start discovering all kinds of things you didn't know you were looking for the first time. And then, suddenly, there it is right in front of you." Campello leans back in his chair, tilts his head to one side studying the range of nearly infinitesimal tics running across Gould's face.

"You sound like your science needs some brushing up, but I suppose I should be impressed you know the Greek and Latin prefixes ante, peri, and post."

"That and a few other things." Campello suddenly leaned forward, looking straight at Gould with an intensity he had not displayed earlier.

"If you're expecting a confession of something, you will be disappointed once again." Gould reflexively pushed back.

"Confession?" asked Campello, a little surprised Gould had gone there on his own. "Oh, no, not yet. We have plenty of time for that later. I was just looking to have a little conversation about some unusual circumstances, but if you want to offer more..."

"No. We're done. As much as I enjoy listening to the repetitive ramblings of a City of Rochester policeman, I'm afraid I have important duties at the university. In any event, I think our period of wild speculation is over," Gould said, standing up.

"And you have been most helpful, indeed," said Campello. "But I hardly think we are done."

"Listen carefully," Gould came close to threatening the cop seated before him. "I came here out of a spirit of cooperation and consideration for a former student who tragically killed himself, but unless you're charging me with something, I'll be leaving you to play with your deck of cards. And I would hate to have to call a lawyer and file harassment charges."

Of course, Gould would not break easily, but then again, Campello was a continual surprise.

"Oh, you may want to call a lawyer, but I'd wait on the charges for a bit. You're free to leave at any time, Professor, but I thought you might want to look at these sections of our puzzle before we fit everything neatly together. It's interesting how these things seem to work out. Just when it looks like the pieces will never come together, one little clue leads us to linking all the others. In fact, I've gotten rather good at this, if you must know. At some point fairly soon, I will have to give a call to your university president to talk about how this picture is forming for us."

An artificial laugh escaped Gould. "Are you seriously imagining that you are threatening me?"

"Wouldn't dream of it," said Campello, stroking his chin with an attitude of satisfaction.

"What do you think you have? Really, I find you somewhat entertaining. Otherwise, I would have already walked out the door." Gould's cynical tone and wry smile are undermined by his gesture of sitting back down.

"We have three young men, and we already have you in the picture with each one of them at their deaths."

Gould's head jerks back at this mention of the third. How did they find out about Finley?

"Three? I believe you have miscounted."

Campello knows Gould is shaken. "Do you mean 'miscalculated? Yes. We haven't talked about the third victim yet, have we? We have three dead young men. There was a Joseph Finley, who everyone assumed jumped out a window. Poor guy was only a sophomore, and there you were, trying unconvincingly apparently, to talk him out of it. Nothing you could have done to keep that little guy from flying out that window, right?"

Shaken, Gould revealed too much, "I don't recall. What are you talking about?"

"Fordham ring a bell? And not to be insulting, Professor, but I thought you had perfect recall?"

Composing himself quickly, Gould rose again and dusted the left sleeve of his suit jacket as if removing the grime of the police station. "I believe your silly little puzzle pieces are what they call circumstantial..."

"Evidence, and funny thing is, when you get enough pieces of evidence, you've got a case, an arrest, a trial, and, eventually, a conviction. May take a while."

Gould shook his head and lifted only one corner of his upper lip. "I am aware of the ratio of arrests to convictions. Not very promising for you, is it? You've got nothing, or you would be arresting me now. While this has certainly been amusing, I have more important things to do, so I'll be leaving. Please, don't get up or disturb yourself in any way. I'll see myself out."

"I wouldn't dream of it," Campello said, smiling. "We'll be in touch." As Gould walked away with seeming confidence, Campello made a note: "Guilty."

Warren did not write all of this, but I had the scene in my head as surely as if I had been that fly on the wall. I had come to appreciate Campello by now, and I knew Roald Gould. Knew his moves, his voice, even the intonations he would use. Now, I needed to figure out a way to have that knowledge work for me.

Chapter Thirty-four
Recognizing a Perfect Fit

Gould had once asked me if I'd read a biography of Shakespeare, and I told him that I'd read Stephen Greenblatt's *Will in the World*.

"Fascinating and so informative. I feel as if I entered Shakespeare's world with Greenblatt. He's such a good writer, and he reminded me that Shakespeare's plays are also set in Italy. Strange that he used Italy as setting rather than have all of the plays set in London."

"Largely speculative and not really biography," he said dismissively, with a touch of scorn that he reserved for other writers of whom he was jealous.

"But still suggestive and rich," I countered. We had attended a Greenblatt lecture, and the idea struck me that Gould's continual criticisms of Greenblatt were constructed out of personal jealousy not professional critique. Discussing Greenblatt led us to discussing doubles, those whom Shakespeare had used, layering his masterworks over others' plots.

"You see, even Greenblatt suggests the yield is not plagiarism," said Gould. "Shakespeare, the master, takes what is his right from the inferior poet/playwright."

"You don't think what he did was plagiarism or theft?"

Gould laughed. "Will's gift to the world."

Only later did I look back on his comments and realize that Gould could have been speaking about himself and Michael, Marc, and Joseph. Gould believed those young men were his inferiors, and he was merely using their work as raw material for something better. How he rationalized their murders was more difficult to understand, but an examination of racism and the history of slavery tells us a lot about what happens when people consider others as lesser beings. Anything becomes possible. Gradually, I began to understand that Gould not only stole their words but acquired power in stealing their lives, like a vampire.

Near the end of my time in Rochester, when I understood with whom I was dealing, I wanted to thwart Gould, even if I could not get his confession of guilt. Surely, Sherlock Holmes would have triumphed somehow. Yet, Gould demonstrated no signs of guilt and was not one to be tripped up.

That afternoon two years ago, after class, he returned to discussing Greenblatt's lecture and comment on age needing youth. "There is nothing to admire about youth except its sexual potency," Gould said, with that slanted half smile he often wore.

"Which is everything," I returned as parry in one of my early, rare moments of insight, honesty, and bravery.

He thought he had dismissed me, so he looked up, slightly curious.

"And nothing," he finished.

At the end, when I was leaving New York, I held only one card, a few seconds of a recording of an obscenity-laced rant by Gould. The threat was enough only to cause his hesitancy. A few words on a recorder were not enough to get him fired or arrested, but I made two copies and mailed one to the university president and one to Campello. Perhaps the record could be added to an expanding file. I could hear Gould's words as I dropped the envelop in the mailbox.

"You think I envied him his poetry? What a little fool you are."

There the word fool was again. If I had been uncertain earlier about the note under my door, I fathomed then that he had slipped the paper there to intimidate and hurt me, the "little fool." I was measuring the distance to his door and eying the letter opener within his reach. The letter opener could be used as both a defensive weapon and a murderous one. Unfortunately, he was closer to the weapon than me.

"That's not true," I said coldly, but my heart was trying to leap up through my mouth. "You wanted to be him."

Gould laughed as if I had told a fine joke. "My, how you've changed, or more likely, I misjudged your talents and abilities, as well as your character."

"Thank you for that."

"Scarcely a compliment. Do you really think you are capable of sparring with me?"

"Spar: a woman enlisted in the Army Reserve during World War II."

"Apparently, you do. How pitiful." He was getting ready for something more, and I took another step toward the door.

"Yes, you had better know the distance and continue to measure that expanse of space carefully, my dear. You have already misjudged me."

"Don't call me 'dear'. You wanted to be Michael for more than his youth, for his future, his talent, too." I almost asked if he wanted Michael sexually, too.

Gould snorted again in what was this time a stifled laugh. "Talent? You know even less than the meager amount with which I credited you. To be him? Well, his future was rather limited, wasn't it?"

"For all that he could have been, for his words, beauty, his poetry which you stole. For what you could not possess, you killed him."

Gould leaned toward me but did not stand. "That's quite an accusation. There are libel laws, of which I'm sure you are aware. You poor, baffled girl, having a nervous breakdown after failing in your program. What was left for you? Should you suddenly go missing, no one will question your decision to end your life. Amazing how easy it is to take one's own life under such dire circumstances as yours."

"Everything is left for me. The real question is what is left for you after you have stooped so l..."

"There is no last word for you in this exchange," he said, rising.

"Justice..."

He laughed mockingly, but I would not let him deter me, "will be the last word."

"Deluded girl."

I backed out his door, never taking my eyes off his malicious ones. In the hallway, there were students moving about indifferent to the danger, the threat of annihilation steps away from them all.

That would not be the last I would hear from Roald Gould, however much I dreaded seeing him again. During those moments, I only wanted to put as much distance between us as possible.

~ * ~

Living in the Italian countryside and along the coast, I looked out as days unfolded with the sun too bright, gleaming off copper roofs, the Tyrrhenian Sea blue with white trails of disappearing boats like written lines. How often had human beings deciphered writing from waves, foam imprints on a beach, driftwood patterns, indentations in the bark of a tree, swirls in a puddle of gasoline, ridges on the skin of a pumpkin, eyes on a potato? I had read about such speculations, but it was unlikely that we would stop searching for patterns even if Socrates woke suddenly to tell us there were none, only the brain seeking definition and solace.

I had left Rome to tour the southern coastline with Elio and then we rented villas from Elio's father. On the hillside where Elio stayed, the long-needled pines with their large cones hid cicadas working their timbals, vibrations of membranes producing a sound that punctuated even the braying of a donkey and festival drums below. The assent up the hill by car would have frightened me once, with roads designed in theory not practicality, but I was no longer scared of such things as geography.

As I sat writing in my journal, a wall lizard scaled the fence post then stopped to survey his escape or hunt. These little green lizards were everywhere, and I had grown used to them after being startled at first. There was a bit of speckled red coloring at their throats that made them seem bloodthirsty, but they were actually very friendly and had grown used to my presence, too. They were likely to appear almost anywhere. After getting over my discomfort, I talked to them to amuse myself at times when the writing came too slowly. How they could scale a straight wall, change direction, and disappear or reappear so suddenly made them a bit of a mystery.

And in that moment of reflection, an image of Roald Gould suddenly appeared before me. I could not get rid of him or hide from him any longer.

Chapter Thirty-five
Where You Love and Hate

Even in the glorious sun of Italy, I continued to look for patterns, for answers to the mysteries. Gould asked his students to look for arrangements, such as those Foucault had pointed out with the idea of author as "author-function", but Gould pushed us to look past the seeming design to also consider intent. He was, after all, a teacher. I began noticing these correspondences and found them in unexpected places by following history, a personal history of a well-known professor and poet. How ironic that Gould unknowingly led me to uncover his crimes.

One evening, I noticed a few fireflies and then, suddenly, they were everywhere, dotting the absoluteness of night with yellow light, as in a scene out of a movie, a fairy tale, a magic show.

"Ah, *lucciola,*" said Elio coming into the room where I was writing and gazing out the window. "Beautiful, no?"

"Yes, very. They appear as if a painter has taken a brush dabbed with sunlight and dropped pearls of yellow across our night canvas."

Elio smiled. "I like that," he said. "Very poetic. What are you working on?"

"An old mystery."

"My lovely Vena, you are the mystery. Let me get some wine for us." Elio disappeared, and I thought about my old mysteries.

~ * ~

Murder in a locked room? I didn't know the answer until Gould

196

appeared at my door; the murderer had a made a duplicate key and simply locked the door on his way out. He had been to Michael's before that fateful night.

I realized what I should have known from the beginning. Gould knew, as well. I sat in a room with a window looking out on a painting of the sea and sky, the vista imagined, as much as demonstrated, by a dimly lit scene of a physical landscape, my room doubling as Howard Nemerov's motel room where I, too, was 'looking in and looking out'. I wrote my encomium of Nemerov's poem, doubled with Michael's poem that Gould had stolen, one inside another.

> You Enter a Room
> as stranger, a hope thief;
> history and memory exiled
> from this staged tableau:
> bed, dresser, and television
> all stand without judgement;
> hyperbolic drone of disembodied voice
> sanctioning details of fake trial of false testimony
> of pedestrian dissertation on lying,
> performed at the foot of a stained bed
> on a scene with cracks in the ceiling,
> opening to the uninvited,
> increasing disorder;
> nothing and everything happens
> in this architectural, metaphoric grid,
> motel's four walls
> absorbing echoes
> of those who once inhabited this amputated space
> while you dream of an encounter,
> yet estranged, far from home

Michael had placed his poem in a book he gave me. For months before I saw Dr. Gould again, anxiety only let me occasionally dress for dinner, nervous tics licking my fork, until I stopped believing he was after me. I allowed myself the luxury of living without fear and forgetting at least some moments of my past. After a time, I decided that Gould had not taken the bait. This thought caused me both disappointment and genuine relief.

Then I got another email from Warren.

~ * ~

Vena,

Gould may know where you are. He's been to the police station, and he contacted me about you. I swear I didn't tell him where you were, but he guessed or someone else told him. I guess the cops interviewed or grilled him. He actually said, 'I know she's in Italy, on the Amalfi Coast.' He left campus suddenly and under a cloud. It's all kind of under the table, but I gather from talking to a few old acquaintances that the university encouraged him to leave. Oh shit, they threw him out.

I gave your address to Campello but no one else. I don't think I told anyone, at least not when I was sober, and I'm mostly sober. Still, I heard from an old classmate of yours, Reggie, he said, that you'd better watch out. Seems Gould referred to you in a "disparaging way" in his class shortly before taking his leave. Take care of yourself. I mean, the guy would have to be really bonkers to cross an ocean to come after you, but better to play it safe.

Here's looking at you, kid.
Warren

Had Warren given Gould more than a cursory answer? I didn't believe he would intentionally betray me, but possibly. Gould went on a fishing expedition, and Warren responded to his cues. All Gould had to say was that he was looking for me and knew I had left the country.

He was wondering if I could be reached in Italy, when Warren would gasp or somehow show that Gould had hit the location right on the nose. From there, too easy for Gould to suggest this or that until he hit on the region, even the town. Warren didn't know that I had baited Gould, hoping he would come. Gould must have found their conversation amusing in that he had so cleverly ferreted out where I was living when a letter arrived from me. Ah, the irony, he would have smiled in that wicked way.

I needed to tell Warren that he was not responsible, no matter what, because I had given Gould my address. That would shock Warren, but perhaps not as much as my missive surprised Gould.

There were a number of things I had to do in preparation. I'd had time to think about my former mentor; consider the kind of man who prefers only male assistants, kills bright, handsome young men, steals their most prized intellectual possessions, and continues to write and publish stolen words with aplomb. There was a sinking feeling when I thought of Gould, and on some level, I think he hated himself. Entirely possible that he was a closeted gay man, but those were questions for a psychologist not me. He did seem attracted to Michael in some way before he decided to kill him.

Using the Internet to the best advantage, I spent considerable time trying to get more information on Gould, but there was limited biographical background on the published poet. A few lines about his short-lived marriage to Margaret Cassill. They were married for less than a year, and the union had been Gould's only marriage. She had never taken his name. Cassill taught English at a small private college in the south and was not widely published. I wondered if Gould had married her to throw off suspicions at a time when coming out as gay was more perilous in terms of employment. Whatever his sexual orientation, Gould was not comfortable in his own skin.

But there were times when he seemed to flirt with me and a few other women, too. He was an enigma, albeit, an evil one. Of course, he could have been bi-sexual, but why were all his victims young men?

Brazenly, I emailed Cassill, asking if she would be willing to be interviewed for a biography I intended to write about Dr. Gould. Surprisingly, she answered back rather quickly and curtly.

"I cannot imagine any endeavor I would rather help with less," Margaret wrote. "Please include the mention of my name as an endnote only in the biography of the narrowly and perversely esteemed (you read that correctly) Roald Gould. We were married for about five minutes, and I scarcely remember. I don't dwell on an unpleasant past. What I do know is that our time together is not extracted with any degree of fondness. He was the rarest of bastards. You do not have permission to quote me on that last sentence."

Clearly, Professor Cassill still harbored animosity for her ex-husband. He had never mentioned her. In fact, most students assumed that he had never married, but everything is searchable today, and there are few secrets left in the world.

Wondering what had happened between them, I guessed that Cassill caught on rather quickly that she was being used as a front or mask to cover Gould's real sexual adventures that allowed him to be with both women and men, or only young men, or only women he actually hated. She must have discovered him in some liaison and then left without making a scene. Cassill was very young and beautiful when she married Gould, and I don't imagine that she dwelled on her mistake for long. Easy to understand why she had first been attracted to him, I thought, remembering the cult of Gould at the University. But what had he done to her? His constant lies and duplicity might be enough.

I thought back to Gould's quick response to favorite mysteries, and his appreciation for *Crime and Punishment*. I reread Dostoyevsky's novel with an entirely different view, examining Raskolnikov's seeming lack of motive for the brutal slaying of Alyona Ivanova. Gould, like Raskolnikov, would see himself as a superior man, but there would not be any redemption for Gould. I suspected then that stealing the poems from Michael and Marc were merely incidental decisions, or perhaps trophies, that he had already planned to kill them regardless. The murders were not about thefts or fear of exposure for plagiarism. The act of taking another life was its own reward for Roald Gould.

One evening, I walked along the narrow streets to a little restaurant. Elio had gone on an errand out of town for his father, but I told him I would be fine. I knew a few of the locals by then, and our three soccer playing student tenants were also very protective of me, I reassured Elio before he left. They were, too. Every evening they would offer to escort me, knock on my door at night to make sure I didn't need anything. They made me feel rather like a princess by the sea.

As I came out of the restaurant near the water, I sensed someone behind me, too close, and I turned. An older couple came toward me from across the street. I greeted them, feeling foolish at my skittishness. They smiled and went on their way. I looked around. Resting on a concrete breaker near me was a copy of *Will in the World*. Frantic for an instant, I took deep breaths and calmed myself again.

Who in this coastal Italian town would be reading Greenblatt in English? The thought of Gould at my back caused me to duck into the restaurant to the bewilderment of the waiter. Near the restaurant door, just inside on a small table, was a copy of Gould's first book of poetry. Whirling around, scanning the restaurant quickly but seeing only unfamiliar faces, I called my dear soccer friends and asked them to meet me. My heart was pounding so hard, I thought it would beat through my chest wall and fall out of my body or open mouth. Finding the Greenblatt text out of place was one thing, but the Gould poetry crossing the ocean on its own?

He was here. I started talking rapidly in English before I recalled myself and broke into Italian again. The poor waiter, a young man who spoke almost no English, must have thought I had lost my mind.

No one would believe me, but I was now sure that Gould was near, biding his time. When Constantine sauntered in first, I ran up and hugged him. He laughed and told his friends that I had finally come to my senses and ditched Elio for him. After a few still breathless moments, I explained what had happened, and they laughed again, a bit nervously this time.

"Show us the book," they said in Italian.

"Books," I said, first handing them Gould's poetry. Constantine turned the slim text over in his large hands then gave the book back to me. Giovanni took the book and stared at the photo of Gould on the back cover then shrugged.

"This is the guy?" he said almost incredulous. "We will beat him silly."

"And the other book he left for you?" asked Constantine.

Together we went back to the place along the breaker where *Will in the World* had been placed. Gone. Gould had found me.

Chapter Thirty-six
Dreaming Transposed as Mystery

As soon as I woke, I searched for Michael's poem. His words must have related to something I had been dreaming, but I could not clearly articulate the vague images, the swirling sensations that were left in the dream world. For some reason, finding that poem became urgent, and I pulled out my notes on Mctigue and Baczkowski, where I had tucked the poem away. There were many explanations as to why I had not read his poem again after that first night of discovery inside the pages of Stephen Jay Gould's book. That first time, I could not grasp what was meant or intended. Yet a dream without form or shape made me seek out Michael's poem again, as if I was finally ready to read his last communication to me.

> You Enter a Room
> A child, a stranger,
> A hope thief,
> Not merely because you are a writer
> Engaging in weird conversations
> In which T.S. Eliot is speaking
> After noticing Jestor's carrot red hair,
> Observing the symmetry.
> You're holding a picture of a painting,
> Finding Mctigue and Baczkowski,
> Discovering a dead poet,
> Noting a balancing act;
> Then standing in judgement

Difficult to accept,
A red herring
In juxtaposition to staged tableau
In which history and memory are exiled
And authorship is constructed from stolen lines;
You, muted and mad,
Are too afraid to peer out,
The room echoing emptiness,
With nothing found after his death;
You standing behind legendary writers
As day falls into night
In an unlit stairwell three stories up,
Only a match to light the room
Where spheres of thought collide
With mounting evidence
Of nothing and nothing more;
Then opening the door,
You venture out,
Apprehensive but determined
To straighten out a few things,
Recognizing a perfect fit
Where you love and hate,
Finding a rope, a knife, a gun,
And learn what you did not know before:
Disturbance in the universe.

And I knew. I understood as clearly as if Michael had been in the room taking me through each line. Why was I so blind before? Michael began writing about doubles, as well, entering the motel room with Howard Nemerov's persona, but from there, Michael began thinking about me, the stranger, the child, and Gould, as the hope thief. He was leaving clues for me. Michael had once loved Gould and grew to hate him. We were characters in his lines, signified by our actions or our pursuits. I was then certain that Michael thought about us not merely because he was a writer, but a man engaging in weird conversations in graduate school, those conversations about authorship, those discussions with living and dead poets. Perhaps he also thought about me because he had fallen in love.

He brought me into his poem with my search into the lives and literature of Mctigue and Baczkowski. Those writers were not Michael's interests, and I had only told him about my obsession once after class. I would not have thought he even remembered until I read the poem again. I also had told him about my fascination with Magritte's painting of a painting and the print in my bedroom. The dead poet, of course, was not Michael but Marc Bennett. By the time Michael wrote "You enter a room," he already knew or at least suspected that Gould had killed Marc. He just couldn't prove Gould's guilt to anyone but himself. Who would believe that a few stolen lines between poets meant anything at all? No one kills for poetry.

Michael was playing the dangerous game of private eye, coming across false clues, those red herrings that had baffled me as well, while trying to piece together what he knew about Gould and Marc, the authorship of stolen lines. He would have figured out, as I did, that Marc was Gould's student and the lines from Marc's poem ended up in Gould's published book. Did Michael already know that Gould had stolen his own lines, as well? He was angry, but afraid and alone as he confessed in the poem. Muted and mad like Hamlet with knowledge of Claudius' murder of King Hamlet. If only Michael had come to me or gone to Campello then, before Gould came to that unlit stairwell.

Perhaps Gould and Michael had a confrontation at the top of the landing leading to his apartment when Gould hit him, knocking him unconscious before putting the rope around his neck. Maybe Gould came over and Michael accused him, facing his mentor three stories up, with facts but not enough of them. Gould would have dismissed the paltry evidence, laughed in Michael's face, but determined then that he had to kill Michael, too. They went into Michael's apartment where Gould brought out the wine, offered contrition, just enough that Michael would have been thrown off balance, started to doubt himself and his speculations.

Gould must have returned on another night when Michael was not expecting him. Had Michael seen Gould with a gun and rope in the past or was he speculating in the poem what would happen when Gould came again? Michael ended his poem with that line about disturbance in the universe, and I had only to add a couple more lines to his poem because the poem couldn't end that way. If I could not change the past, I could invent an alternative, providing a different conclusion in fiction for Michael, for Marc, and poor Joe Finley. They all deserved a very different ending.

Funny, but I thought about Rebecca Solnit's book *Wanderlust* as I completed Michael's poem with my own last lines. Solnit's words fell across the page of my memory: "Language is like a road; it cannot be perceived all at once because it unfolds in time." My road was finally unfolding, and I slipped Michael's poem away again and went out for a walk.

In such a beautiful country as Italia, living with a lovely, even if occasionally unfaithful man, you might assume I would never think of death or have such thoughts cross my mind. But that would not be true. I foresee death just as I think about life every day and night.

According to his student Plato in *The Apology*, Socrates said during his last moments of physical life, "For the state of death is one of two things: either the dead man wholly ceases to be and loses all consciousness or, as we are told, it is a change and a migration of the soul to another place. And if death is the absence of all consciousness, and like the sleep of one whose slumbers are unbroken by any dreams, it will be a wonderful gain." Soothing, right?

I would like to be able to say such perfectly logical and poetic things during my most aware moments, but this kind of eloquence escapes me, evading most of us. Even if we are clever and good with language, there is a higher plane to which the intellect must rise where the soul is met in correspondence: that perfect generative collision reorganized as words on a page. Socrates, naturally, had no words on a page. Only by the grace of Plato do we even know what he supposedly said. Plato claims to have given us a verbatim account.

Could Socrates have been this serene as he waited for the poison to work its way to his heart, the execution a slow-moving sentence? But what inspired all those students, those young Athenians around the dying man was his ability to harness fear, reflect calmly, and continue dispensing wisdom until his last breaths. At least that is the portrait we were given.

Intriguing to speculate how many of those words were, in fact, uttered by Socrates and how many were the creation or addition of Plato, Socrates' student who had become master, disappearing inside the symbolizations of his teacher.

Somehow, wise old Socrates gave death a better spin than human history usually seems to suggest, but I like his two choices that preclude anything very negative. And, within them, a host of possibilities could be explored. I can't imagine standing beside Plato, taking down every last word from the great philosopher, and I can't conceive of the scene only because a woman would not have been allowed at such a proceeding.

But even if I had somehow disguised myself and gained entrance, I would have been unable to finish. More than likely, I would have acted conspicuously, likely been arrested on some ridiculous charge, such as impiety, the following day. There was Plato, however; dispassionate, resolute, creating, and preserving while almost invisible to those around him. Plato was the fly on the wall to the Athenian accusers, to Anytus, to Lycon, to Meletus, yet this intelligent little fly would condemn Socrates' accusers to ignominy.

Plato, too, has disappeared in the physical sense, and even history must fight and claw to be heard in our noisy world of the moment, of now. Where would our philosophy, our sense of justice, be without Plato's cool head in such a crisis? Our inexact and mistaken certitude would overpower better judgement. Plato's talented art allowed Socrates the kind of immortality the old master—as antithesis to the sophist—would have been surprised at finding.

Even if death is benign, the longest night remains incredibly hard for most of us living to contemplate, even if death feels like the best, long, undisturbed sleep in life. Of course, I remember Michael, but the image created by Socrates gives me some peace to think of him sleeping deeply in that last long sleep. The sleep of death is far easier to contemplate than the slow tortures Gould enacted upon his victims, long before he ended their lives. Gould, too, must face that last sleep someday, but he will likely go kicking and yelling, terrified and wildly angry.

Unfair of me not to concede that Gould gave his students something, brought gifts into his classrooms. He was evil, but he had incredible genius and knowledge. I will never understand why he chose to act perversely with them. Without Gould, I would never have read many of the texts that enrich my life. I certainly would not have read Foucault or Simon During's interpretation of his writing, come across During's statement, "Language is, as it were, its own ground—a notion that points to a strange fold or doubling which limits any account of a discursive practice's preconditions." Or During interpreting Foucault in that, "absence as such carries death's traces. If that were not the case, there would be no writing, as writing is to be regarded…[as] the attempt to incorporate absence."

Wasn't that, to some degree, what all of us writers are trying to do? Gould led us and opened our eyes, but he also wanted to control everything, control his students and their desires, subvert them to his own.

I cannot conceive of a death in which Gould's sleep is undisturbed by nightmares. I wish him all of those torments that Socrates denies the wicked, as well as the holy. If given that luxury, I would place Gould in Dante's *Inferno*. I would have Ugolino eating the back of Gould's head in the 9th Circle of Hell. But it's not up to me. I could only dream.

When Elio returns, I tell him of my plan to trap Gould. I am not the least heroic, but I had a moment in which I anticipated the rush of that experience. To be frightened and to go forward because that movement feels like the right thing to do is at least something approximating bravery. Elio claims I am the bravest woman he knows. I laugh and say that is because he doesn't know a lot of women, but he does. Women love Elio as much as he loves them.

Last night, my slumber was once again interrupted by dreams, many of which were disturbing, but only one was beautiful. I woke with the distorted images still on my eyes, on my tongue, running over my bare skin. I would like to add a sub-category to Socrates' two choices: death, in which the long sleep allows for dreams, even those which are unsettling, dreams in which we are swimming under water, through water, past everyone and everything, as I was last night.

Light is only a memory on that darkest of nights in which even the sliver of moon's arc is absent, yet I found my way in cold blackness. I should have been terrified as I recalled no boundaries or solid points of reference, descending into ever deepening waters. I wasn't swimming to the bottom because I understood there was no nadir to this lake. No one, not Elio or Bill or Warren or Michael or anyone else is with me, but I continued.

In the dream, I am alone, unafraid, still seeking answers to our mysteries. I wake.

Picking up a pen, I added two final lines to Michael's poem:

Stories of writers/Dreaming transposed as mystery.

I hoped he would have liked the additions. Really, I did not want to leave his poem with that "disturbance in the universe" to end everything, even if that is what human beings do and have done throughout history.

I wanted to forget about Gould, imagine that he would drop his obsession with his search for revenge or whatever drove him. I tried valiantly to place all of that behind me. I was engaged again with the pedestrian, mundane, the working life, the tragic and sorrowful, and still, every day, discoveries of the absolutely extraordinary. Yet, behind it, Gould waited for the right moment.

Chapter Thirty-seven
Finding a Rope, a Knife, a Gun

Then Gould was at the door of my little rental house, knocking respectably at first. In another instant he began increasing the intensity and urgency until he was pounding with both fists. He stopped.

I could hear him, and I froze. Should I warn the boys again? My voice left me as if I was dreaming and unable to utter a sound. My stomach turned. Breathing was difficult and suddenly became a conscious choice.

Fingering a knife inside his pocket, Gould yelled out, "I'm here, Advena." He was done with subtlety and lifted his foot to kick in the door. "I have found you, my little bitch. You have nowhere left to hide now, you cunt," he yelled. So unlike him to reveal his nature, but perhaps crossing an ocean and pursuing me in a foreign land had caused him to lose his reserve. "All your clever machinations for nothing; you were never a challenge, ultimately, no match." With that last remark, Roald Gould kicked down my door, old wood splintering and sticking out like abandoned swords. He threw himself forward, disappearing inside my doorway.

I listened with a kitchen knife in my hand, heard, then watched the scene unfold below me as Gould appeared outside again, stomped and beaten by two brothers, Giovanni and Sergio, and their friend Constantin. Good someone had warned those young men about a crazy, violent American who might try to break into their apartment.

I had sublet my flat to these three Italian youths who played soccer, lifted weights, and were now dragging their intruder further into the street. Gould held his head with both hands and yelled something unintelligible.

His fury had been somewhat subdued as Constantine pulled his arms back behind his body.

Someone must have had the foresight to call the Carabinieri before the tableau released itself on the stunned village, because the Carabinieri were already running over to arrest the foreign intruder and thief. Someone must have known one of the Carabinieri personally because he was taking Gould's response that way. On the abused body of the stunned and confused American, the sharp looking Italians, in their dark blue uniforms with the red-stripped trousers, found a knife, gun, and rope Gould intended to use. Impossible for him to deny. He only screamed, "Fucking bitch," over and over. "I'll get that little bitch." How he had smuggled the gun into the country or obtained the weapon in Italy was a mystery. He struggled briefly only to find himself face down again.

When asked in English what he planned to do with the knife and gun, Gould hung himself: "I will kill that little bitch."

Five additional witnesses to the break-in were on hand to give testimony to the local polizia who joined the scene: this crazy, uncivilized American kicked in the door as he shouted obscenities. There was much talking at once.

Three credible young Italians, who are well liked and respected, gave testimony, describing the break-in on the narrow street. The Carabinieri took note, as I walked outside and faced the mask Gould wore.

"I knew it, knew it," he said, triumphant for only a moment again. "You fucking little cunt. I will get you yet."

"Careful, Gould, these Carabinieri know English."

They nodded their heads because I had signaled to them with my own nod, but Gould was not certain. He stopped speaking for a moment. "It could mean anything," he said. "I will get you yet. You'll never get your poems back."

I tried to laugh although nothing was really funny. "I don't want anything from you. How do you feel? Perhaps you are not as smart as you thought."

Gould stared at me as though he could bore a hole in my brain. "This is nothing," he said at length. "I will be free as soon as my lawyer arrives. I will find you again. Alone."

"That could be months before you see your lawyer, and then he will discover that only an Italian can represent you. These Italian courts, I'm afraid, are a bit slow."

"I know rather well how to wait. Revenge is best served cold." Gould somehow seemed less menacing with his hands tied behind him.

"Well, you may be colder than you can yet imagine. Why did you do it?" I asked as the Italian police picked him up and started to take him away. They stopped and allowed me the indulgence of questioning him.

"Why?" He laughed, blood spraying from his nose and mouth from his exertion and wounds.

"Why did you kill Michael?"

Gould smiled, but the need to contort his lips upward must have hurt because he choked at the same time, spitting up. Blood dripped down his face and hands. Then he looked at me one last time before they dragged him away to a police car. In that long, last look, he said everything. "Michael was nothing. Weak, a stupid boy. Weaker still as a poet," he yelled as they pushed him into the car. "You're nothing."

That Michael had meant nothing to him, that killing him was easy, was clear, but Gould would find prison was less accommodating than his life had been. He might even find that his life meant less than nothing to those who would surround him for the next several months or years.

As he was driven away, I began trembling for the first time, the adrenaline finally kicking in. I wasn't sure if the shakes were caused by fear subsiding, anger, or the horror of the experience relived.

~ * ~

Our tenants, the soccer players, offer their tale again in court as the Professor is roughly led into a very complicated network. The Italian legal system is known as a maze that has one law for foreigners and another for Italians, I'm told. Gould would find the Italian courts less forgiving and very, very slow. Further, he would discover that he had no rights to a lawyer or *avvocato* before his hearing. I'm told by a particularly well-connected policeman that Gould screamed and yelled, banged his fist, and demanded, grew red in the face, his curly gray hair flying in multiple directions—all to no avail. "Idiots. You're all fucking idiots," he shouted in court, much to the public officials' displeasure. His behavior made the punishment harder on him, but he was so unused to being captured, to being insulted, to being less than, that he could not stop himself.

I imagined that Roald Gould would discover, after taking the lives of those young men, as if they were nothing, that life, in fact, was something very dear to lose. For the first time in his privileged life, he would know absence and want.

It is one-sided at his eventual trial. They do not take kindly to the violent American's insults or his arrogance. He is unable to sway the court with his stylish prison uniform or his books of poetry. His condescension and ability to memorize vast quantities of other people's words do him no good in these circumstances.

Apparently, no one in town knew a blue-haired American girl with short cropped hair about whom Gould continued to rave during and after his trial. "She dyed her hair, you idiots. She was here all the time, and you didn't know!" Elio's brother said it appeared Gould was mentally ill, in the way he ranted and swore in English. The trial in which he angrily, even hysterically, protested his innocence, took a long time before they led him off to prison.

There would be beatings in prison, as well, Gould not a model prisoner, not one to get along with other inmates. But this is not the account of the victimization of an innocent man. Gould was never innocent.

Roald Gould's life was greatly shortened by his time in the Italian prisons, his sentence extended more than once due to violent outbursts with guards and other prisoners. He was quite simply not a man used to deprivation and denial, so incarceration led to behaviors that surprised even him. A surprisingly harsh first sentence led to a second one.

Although I had given Elio my explanation, Gould's murders still made little sense to me. He was more than capable of creating his own poetry, so the mystery of why he killed Michael and Marc remained. In all likelihood, he had killed Joe Finley for the same reasons or lack of reason. Should Gould ever be tried for his real crimes, a jury just might be convinced that he had sufficient motive. Who knew how hard it was to create a good poem? I began to feel more confident in my theory that, perhaps, Gould killed Michael, Marc, and Joe for something other than their words; stealing their poetry was almost incidental, an opportunity presented in the act. Those young poets had the audacity to hold themselves as equals to the master. They had made the mistake of tipping an unbalanced scale. Gould found gratification in taking another's life. I wondered if his hatred of these young men began as an attraction, lustful desire that had to be repressed. Gould must have hated himself on some subconscious level.

For Gould, every action had always been about power, as Foucault had written, "the pleasure that power excites." Until the moment of his arrest in Italy, everything, every action for Gould was an abstraction, even the lives he took. Unlike his philosophical nemesis-counterpoint, Foucault, Gould saw no victims, only power-relations and gamesmanship in which he always—until very recently—emerged as victor.

Even after his eventual release from the Italian prison and his hasty flight back to the U.S., he was surprised to be greeted at the airport by the New York State Police. To his astonishment, he was wanted and extradited. He was going back to Rochester, of all places, without fanfare this time, without so much as an audience of naïve young students.

Warren had given Campello my new address in Rome, and Campello sent me a note sometime later.

~ * ~

Dear Miss Goodwin,

Your friend Warren and I have spoken often recently, and he gives a good account of you. I thought you might like to know a little about the resolution of our case.

Turns out that bodies do reveal their stories, even after a long time. Your friend Michael Lawler was found to have ingested an incapacitating agent at the time of death and his body showed a large perimortem bruise at the back of his skull which would have made it impossible for him to have hung himself.

There were also fingerprints and DNA evidence left by Gould at the scene of Lawler's apartment. I went back to the scene immediately after the first time you came to the station. Unfortunately, telling you at that time would have been impossible for me to share. We can't give away all our secrets...

~ * ~

I hated imagining Michael's last moments, but I saw the murder in my head, even when I tried to drive away the images. Michael drugged and smashed over the head, unconscious or nearly dead from the blow, then yanked to the stairwell where Gould pulled a rope over his neck, cruelly hoisting him up like a sail. I wanted to cut Michael down, save him, push the smiling Gould down those stairs to his death, but I could only do what little I could do.

Campello's note continued by describing the additional results they discovered.

~ * ~

Marc Bennett, turned out, also had a skull fracture most likely caused by the claw end of a hammer rather than a rock. His death was not the result of a fall in the river, the indentation still distinguishable in the bone even after all this time. He was unconscious when he drowned.

~ * ~

Campello offered me some insight into the murders. On the bank, I knew, was a smiling Gould stepping into the shadows again. This time, however, Campello was seeing Gould at the scene, just as I was.

Campello was not one to write letters, he noted, but he was almost eloquent in his elaboration of the trail left by the murderer once they began the investigation in earnest. His letter continued.

Unfortunately, Joe Finley was cremated, his aunt and uncle related to us, cremation paid for by none other than Roald Gould. Finley's aunt and uncle said they were grateful for all of the attention his professor gave their nephew, particularly this attention after death.

~ * ~

I read greedily and realized my suspicions that Gould had been at each funeral, paying for expenses, getting the bodies buried quickly, or in the case of Joe, burning the evidence, looking like the deeply concerned professor. Apparently, Gould had offered to have all the young men cremated, but relatives appeared out of nowhere, contesting that type of disposal. All of that false, bizarre concern, yet no one was suspicious until I had walked into the Rochester City police station.

Thanks to you, wrote Campello, I grew skeptical of the official version of the "suicides" and that accidental death finding.

~ * ~

I had figured out a little more of Finley's story than Campello, however. Never giving up, I had written to his aunt months ago, and Joe's story kept unfolding. His aunt found a letter Joe wrote to his dead mother and addressed to her. The missive his aunt had not wanted to open because of the pain of Joe's death, but when she finally did, she discovered a poem. I had previously asked her for any of Joe's writing for my book of remembrance of young poets, and she sent me a note with, "this is a poem he had written while in college," a poem that not-so-strangely appeared in Roald Gould's second book of poetry.

Only then did I begin to wonder how many other young men were buried with the mark of Roald Gould.

If police investigators followed his history, looked deep into Gould's past, they would discover that Gould had witnessed the suicide of a classmate while in high school. Reading about the event sickened me. What or whose words were in Gould's first book? This would be a pathway for Campello to follow, however, not me. I was done with unearthing Gould's crimes. Once the gates were opened, the waters began flowing and would lead to all kinds of places no one had previously imagined. I suspected that Gould had killed long before he was famous, before there was even the slightest inclination to steal another's words.

Campello's letter ended with the line, "Good work, Detective Goodwin." I saved this missive.

Sipping from my glass, a light Moscato, as Elio stroked my shoulder-length brown hair, I continued looking out through the doorway when Elio wrapped his arms around me.

"You got your man," Elio said, intending the pun.

"With a little help from my friends. No," I corrected myself, "with a lot of help from my friends." Ironically, Gould had tremendously helped in his own arrest and fall. His mocking dismissal of me because I am a woman allowed him to believe I could not possibly be a threat. "His own sexism worked against him."

"Serves him right," said Elio with dramatic flair. "Now what's next?"

"My dissertation if I can get the topic accepted."

"Your dissertation? You will finish the paper now? In Rome?"

"I will try, beginning tomorrow."

"Of course, I mean, what is your next case? Maybe on the side, while you finish writing, you will solve another crime here? Your detective skills will not go unnoticed."

"Hardly," I said, then... wondering.

"Che cosa dobbiamo fare oggi, mio amore?" Elio whispers in my ear, causing me to wonder where I really did want to go next. Then I knew. I just wanted to go down to the sea.

"Andiamo verso il mare."

Chapter Thirty-eight
And Learn What You Did Not Know Before

A year after Gould's arrest, I was working two jobs in Rome: teaching and tutoring in English, and had managed to save enough money to pay back Bill. Of course, Elio's generous father made paying rent a little easier, giving us a greatly reduced price. How could I not like Vincenzo Canestrini? Just as Elio, however, I did not forget his choice to leave his family. I was aware that Vincenzo was buying something in return for his magnanimous gestures.

Elio introduced his father, and I found him as charming as his son. With graying curly hair and a broad smile, he had dimples like a boy and beautiful white teeth that were most likely not his own. Vincenzo had earned his money in real estate deals in other countries, he said, and returned to Italy to live as he wished. Of course, he had money to begin with, Elio's brothers reminded us. Elio was his youngest son from Vincenzo's first wife, but his subsequent wives had no children. Vincenzo had a penchant for Eastern European models but always drew up prenuptial contracts. When they left him, they were often no better off than when he first proposed.

There was no question that Vincenzo favored his youngest child. The two elder sons were estranged from their father, and they only occasionally visited their little brother. Even in families, there are deeply divisive politics. From just my brief interaction with each of them, I could see they loved their little brother but could not bury their resentment entirely. They were, however, surprisingly pleasant to me.

Elio could have done anything or nothing, but he chose to live a life trying to help others, becoming a teacher and working hard. I watched his brothers' interactions and the obvious affection between father and son and wondered about my own relationship with my parents.

Bill wasn't graceful or charming like Vincenzo. He didn't have a shock of beautiful, curly gray hair. In fact, the few gray strands that lay across the top of his head were usually covered by a cap, but he had been there for me all those years, paying bills, instructing, cleaning, calling teachers, cooking even though he had no idea how to go about it. He held back my long hair with one hand while holding a pail with the other when I lied about drinking at an after party for the celebration of a play's performance. I told him I had the flu, vomiting half the night. And he stayed by the side of my bed, sleeping in a stiff chair when I was in the hospital with pneumonia when I was nine years old.

Like Greta, Bill had no idea how to be a parent, but unlike my biological mother, he never gave up on me or gave up trying to do the right thing even when he didn't know what the right thing to do was. Miles and years allowed me the luxury of looking back on my childhood with a slightly different lens. Bill wasn't cool, and he was never a lot of fun, but he was much more present in my life than I had given him credit for.

Not the first note I had sent to Bill, this one contained a surprise. Our correspondence was infrequent and brief, much as it had been while I was living in Rochester. I sent him a cashier's check for the full amount of the loan plus interest, as I had promised. Even though paying him back would stretch me to continue to live frugally, the act felt good and right to send the check. Living cheaply was somehow easier in Italy than living in New York, even upstate.

Let me be perfectly honest here, living in Rome was also easier because Elio and I were together in one of his father's many apartments. We paid a greatly reduced rental fee to Vincenzo in exchange for helping to manage a few properties. I found I was rather good at redecorating places and painting. Elio was nearly as handy as a carpenter. The best part of the arrangement, however, was meeting and getting to be friends with all of the tenants. I was finally becoming conversationally proficient in Italian and writing my own poetry again in a second language. Yet, somehow, my first poem written in Rome led me back to America.

"Ginevra de' Benci"
Considered austere and chaste,
Ginevra de' Benci, even at 16 years, knew
what was expected of her in marriage
to Luigi Niccolini, her mouth turned
ever-so-slightly downward; the lids
of her light brown eyes lowered, but
not demurely, rather, in resignation
or disinterest. They have said
she was admired for her restraint,
even as Leonardo slowly mixed colors,
would she have been thinking of escape?
As he painted juniper tree in background,
surrounding Ginevra's delicate face
and reddish-brown hair, the leaves
of the ginepro seeming to sprout
from her flowering head that contained
such intelligence. "To what end?"
she must have asked when her father
praised her acumen before telling
her of his perfect arrangement for her.
Ginevra's keen intelligence
would have had to wait another 400
years for it to matter, she thought,
wandering into the future as a clever
witch. Leonardo cognizant of this woman's
gifts and fate in the way that he knew
airplanes would one day carry men
in the skies. As he inscribed the painting
with the words, "Beauty adorns Virtue"
on reverse of the painting on wood,
Leonardo continued softening the edges,
mixing colors with his fingers as well as brush,
taking care to suggest her discernment

even in the pose of her hands, which
were later cut off the wooden portrait by accident,
lower third sawed away, lost to history,
a mystery like his well-known Mona Lisa
who even the impossibly gifted genius
could not fully illuminate. The world
captured by his Mona Lisa while Ginevra
de Benci's gaze beyond the painter
made her passage across
an ocean to the Americas.

~ * ~

After everything that had happened, I still wondered for a moment what Gould would think of my new poem. Then I was angry with myself for even considering his warped opinion to be of any value. I suppose all those years of schooling, looking up to the teacher and then professor, I had come to give them more gravitas and expertise than they may have deserved.

My life would never be the same, but then, whose life is? We're not static creatures. I returned to some relatively normal activities; teaching, reading, and writing. I'd even begun relaunching my search into the mystery of Mctigue and Baczkowski.

Elio turned out to be more than a friend, more than a lover. We spoke each other's languages and language. Of course, he still loved all beautiful girls and women and looked at them with a sigh and probably more than a little longing. Yet, he never ceased to make me feel special. Sometimes we fought and got jealous, but the tug of war was the kind of fighting that leads somewhere and nowhere and suggested our connection began far before we moved into together. Our arguments merely betrayed our very human insecurities.

"Would you still love me if you didn't think I was beautiful?"

"But you are and I do."

"I'm asking a hypothetical here."

"Then hypothetically, I would love you even if you weren't

beautiful."

"That's not fair and not what I meant."

"Yes, it's exactly what you meant. You want to trick me into something, so you get mad at me, storm off, and then I have to work very hard to win you back. If you offer a hypothetical, then I get one, too. Would you love me if I was not handsome and rich?"

"Yes. Suppose I was suddenly disfigured? Would you love me still?"

"You answered too quickly. If I was ugly and poor, you would still love me? And I would be very sad if you were disfigured."

"I would still love you. We are being ridiculous, aren't we?" It occurred to me that I might by lying, as well. Would I really love Elio if he was ugly and poor? Was I really a shallow person?

"Right now, I can't imagine not loving you. Is this a failure of my imagination or an admittance of my guilt?"

He drew me toward him, and I didn't resist. This act should have been the ending, but I knew we were destined to continually repeat our tug-of-war.

Elio decided he didn't like Warren even though he had never met him. "You don't need to write to this Warren any more. He is history." Elio was always proud of his mastery of English slang.

"Sorry, but Warren will always be my friend," I said defensively.

"I don't know about this, this character," Elio brooded, refusing to go to coffee with me the morning after I read Warren's letter. "You have me. Why do you need this Warren?"

"Don't you remember that girl in grade school?" I said, coaxing him back. He shook his head but listened. "You know, the one whose pigtails you pulled?"

"Pigtails?"

"Okay, the braid you held a little too long, and she got angry with you?"

"They were never angry with me," he shrugged, innocently enough.

"No, I don't suppose they were, but the girls you really liked a lot, yet you knew you would not marry them?"

"Ah, yes, all those pretty girls."

"Warren was my first real love, but we knew we weren't right for each other. Still, we remain friends. A good thing, nothing to be jealous of, don't you see? I left Warren more than once." Elio lowered his shoulders and reached out for me, pulling me to kiss him.

"Okay. Then we go for coffee?"

"Then we go wherever you like."

My darling Elio stormed out on more than one occasion, but being in love with a passionate Italian has to have a few drawbacks. There was much to be grateful for in my relationship with him.

One Sunday morning, I asked Elio if he would read Mctigue's play and Baczkowski's novel and let me know what he thought before I shared my theories with him. He knew by then that I was impatient but willing to let him take his time. As a kindness, he started in on Mctigue's play as soon as I gave the book to him.

While he read, I determined to come up with at least a plausible theory for doubling in their literature. I had researched to the extent possible to find tangible evidence. That trail was cold, but the one in my imagination was warm enough.

Chapter Thirty-nine
Stories of Writers

This was a story of two young men who would meet in the beautiful City of Paris, fall passionately in love at a time when such love was still forbidden. For Mctigue, his relationship with Baczkowski was not only taboo but burdened with enormous guilt, even shame. Mctigue's Irish Catholic upbringing fought with his identity, his sexuality, until the author successfully or unsuccessfully according to your point of view, buried it all; his guilt, lust, homosexuality, cynicism, disappointment, unrequited passions, in layers within his art, until the emotional turmoil was almost entirely lost to his physical body. Yet some memory emerged in the work itself. There were whispers and discordant notes that came out of dialogue, description, even the structure of a piece.

Mctigue had turned away from Baczkowski who was, after all, willing to go wherever their affair took them, even death. I wondered if Mctigue considered he also turned his back on himself. But when Mctigue shut the door on his face, Baczkowski didn't break down the narrow wooden door or run away, yelling angrily through the lovely little side streets in the city of light and love. The young Pole pulled down the pliable brim of his hat, turned and walked slowly to his little, rented flat in the rain, cheered himself on the way with a good wine and a ruddy young man he met in a bar that evening.

Within the hour, he was fucking and smiling again. For Baczkowski, all of society was a moralizing, hypocritical, cruel parent very much like his own father who cut him off even with his wife begging him not to leave their only son stranded in a foreign country. Baczkowski had learned to find his way in the world without needing that affirmation from anyone but himself. He was always quite sure exactly who he was and what he wanted to be.

Baczkowski woke early after his break with Mctigue, cleaned up, made breakfast for the young man whose name he had already forgotten, and then packed his light bag to head back to Poland where his life would be in greater jeopardy if he allowed it. He didn't allow it, however. Within a short time, Baczkowski had borrowed from friends and ex-lovers and left Europe to board a boat bound for Argentina where everything changed for him yet again.

The young Argentineans Baczkowski met were warm, friendly, and relaxed about their sexuality, engaging in affairs with men or women. There in the Buenos Aires' cafes or on the streets, Baczkowski found his home, his art, and his pacing in life. With scores of lovers, both male and female, Baczkowski lived as he loved—to the fullest, yet with a fickle heart always. He never forgot Mctigue and held his memory with fondness tinged with bitterness buried in the shallowest of graves and mockery in his art. The doubling was deliberate but intended with a wink or, more likely, a smirk.

Mctigue, for his part, became an aesthete, delving deeper into philosophy, language play, and satire where he would make his home. He never forgot Baczkowski, however, refusing to speculate or consider another alternative to the path either had chosen. Only near the end of his life, when he had grown deaf to the whispers of his buried life did he ask a woman to marry him in order to assign the rights and royalties from his plays. For Mctigue, the interaction was a business matter as much as a matter of loyalty.

"Good morning, Alice." She was always punctual with her work and her timing. Her brown hair neatly tied in a bun at the nape of her thin neck. She was pretty, however, but delicate, frail. The two of them together ate less in a day than one stout man at a meal.

"Good day, Dailan," she said brightly, as she always did, regardless of his mood or temperament that day.

"Alice, have I ever told you how much I appreciate what you do for me?" Mctigue rose slowly from his large, overstuffed arm chair where he typically sat to write. He had to use one arm to push off and realized that his stance was not entirely steady.

"Of course, you have. You are very generous and kind." She was suddenly worried because she did not know what precipitated this change of direction. Perhaps he was going to dispense with her services, and she would have to leave. The thought terrified her, but she could not let that show.

"Alice, I'm not a romantic, as you know well, but would you be willing to consider my proposal?"

"Of what, sir?" Alice was not a fool but neither could she contemplate a day when her employer would ask to marry her.

"Of your hand in marriage, of course, if that's how they still say it."

"Why, I." Alice dropped Mctigue's recent manuscript, then scrambled to pick up the papers quickly. Fortunately, she had clipped the pages together, so they did not spill across the ancient wood floor.

"Oh, let it go, for now," Mctigue took her hand and lifted her, raising her eyes as he did so. One of the traits he most admired in Alice was her attention to detail and inability to let things go, yet at that moment, he wanted her to forget everything except his words. "I don't mean to be abrupt, but I'm too old for this dance. We could be very comfortable with each other. We could be... What do you say?"

Alice moved from nervousness to slight panic all the way to resolve in a matter of seconds. "Then, the answer is 'yes'," she said with just the hint of a smile. She was careful not to express joy that would startle them both.

"Good. Settled," he said, and the matter was. They were married within the week, and, eventually, Alice inherited a small fortune in royalties. Mctigue was to die a few years later, but he was never as demanding in his marriage as he was as Alice's employer. For all of her insight into Dailan, however, Alice never knew for certain what role Baczkowski played in her new husband's art or his heart.

That was why their works were found one inside the other. Mctigue and Baczkowski had been writing together even when apart. Neither had found another partner in life who could match the one they had willingly given up years before.

Chapter Forty
Disturbance in the Universe

For a few weeks, Elio said nothing about the authors or their literature. I'd even forgotten that he was reading my two favorites. Then Elio sat up in bed one morning and read aloud a passage from Baczkowski. "Hey, Sherlock," he yelled, "I don't know what this means, but—" He jumped up, excited, as I turned my head from the writing piled high on my desk. "I just read Mctigue, and I was in the middle of Baczkowski's novel. One inside the other. It's really strange."

"Ah, yes," was all I said because I appreciated that he knew. I was still working on a long poem that was a struggle. Recently, I had begun writing as well as teaching poetry again. Tentatively, I titled my poem, "The Idea of Order at Molise," and I could feel Wallace Stevens looking out at me, not particularly pleased with the allusion.

~ * ~

Long before Michael's murder, my detective work started with books. More than analogs, these fictions spoke to—had full-on, late-night conversations with—each other, as much as they did to me and other readers. These particular homologous texts had become my obsession until everything changed. Even after Michael's death, even then, their stories called me back and asked me to uncover the face behind aspect.

As I crossed out a line in my poem, Elio wrapped his arms around me and coaxed me back to bed, not all that difficult for him to do. I tried very hard never to be late to my classes and managed rather well, despite

Elio's suggestion that we remain in bed for the next five years.

"So now, do I get to hear your theories about these two writers?"

"Yes, you do." I set out my careful evidence with Elio nodding his head, examining the notes, flipping them over to add his own observations. When I finally wrapped up all my imaginative speculations, Elio approved.

"Will you write about this?"

"No," I said, and I meant it. "It is our secret and, of course, Mctigue's and Baczkowski's. I don't know why, but I wanted you to know."

"This is one of the nicest things you have ever said to me," he said solemnly.

To show his appreciation, Elio got a second job, and I was proud of him although his father continued his generous support of his son. Sometimes you have to accept help, we both reasoned.

"Maybe I will give some to my brothers."

"Really? Would they take the money, knowing it is from the father they despise?"

"I won't tell them."

"They'll know. Teachers and tutors don't make much money."

"You're right, but I will do something for them, you'll see." I had no doubt that Elio would make good on his word and find a way to help his brothers without them knowing the gift was a result of their father's generosity.

I don't really know why I was so comfortable and at home in Rome even before meeting Elio, but I was as comfortable as a cat curled in front of a fireplace. The feline metaphor came easily in a city in which cats roamed freely, were fed, and treated as if they would always belong. Maybe the ancient layers of the city made her seem like another mystery to me. Every time a construction project began, work was temporarily halted. They would find artifacts a thousand years old or more as they sifted through the ages. But quite often, ruins were built over, burying the past a little deeper. Italians took their history for granted to some extent, of course, but I couldn't help getting excited walking on 2,000-plus-year-old stones, a foot path walked by Caesar, as well as his assassins.

"Look," I shouted to Elio, "I'm standing where Caesar once stood."

"No, no, no," he laughed. "Caesar was a little to the right of where you're standing."

Italy's colors drew me in anew every day. Ochre shading suggested depth; there was symbolization everywhere. Green shutters setting off open windows to our views of one another. There is a painterly quality in the Mediterranean region that must have inspired all the masters. My favorite locations were on the streets or sitting in the open-air restaurants with checkered table cloths, even the plastic ones, and watching all of the people. On my face, a new pair of sunglasses, my third since arriving in Italy, rested comfortably.

"You look like a movie star," said Elio touching my cheek.

"Just a teacher and a middling poet," I responded.

"Ah, then a wonderful teacher and poet."

Elio had his favorite spots and I had mine, but we both agreed to linger when the mood struck either one of us. Strangely accommodating to his whims, I found the action of giving in to Elio was easy.

Although he considered some of my responses silly, such as when I was so fascinated with the life-like mannequins in the high-end store windows in the city, he indulged me. I stood in front of one Italian youth with a Roman laurel wreath around his black locks, the young mannequin who was wearing the latest swimwear. "His eyes," I said, "It is as if he could step out into the street and leave his plaster cast days behind." Elio shook his head. As a foreigner, I was unused to these life-like mannequins, only later finding a bit of their history and story after reading about the character Galip in Orhan Pamuk's novel *The Black Book*. Pamuk's Galip wandered around Istanbul, discovering the eerie dummies beneath the city in catacombs, as he looked despondently for his missing wife.

"Really, Elio, I think this one escaped." The wonder of Elio is that he sometimes thought I was ridiculous about my fascination with the mannequins but still played along.

"Well, let's not stare at him, then. We don't want to draw others' attention if he is planning a get-away." We tried to be surreptitious, but I kept looking back. "You're hopeless," said Elio. "A wonderful, hopeless romantic."

"Not at all," I answered. "In fact, I have an inordinate amount of hope, but I may be a romantic."

"Good. I like romantic very much." He wrapped an arm around my shoulders, and we walked on as intimate and casual as if we had known each other and been lovers for years.

On a weekend adventure, Elio and I went to the ruins at Paestum, the ancient Roman city built on the older ruins of the Greek Poseidonia. "Here is the real secret," Elio said. "We Italians don't like to promote this historic site because Paestum is really a Greek ruin, that of Poseidonia. We Romans built right on top of the Greeks. Let them do their own advertising, is the thinking, but let's go anyway," so we did.

"Of course, when we go to our Pompeii ruins, you will see how grand they are."

"I want to see Pompeii," I said, half in protest. I wondered why he had chosen Paestum instead and asked him that question.

"To be honest, Pompeii will be very crowded and hot today. So many tourists that we won't be able to move about, but at Paestum, quiet, all will be empty, no, I mean, there will be no one there but the two of us."

He was nearly right. The ruins were deserted with only an elderly couple across the field and a family with two children resting on the grass nearby. Elio took my photo in front of the Doric temple of Athena found there, and the white against my newly browned skin made a beautiful high contrast, he told me. The paintings from the uncovered tombs were the most fascinating to me, particularly the one of a youth leaping from the wall of human knowledge into the unknown, that "undiscovered country" that Shakespeare would use as metaphor for death. I was struck by the youth's willingness, no, eagerness to dive into that other realm.

"That picture is like you," Elio said as I showed him the photo I took of the youth joyfully leaping beyond the wall into blue waters far below.

"I don't know. I'm much too afraid. My picture would have me climbing down a ladder leaned against the wall and dipping one foot in tentatively."

"What are you saying? I have already seen you dive into everything here. You were fearless with Gould and with me."

I liked the fact he added "with me" because I really was rather brave with my heart almost immediately after meeting Elio. My time in Italy might easily have turned out differently, very badly even. "Thank you, Elio, but you'll recall I was standing in your apartment for days, waiting to see if Gould would show up. I am a little ashamed that I might have put those boys in danger. I had a safe vantage point to watch any proceedings."

"No, I don't accept that. Those boys? Those men are the best athletes around and would beat up anyone if they felt like it. And you told them about Gould and what he might do. You warned them and prepared them well ahead of time. We even called my brother."

"It's still not the same as facing him myself, by myself."

"I disagree. You knew your letter would bring him to you. You waited, yes, but with a clever trap, and one that required great patience. Not all bravery must be with swords or other weapons. You used your brain." Elio pointed to his own head for effect.

"If I lack for confidence, I will just let you flatter me." He wrapped me up in his arms.

"That is good. But no flattery. I am telling you truth." I let Elio convince me that what I had done was enough, at least things had ended well in terms of my simple plan. Nothing as sacrificial as throwing myself over like Sherlock did to end the threat of Moriarty at Reichenbach Falls. Gould was in prison, the three, strong young men had become our friends and were now working on fixing apartments for Elio's father.

"Your old professor, why do you think he did it?"

"Killed Michael and the other young men?"

"Yes."

"I can only speculate. Gould murdered not really for their poetry although he stole their words. I'm not really sure I want to get into the mind of that kind of killer."

"But you did," Elio says smiling. "You wrote the letter that brought him to you and his arrest. How did you know he would come?

"I didn't know. I tried to imagine what he thought I was looking for and wanted, and then I did the opposite. A dark, uncomfortable place."

"So, your speculations?"

"Gould thought, thinks, of himself as a superior man. On some level, I'm convinced he was sexually attracted to those young poets, as well as drawn to their challenge to his intellect but disgusted by his own attraction. He hated them because he hated himself."

"He is gay?"

"Angry, repressed homosexual, I believe. He was also attracted to their minds and talents, but he could not tolerate anyone other than himself having that kind of ability, especially someone he was impulsively drawn to. He was, ultimately, immensely, delusional."

"What will you do now, Sherlock?" Elio had recently taken to joking with me about my amateur investigative skills.

"There are always more mysteries to discover," I said, and we headed back to Rome where there are cities beneath cities and depths below our depths.

~ * ~

Back in Rome, there were things to attend to, not the least of which was getting in touch with Bill again. Weeks after sending my note to him, Bill wrote back. "I'm coming. Need directions. Where do I meet you? At the airport, I hope?" He had used the money I returned to him to buy a plane ticket and was on his way. Even though Bill was one of the most well-read individuals I had ever met, he had not traveled far, preferring to do his traveling "through imagination," as he said. I wondered if he would be worried on the long flight. For the first time in a long time, I was nervous for him.

With Elio behind the wheel on the way to the airport, I thought about how much my life had changed since leaving Rochester, New York. I wondered if Bill would recognize me. Would he be critical of Elio? Of me?

I did meet him at the airport, holding one of those signs that read in big, bold letters: "Godot?" I got a few stares and more than one person smiled, but Bill knew the allusion was for him right away, weaving his way through a crowd, waving at me like a madman. Then in something out of a movie, he ran up and wrapped his arms around me in an old-fashioned hug.

Turns out I was his daughter, after all.

"And this must be Elio? Good to meet you, young man. Vena writes fondly about you." They shook hands and smiled at me.

Everything was, for the briefest of moments, perfect.

About the Author

Writer, poet, and educator Nancy Avery Dafoe, Homer, NY, has published books on teaching writing, Breaking Open the Box and Writing Creatively: A Guided Journal through Rowman & Littlefield Educatio n in 2013 and 2014, respectively. Her latest book on education policy, The Misdirection of Education Policy: Raising Questions about School Reform was published by Rowman & Littlefield in June 2016. Her first chapbook of poetry, Poets Diving in the Night, is due out from Finishing Line Press in January 2017.

She recently won the William Faulkner-William Wisdom creative writing award in poetry for 2016 and previously won the New Century Writer award for short stories. Dafoe's poems, essays, and stories have appeared in numerous literary publications. Her fiction work also appears in the anthology Lost Orchard, published by SUNY Press in 2014.